The Excursionist

The Excursionist

J. D. Sumner

ISBN: 978-1-911195-28-3

Also available as an ebook
ISBN: 978-1-911195-27-6

Typeset by Agnesi Text
Cover design by Emma Rogers

Printed in Great Britain by Clays Ltd, St Ives plc

The Excursionist, Being an Account of
the Attempt of Jack Kaganagh to Visit
his ninety-eighth, ninety-ninth and one
hundredth Countries and Thereby Ensure
Membership of the Travelers' Century Club

Part One

At the age of thirty-five one needs to go to
the moon, or some such place, to recapture
the excitement with which one first landed
at Calais.

EVELYN WAUGH

Part One

CHAPTER ONE

Silver Machine

Ladies and gentlemen, this is your Captain Nigel Cruttwell speaking, welcoming you all aboard the Coronation Islands Airways flight number 017 from London Heathrow to Placentia. The flight time today is eleven hours; we've just been given the go-ahead from Air Traffic Control so we'll be pushing off from our stand any moment now. We'll be flying at around 37,000 feet; we've got a good tailwind behind us today so we don't anticipate any problems. I am sure you'll be well looked after by Jeremy Sizemore, our in-flight Client Service Team Leader, who will be ably assisted on deck today by Diego Garcia and Jenny Clapp, so please, sit back, relax and enjoy the flight. We know you have a choice of flight carriers when you fly, so thank you, once again, for choosing CIA and we do hope you enjoy the flight . . .

CHAPTER TWO

Whole Wide World

The Coronation Islands lie between Madagascar and Sri Lanka. I was flying to Placentia, Kilrush and Fulgary to join the Travelers' Century Club. I wanted to visit one hundred countries before my forty-fifth birthday. I am very goal-orientated, and if I say I have to do something then I won't be able to relax until the task is completed. I have been from Angola and Anguilla to Zambia and Zimbabwe, and I have the hatpins to show for it. I was keen to get these three countries ticked off before my forty-fifth birthday. It would have been great if Kay had been able to visit fifty countries before my birthday, so we could accomplish something together. I had to tick off three countries rather than two, as my planned flight to the Faroe Islands, for Ireland's World Cup Qualifier, was re-routed from Denmark to Norway due to poor visibility. I never got to see the Faroes. Instead I was marooned with the boys in green at Bergen with only my Black and Red notebook for company.

Having spent the night in a Norwegian truck stop, in a room with grey walls and a view over a burger bar, I discovered the next morning there were still no flights to the Faroe Islands, so I went home. I watched the match on TV, sitting on the sofa, wearing my new replica shirt and eating a Pad Thai takeaway. I shouldn't have tried, really. The airfare cost a fortune and I didn't get to the match or the country. This is why the Faroe Islands are called the Maybe Islands: maybe you get there and maybe you don't.

Now I had to visit three countries before my forty-fifth. The Coronation Islands of Placentia, Kilrush and Fulgary would not have been my first choice; in fact, they were my ninety-eighth, ninety-ninth and one-hundredth choices. They were doable in the way Macau could be done on a ferry from Hong Kong and Paraguay on a coach from Buenos Aires. As far as the TCC was concerned, even the most fleeting of visits counted towards the total number of countries 'even if only a port-of-call, or a plane fuel stop'. The point is I can tick off a country while I am on the way to do something interesting. The TCC was inaugurated in 1954 and is limited to travellers who have visited one hundred or more countries. The benefits are 'more self-satisfying than anything tangible'. The website offers 'camaraderie and friendship among the members as well as networking opportunities', 'worldwide recognition of "bragging rights"', as well as 'members-only pins which are updated when a member reaches higher levels of country visitations'. Besides which, they have got a branch in London, and I could do with meeting some new people.

Booking a holiday or a trip gives me something to look forward to, whereby I can escape the life-shortening drudgery of knowing exactly what, when and where. This is the reason why I felt it was time to move on. I had been offered a job trading the VIX in a new start-up operation. The VIX is the Volatility Index for the S+P 500 (SPY) and measures how volatile the market believes the next thirty days will be. Put simply, it is the output of a mathematical equation based on the perceived future. I had promised to give them an answer upon my return.

It becomes more difficult to take on new challenges as you get older – you tend to look at the downside rather than the upside, which was why I needed to take up the new job offer. There is a part of me that thrives on routine as it keeps my head straight. I believe the holiday starts when you first allow yourself to think there is a next time and that you are going to go away. Can I afford it? Can I book time off work? Would some sly bastard put his dates on the office holiday-calendar to thwart me? At work I can tell myself, 'Blimey, soon I'll be in Placentia with a searchlight tied to my canister, looking for dugong.'

There are so many decisions to make: how do you book the holiday? What are you looking for? What do you want to do? Do you want to go and do nothing? Is it the right time of the year to visit? Are you thinking 'beach' when the calendar is telling you monsoon? If I have been bored on a beach on my last holiday, then I am more likely to book a trip where I'll have new experiences: rainforests, jungle, historical cities, wildlife. Having come back from holiday, shattered from all my excursions, I fantasise about just lying down, getting tanned and relaxed. My previous holiday was to Mauritius, a tropical island of fine dining, sand-flies and hydroponic vegetables, so the Coronation Islands and their wildlife, temples and history offered a contrast.

I had done some research and had looked up the best places to stay – the Nick Leeson suite here, the Imelda Marcos ocean-view junior suite there – and I asked several operators for a quote. They gave me conflicting itineraries, hotels and dates. When the quotations arrived, I knew I shouldn't have bothered. These people were tomb-raiding me while I was still alive. I only wanted to go to the Coronation Islands to tick them off my list. And then I could relax. I don't like receiving personal calls in the office.

'Oh hello, Mr Kaganagh,' I said.

'It's Kaganagh,' I said.

'Hi, Mr Kavanagh, it's Suzie from Porpoise Travel.'

'Suzie.'

'It's about your trip to the Coronation Islands; just to say it's booked.'

'Are you sure? I was really just making an enquiry.'

'I know but I'm holding flights for you. Flights to Placentia get very busy at this time of year,' she said.

'But it's after the schools go back and well before Christmas,' I said.

'The Coronation Islands are inaccessible, there are very few direct flights and even fewer with connections. If, for example, you miss your flight from Kilrush to Fulgary, you have to wait another week. And unless you want to spend your birthday on your own in Fulgary then this really is the only option.'

Three interchangeable voices on the end of a phone (two Suzies and a Lucy) began to hassle me for a deposit. They booked, changed and reserved planes without asking and pushed me to confirm. They spoke to me as if they knew me. How could they tell me what I wanted when I didn't even know myself? I didn't know which Suzie worked for which company, but didn't want them to guess from my tone.

'Hello, Mr Kavanagh, it's Suzie.'

'Kaganagh, it's Kaganagh. Hi Suzie, sorry, where are you ringing from?'

'We can only hold the flights till the 7th; are you able to confirm?'

'I can confirm that I didn't ask you to hold flights,' I said.

'Right. But you wanted to go out to Placentia, on to Kilrush and arrive in Fulgary and return home in time for your birthday on the 26th, is that still correct?'

'Well, yes,' I said.

'I can take a deposit now to secure the seat. Availability is very limited.'

I coughed up the 15 per cent deposit. I paid a price that bore no resemblance to the three weeks, five-star hotel, including flight upgrades and we'll-give-you-a-fiver-back deals, that were advertised on the Internet. I spoke to some bloke in Mysore about booking a heavily discounted club-class flight to Placentia from London Heathrow.

'Heathrow, sir?' he said.

'Yes,' I said.

'Heathrow?'

'Yes, Heathrow, London Heathrow.'

'London Heathrow . . . which country is that?'

I have visited ninety-seven countries, but, I still don't understand how, having paid a deposit based on an agreed itinerary, you find the holiday you think you have booked bears no resemblance to the one you have bought.

'Oh hi, Mr Kavanagh,' Suzie said.

'Kaganagh. My name is Kag-an-agh,' I said.

'Good news, we've managed to book Turtle Lodge in Placentia, the Fenix in Kilrush, finishing off at The Omanalak in Fulgary,' she said.

'What about the Hotel Wellington in Kilrush?'

'Right, I'm afraid the Hotel Wellington is fully booked,' Suzie said.

'But I've just given you the deposit for the Wellington.'

'I know but we've just been told it's fully booked.'

'Why did you let me pay you then?'

'We don't confirm availability until we receive your deposit, and our agents have just told us it's fully booked,' she said.

'So where do you suggest?' I asked.

'We've booked the Hotel Fenix for your second stop?'

'The one you said is not in the same league as the Wellington and has the view over a speedway stadium?'

'You remember it?'

'Is that really the best you can do?'

'The only other option is the Golden Temple, and we have had some clients return with gastric complaints,' she said.

'You win.'

'Thank you, no problem; I'll just pop this in an email for you.'

So yes, one of the Suzies got the order, my deposit and probably her Christmas bonus all in one call. I imagined her sitting there, with her collar turned up on her stripy shirt, picking her teeth with an Amex platinum card.

By the time I had spoken to three travel agents, read Frottager's guidebook, had my jabs for polio, tetanus and hepatitis, cancelled the newspapers and fitted timers to all my lamp sockets, it was the prospect of not going that seemed most relaxing. I hate travel agents, luggage trolleys, queues, tannoy announcers, airports,

British Airways and people who wear sunglasses at airports to look like a celebrity. Check-in desks are the mosh pits of international travel. Kay forbade me to speak to check-in staff. She said I was rude and impatient. Kay had travelled a lot. One of her previous boyfriends had been a pilot. I am not someone who will take 'yes' for an answer. That's what Kay used to say. She is dead now. At least I think she is.

CHAPTER THREE

Money In My Pocket

I am a stockbroker. I work on the trading desk at Fundamental Capital, Britain's largest provider of non-ethical funds, which was how I can afford to gad about clocking up the countries. Fundamental Capital is a great place to work. The people are friendly, the company looks after its employees – and that is why I've stayed here a while. Some smart cookies run it too. While everyone else was ploughing into ethical stocks and pushing prices up to ridiculous levels, we stepped back and stuffed everyone into non-ethicals like tobacco, booze, defence and gaming. Non-ethical investments will always outperform ethical ones over time. It's the difference between wants and needs.

I was attracted by the image of the 1980s' stockbroker: black Porsches, red wacky braces and house-brick mobile telephones. I never bought a Porsche, don't carry a mobile phone and am still waiting to wear my braces (or if you prefer, suspenders) ironically. These young oiks were earning shed-loads of cash for doing nothing more than gambling with other people's money. If the stocks went up they were paid a handsome bonus, if they went down it was market conditions. Being paid large wads of cash to hang out with a load of arrogant, ill-educated, opinionated, irresponsible, selfish, immodest, showy, self-serving clowns seemed like a once-in-a-lifetime opportunity. But there was a downside: the early-morning meetings at 7.30, which meant getting up at 6:05 to catch the 6:39, stopping at Seer Green and Jordans, Ryan's Chip and West Ruislip, alighting at Marylebone at 7:05, walking to Baker Street, then two hot, milky coffees and straight into the meeting. If you have to get up that early, you may as well get paid for it. My new job offer pays, on basic alone excluding bonus, 40 per cent more. Money isn't the most important thing: it's the only thing. To paraphrase Woody Allen, money can't buy you happiness but I've never seen an ecstatically happy poor person.

My view is persistence beats resistance. And that is how I built up my client base. I rang people every day. Most days they won't speak to you. But sometimes you get through, and, if you do, you have to make them listen. After a while, the clients feel sorry for you, and they throw you an order. You only lose when you stop calling them. If you don't give up, they remain a prospect.

I boxed as a kid. In the Easter term, you had to do cross-country or boxing. I didn't fancy running around for hours in mud and gulping for air, so I boxed. Every day, I'd train with an Italian. He had got through to the ABA semi-finals. He had jet-black hair, regular features, a toned abdomen and olive skin. He was a good-looking boy but a better-looking boxer. He had quick hands, moved his head slickly and had dancing, nimble feet. He would punch me in the face and ribs for three two-minute rounds. Kids used to come and watch him hit me every day. But he never knocked me down onto the canvas. And that is like life in the City. I have taken punishment, could and should have been stopped, but I am still standing.

Getting a job in the City is like getting a girl. The less interest and enthusiasm you show, the better chance you have. I sussed out that the way to make money was to move into any area where there was a shortage of people with experience. Employers tend to bid up for someone if they think you might go somewhere else.

One of my ex-colleagues, Robin Hunt, had asked me to set up the VIX trading desk. The VIX was not backed by anything tangible as positions are held merely as a prediction of the future. The VIX is referred to as the Fear Index. My current job was getting a little too cosy, but I wasn't pushing myself forward for the job with Robin Hunt, which made me more attractive in his eyes. I had to go away and mull things over.

I was still paying for my ex-wife's house. She had taken me for a mug, then a Merc, then a million. I did quite well out of the divorce settlement; I kept most of the back garden and some of the roof tiles. I wouldn't have minded if I hadn't come home to find somebody else's kippers under the grill. I should have twigged when he helped move her stuff out when she 'just needed some space'. Having provided my ex-wife with a property, it would have been too upsetting if I hadn't maintained at least a token presence, a foothold, in the property market. It was nothing like the mock-Roman Palladian palaces I was used to purchasing but a pied-à-terre in a reasonable area. I calculated that, allowing for mortgage and alimony payments, it was the second week in September before I earned any money for myself. One way of saving money is not to take any holidays. But if I don't take holidays, what is the point of working? If I don't work, how can I provide for my ex-wife and her current husband Graham? It isn't as if Graham has found it difficult to work since the divorce. It's just he hasn't needed to. He must have put his back out carrying my ex-wife over the threshold of their new faux-Tudor, five-bedroom home with under-floor heating.

I had reached an agreement over visiting rights for my daughter from my ex-wife. But, having paid for two sets of legal fees in order to agree a financial settlement, every time I went round to their new house, the ex asked me for more. I was paying her lawyer to write to my lawyer to ask for more money. And if I said no to her demands, I would get a call saying my daughter was ill or had been invited to a toddler's party on the day I was supposed to visit. Her other trick was to pretend I had got the dates or the times wrong. It was easier just to give up. People only change in books or in films, not in real life. I stopped seeing my daughter as regularly when my folks told me she had started to call Graham 'Daddy'.

CHAPTER FOUR

I Travel Alone

Increasingly, as I travel and the day of departure draws near, I become anxious about saying goodbye to friends and family, worry about whether I will be burgled and fret whether the flight will be delayed and my luggage will arrive. Having experienced the Indian Ocean tsunami in 2004, I realise that nothing is guaranteed.

It is stressful going on holiday. As soon as the cab picks me up, I fret about what I have forgotten to pack. It is only when I can remember what I have forgotten that I can relax. Packing is not my forte. I try to predict what is superfluous, what will be the one thing I'll unpack and say, 'Well, that was daft wasn't it?' Do you go for the one-of-everything-in-case-of-emergency approach or the five-white-T-shirts-two-pairs-of-blue-denim approach? Frottager's *Guide to the Coronation Islands* (2009) offers another perspective: 'You should remember to pack dull colours for wildlife spotting. Bright colours put off mosquitoes, so make sure you pack carefully.' For this trip I packed my Vilebrequin linen shirt with the navy background and pale blue leaves and the red, orange, yellow and purple hibiscus. It was still in the wrapper from when I bought it, on my last holiday with Kay.

The highlight of any holiday is waiting to take off. It's when you leave behind the drudgery of everyday living and swap routine for excitement. I looked out of the window and watched the planes backed up in a queue like long jumpers in the Olympics. We had a Qantas and a Lufthansa in front of us, and then it would be plain sailing, as it were. The stewardess gave the obligatory, dull, lifesaving spiel but she knew nobody was listening. She made the recovery position more complicated than it needed to be; all it should involve is two Nurofen and a glass of water. I nodded, established eye contact with her, and read the in-flight magazine to see what films they had.

I'm one of those who scramble about for books and a change of shoes in the overhead locker whenever a plane is about to take off. I could sit down in a seat for an hour and a half not needing anything at all, but, as soon as the zip-up-and-shut-up lights come on, I'm like a junkie separated from his needle. As soon as I am told I can't pee, drink alcohol or rummage about I discover a new sense of purpose. I spend the first hour asking the stewardess for things I don't need only to find out I'm sitting on them. I get bored. I used to annoy Kay by asking questions when she was watching her films. I miss Kay when I fly. She took care of everything.

CHAPTER FIVE

Us And Them

There was nobody to talk to on my flight from London to Placentia so I read Frottager's *Guide to the Coronation Islands* (2009). Placentia's civil war lasted eight months. Placentia's GDP per capita is one of the lowest in the world and similar to Western and Central African countries. It has never been a rich country, and it is also one of those that has only ever been known for one thing. Grenada is known for nutmeg, and Placentia is known for rhubarb.

Rhubarb was first introduced into Europe by Portuguese traders who sailed to Southern India to pick up spices, especially pepper, and then nipped over to Placentia for their rhubarb. We tend to take rhubarb for granted. As Nigel Slater writes in the January 2009 edition of *The Garden*, 'Apart from a deep winter mulch of manure (it has an appetite for nitrogen), this is a garden fruit that is very undemanding for the gardener.' Commercially produced rhubarb is grown in heated, windowless sheds mostly around Wakefield in Yorkshire, an area known as the 'Rhubarb Triangle'. 'In order to prevent the light from infiltrating the sheds and sending the pale yellow leaves green as they unfurl, the stalks are picked by candlelight. Choose the right night to visit, and you can hear the whispered cackle of the leaves unfurling.'

While the Rhubarb Riots in the Coronation Islands did not cause as much of a stir as the Dutch Tulip Crisis of the 1630s, the two events are integrally linked. As has been documented elsewhere, a mere tulip at one point was worth 76,000 dollars. The famous Dutch horticulturist, Gotthard van Moorsel visited Placentia as a student at the University of Leiden, the same university where Carolus Clusius conducted tulip research in

1593. The Dutch middle classes were keen to exploit the next big thing, as were the Portuguese. Both the Portuguese and the Dutch aligned themselves with different factions. According to Frottager's *Guide to the Coronation Islands* (2009), the first settlers were the Dutch, which led to the deaths of thousands of indigenous people from diseases brought over by them. The early settlers were keen to plunder Placentia's rhubarb supplies; a power struggle ensued between the decrepit monarchy led by King Fulsom, backed by Dutch money, and political groups financed by Portuguese interests. King Fulsom was kept in power by the land barons who owned the fertile rhubarb farms in the northeast. King Fulsom used civil disobedience, imagined or real, to tighten his grip on the people. The royal family was alarmed at reports of well-attended public meetings and imposed a curfew to thwart civil disobedience. The curfew was used by the government to fix a price for the farmers' produce whereby the rhubarb was bought from the collective farms at an artificially low price and sold at a considerably higher price on the international market. Farmers' income fell below subsistence level and 'the Rhubarb Riots' raged, followed by three years of fighting with both monarchists and farmers incurring heavy losses. In the end, both sides ran out of cash to buy guns and an uneasy truce was called. The civil war had been a disaster for every Placentian. While the country was aware they could not undo the injustices of the past, they could do something about the future. A deal was successfully brokered between the warring factions by Sir Roger Dewy, the Governor General of the British Indian Ocean Territories, and in 1946, or 1947, depending on which source you use, the Placentian People's Party and King Fulsom came to an agreement to ban war from the island.

The country's economy, unimpeded by spending on munitions and defence, invested any budgetary surplus in health and education. Placentia's decision to ban war, the so-called war-against-war policy, was the envy of neighbouring islands. International lobbyists, themselves bankrolled by defence companies, harangued the government to reject this overtly undemocratic policy. Bowing to international pressure, the politicians began to detain those who were caught in the act of, or suspected of, agitating for peace, and hundreds were arrested. Those found guilty of agitating for peace, and acting contrary to the interests of their fellow countrymen, were summarily executed. The pro-peace agitators, with their radical agenda of health and education, were forced to flee the island, leaving behind both friends and family. Many of the agitators drowned in their attempt to leave Placentia, as is documented in the small museum on the main coastal road. The small museum in Petioles is still open today and remains Placentia's premier tourist attraction.

CHAPTER SIX

Bring Me Sunshine

Having cast my experienced eye over King Fulsom in my well-thumbed copy of Frottager, I reached out for the other stock-in-trade standby for aeronautical tedium – the Coronation Islands Airways in-flight magazine. There are 'three seasons in the Coronation Islands: humid and dry from May to August, hot and dry from September to November and warm and wet from December to April'. I was arriving between the hot and dry and the warm and wet season and didn't really need my ski jacket.

Most of the articles were dedicated to the intellectual challenge of trying to crowbar any cheesy journalistic link between, for example, a jewellers and a coronation. Thus we had an advertisement for the Crown Jewels boutique with 'Crown Jewels fit for a King'. The magazine was called *The Coronation Islands Guide to Regal Pleasures*. It had the usual features on where to eat the freshest fish, the hottest new nightclubs where you could mix with the locals, beach bars showing you a coastal infinity of crystal blue and beaches where the gentle waves caressed miles of virgin white sand. This was a land of contrasts where everything was either 'exquisite' or 'award-winning'. And where a bite to eat would appeal to the gourmet in you in a land where everything was a taste explosion. There was a noticeable absence of a taste explosion in the back of the in-flight magazine: I searched the *Shopping Mall in the Sky* for gift ideas, but all they sold were model aeroplanes with the CIA insignia, eight-foot inflatable dugong and benches with maudlin descriptions dedicated to deceased family members.

Coronation Islands Airways presented you with 'the sommelier's Carte du Vin, with some of the world's most exciting, prestigious and innovative wines'. I blind-tasted a Crozes-Hermitage, a Malbec, a Ribera Del Duero and a Meursault, which isn't easy to do on your own with a very small tray. The air hostess was obliging to begin with, bent down, smiled, called me 'sir,' but the more wine I asked her for, the less hospitable she became. With every glass, I asked for fizzy mineral water to avoid dehydration but she only eked out an eggcup-sized measure.

'Could I please have one of those bottles of fizzy mineral water?' I said.

'I am sorry, sir, we are not allowed to give them out.' She bent down so close to my face I was worried she was going to kiss me.

'I don't want to bother you all the time, asking you for water. Can you leave me the bottle; I don't want to make a nuisance of myself.'

'I am afraid we can't do that, sir.'

'Why?' I asked.

'It's against regulations. I am sorry, sir.'

'But your in-flight magazine says quite clearly on page twenty-eight, that passengers should make sure they remain hydrated.'

'I know, sir. I am sorry but they are the regulations.'

'I am only asking for a bottle of fizzy water. I have spent thousands of pounds flying Business Class with you. I'm thirsty,' I said.

'I am sorry, sir. It's the rules.'

'The rules... what airline has rules to prevent passengers from drinking water? Why advertise what a great service you provide, if you won't give water to a thirsty passenger? What's the point of pouring an eggcup-sized measure of water if I can jug down full glasses of wine? You do this because, as you know, the less weight you carry the less fuel you need, which means lower fuel costs and better profit.' And with this, the hostess began to take away my empties.

CHAPTER SEVEN

Big Seven

Ladies and gentlemen, we will soon be arriving at King Fulsom International Airport. Please have your headsets ready to hand over to our cabin staff, along with any rubbish you may have, and put your seat back in the upright position. We will be asking passengers who are visiting Placentia, who are neither nationals, nor in transit, to fill out a disembarkation form.

The form asked me a list of questions, the answers to which were provided by my passport, which I was going to present to the passport official at the same time as the disembarkation form. Kay used to take care of all form filling. She used to fill in every embarkation and disembarkation form, visa application, customer-satisfaction survey or any of those other forms you have to fill in at check-in. I had to make do with putting down 'Radio ventriloquist' as my 'Occupation', 'Graceland' as my 'Address' and 'Unlikely' as an answer to 'Sex'.

At immigration, a bored-looking gentleman in a black pointy hat and a beige uniform took my passport with his right hand while talking to his colleague in an adjoining booth. He looked at my passport, without looking at me, and flicked his hand like he was chasing flies off his food.

'What does that mean?' I asked.

The immigration official ignored me and flicked his hand again.

'What do you want me to do? Do-you-speak-English?'

'Yes, thanks. Can-you-read-English?' He pointed to a sign saying *Cabin Crew Only*.

Arriving in any country with a hangover just makes things worse. I had arranged a private transfer and was supposed to have been met by a man standing by the information desk. I knew the driver would be lolling about outside in the heat rather than where we had agreed to meet. When I eventually found him I asked why he hadn't come inside but he just smiled weakly, so I frowned while he drove.

I was dehydrated, certainly sticky, possibly smelly and didn't know whether I fancied breakfast, lunch or dinner. The drive was conducted in silence. I put Nelson, my driver, off any conversation with a few gruff answers prefixed with 'Sorry?' I was lucky everyone in the Coronation Islands spoke English.

After forty minutes or so, Nelson took a left down some unmade road and followed the sign to Turtle Bay Eco-Lodge. The lodge was just beyond the back of beyond. The anticipation was building, as was my concern as to how much to tip Nelson and the guy who would take my bags to the room. Would I tip the driver now or ask if he was the guy who would take me from Turtle Bay back to Fatty Fulsom's Fab Airport. Experience taught me that if Nelson said it was himself picking me up on the way back to the airport that he would a) turn up and b) turn up on time and c) it would cost me less in tips. I don't come from a tipping culture; it is one of the reasons I never answer the doorbell on Halloween.

The lodge was located on the sandy banks of the Essandoh, in the traditional main house of a farm, with a view over the mangroves. It only had eight rooms and accommodation was very basic but it was also the best lodge in Placentia that was available at the time of booking.

The receptionist/owner/bellboy, Kurt, smiled, printed something off his computer and pushed a form towards me over the wooden counter.

'Do I have to fill that in?' I asked.

'Yes, please,' he said.

'Why? Don't you have the emails from my travel agent?'

'Yep, should do. Yep, we have it all here.' Kurt showed me the paperwork.

'So, sorry, why do want me to give you this information again? I've just written it out in duplicate for your chums at the airport,' I said.

'Yes, please, if you will.' Kurt disappeared behind the counter.

I sighed and made my handwriting look spidery.

'Have you stayed here before?' He put my form away without a glance.

'No.' I looked down at the desk and drummed my fingers.

'Have you been to Placentia before? Will you want an early alarm call?'

'No and no.' I nudged my luggage towards me with my feet.

'So, you're a keen twitcher?' Kurt asked.

I shook my head and picked up my hand luggage.

'We've got Japanese guests at the moment.'

'Great,' I said.

'You want to know why they are here?'

'Why are they here?' I said.

'Black-tailed Godwits, Eurasian Thick-Knees and Brown Boobies...'

'Have they seen any Brown Boobies?'

'They've seen Woolly-necked Storks, Northern Shovelers, White-bellied Drongos and three Brown Boobies.' Kurt nodded.

'Impressive. Three Brown Boobies, you say.'

'Yep, all at the same time.'

'I'm glad I brought my camera,' I said.

'What they really want is to tick off Eurasian Thick-Knee. Perhaps you'd like to go birding with them?'

'Not really my thing.'

'Fishing? Riding? Canoeing? Photography? Walking? Painting?'

'Not really, just here to catch up with some sleep,' I said.

'The best time to catch all the wildlife is daybreak so we advise that our guests have breakfast when they get back from their excursions. There is coffee and tea provided in the breakfast room from about 5 a.m. onwards. It would be a great shame to miss out on all our wildlife, wouldn't it? I am sure you will love it.'

'Did you go today, Kurt?'

'No,' he said.

'I don't suppose you know any football results?'

'No.'

'Do you know how I can find out?'

'Not really, not here,' Kurt said.

'Right, well, if you'll excuse me, I'll take my stuff to the room.' I picked up my bags. It was too hot to wear a ski jacket.

'Let me get you some help with your bags.'

'Don't worry,' I said.

'They look heavy.'

'No, really – while I can, I may as well,' I said.

'Let me help.'

'No, really, it's fine. Really,' I said.

I struggled with my bags as they banged against my fat, hot legs. I was terrified about losing my hand luggage which had everything including my money, passport and travel documents. I always guard my luggage so the first impression I give to strangers is that I think everyone is a thief.

The lodge had tiled floors, heavy ceiling beams, and lots of dark colonial furniture. Everywhere was swathed in mosquito netting including an outside dining area and a reception room with a television that doubled up as a bar. There was a room indoors where you could watch wildlife and outside was a barbed-wire fence from where, at night time, you could see the turtles waddle onto the beach to bury their eggs.

There is always a sense of excitement when you get to the room. All the rooms were different and some were spacious and had verandas. The décor was understated but not in a good way. They just didn't have any; it was just shite altogether and the size of the spider clambering out of the toilet bowl had to be seen to be believed.

Kurt showed me the facilities:

'This is the bed,' Kurt said.

'Yes.'

'And the phone,' he said.

'Yes.'

'And this is the air-conditioning.'

I wiped sweat off my forehead with the back of my hand.

'The shower.'

'Okay,' I couldn't look at him.

'This is the toilet.'

'It looks like it,' I said.

'Everything okay for you?'

'Perfect. Thank you. Where is the safety-deposit box?' I asked.

'We don't have that. We don't even have room keys,' Kurt said.

'Do you have a safe in reception?' I asked.

'Yes, of course,' Kurt said.

'Why of course?'

'Yes, of course, for security.'

I had a lukewarm shower and dried myself on a small, anti-absorbent towel. I flushed the toilet; it smelt strongly of drains. I tried to shave in the tepid water but the sink didn't have a plughole. Or, rather, it had a plughole but not a plug. The fan in the bathroom was positioned at throat height. I kicked my travel clothes into the corner of the bathroom, donned my khaki shorts, short-sleeved white linen shirt and dark brown moccasins, stuck my hair down, cleaned my teeth and squirted myself under my arms. I trawled through my luggage looking for stuff to put in the Turtle Bay safe before leaving my room unlocked.

I pulled my Tilley hat from my hand luggage. Tilley hats are the best-marketed products I have ever come across. The hats have brag tags, which can be given out to anyone who shows any interest in them. The tags carry the message that Tilley hat wearers are 'interesting people of sterling character' and that 'it is customary to provide the giver of Tilley Hat procurement information with A WARM HUG, OR STAND HIM OR HER TO A DRINK'. Tilley hats last a lifetime, float, block 98 per cent of the sun's harmful UV rays and have a secret compartment and an adjustable wind cord. If you buy a Tilley then you never need to buy another sun hat again. I keep some red thread I was given by the Wailing Wall in Jerusalem in the secret compartment, which also comes in handy if you are trying to stow away some cash or credit cards.

As soon as I put my hat on, I felt as if I was on holiday. Placentia, the celebrated home of the Rhubarb Riots, is the most westerly of the Coronation Islands. I had ticked off country number ninety-eight, and I was still on track to have visited one hundred before my forty-fifth birthday. As I said, I had hoped Kay could have visited fifty countries with me before my birthday but she wasn't as keen as I was.

But while I was very happy to be in Placentia, I couldn't help but think about Kilrush and Fulgary; Kilrush, with its history and temples, and 'Fly and Flop' Fulgary with the pinkish sands of the Omanalak Resort on Meelick Bay and the super-deluxe, sunset-beach, over-water cabana. I couldn't wait. Placentia is a place for wildlife and birdlife enthusiasts. In fact, with the exception of Thursday's late-night opening in peak season down at the museum in Petioles (a must-see for those interested in the history and production of rhubarb), there were no nightlife, architecture, clubs, waterfalls, mountains, salt lakes, cave paintings, volcanoes, beaches, temples, churches, or indeed anything worthy of mention apart from the plant life, birdlife and wildlife. If you didn't like those, you didn't like Placentia. I knew I didn't want to get up at 5.15 a.m. on the off chance I might meet a Masked Booby or a Yellow-eyed Babbler.

I unpacked, read some magazines and, feeling drowsy, I must have fallen asleep. Waking up in a strange bed, in the pitch black, hearing cicadas gave me quite a jolt. I'd had a dream that started with me almost going to prison and then partying with Lady Di and members of the Saudi royal family.

I looked at my watch – I was late for supper. Drinks were served at 7.30 and supper at 8 p.m. I didn't have time for, or the desire for, another shower. I walked into the bar-cum-television room where I met the Japanese family (a dad, a granddad and two boys), a young French couple (who didn't speak English) and a powerfully built South African gentleman with grey hair. Terrific. I had absolutely nothing in common with any of them. I acknowledged them with a cursory smile and a nod, just in case they were looking at me (which they weren't), sat down and scribbled anxiously in my Red and Black notebook. The good news – I was on holiday; the bad news – I was on my own.

The dining room was already set up. I was sharing a table with the grey-haired South African and a Placentian by the name of Bendy. Terry, the South African, introduced himself.

'What are you doing tomorrow, Jack?'

'To be honest, Terry, catching up with some sleep,' I said.

'The wildlife is best at daybreak. We'd some luck today, didn't we?'

'We did,' Bendy said. 'We saw lots, didn't we?'

'Yah, we saw sambhurs, chitals and spotted deer…'

'A pair of Red-billed Tropicbirds,' said Bendy.

'Yah, a pair of Red-billed Tropicbirds,' said Terry. 'What will you do tomorrow morning Jack?'

'Bit of a lie-in tomorrow, I'm on holiday. Just sit around and relax.'

'The morning's the best time before it gets too hot,' said Terry.

'I'll think about it,' I said.

'Okay, well, I'm turning in,' said Bendy.

'Yep, so am I,' said Terry.

Terry and Bendy got up and left. It was only 9.15 p.m. What the hell was I going to do now? I went back to my room so nobody could see me sitting on my own and read Frottager: 'The Rhubarb Riots were all the more remarkable because they were fought in spite of the laxative powers of the giant rhubarb and its astringent effect on mucous membranes and the nasal cavities. The national flag of Placentia is similar to a Union Jack design but with purple to represent the stem of the rhubarb, the green to represent the leaves of the rhubarb and the white to represent the peace of the war-against-war policy.'

It was the first night of my first holiday since Kay slipped away, and I was tucked up in bed, on my own, and had turned off the light shortly before 10.30 p.m. I hoped things would liven up before my return to England.

CHAPTER EIGHT

Monkey Man

I read the preface to Louis Chagrin's *In Placentia* (1971) and fell asleep. I woke up in the middle of the night when a frog fell on the floor. It sounded like someone spitting catarrh into a toilet bowl. This interrupted my dream that Paul 'Gazza' Gascoigne had been appointed manager of the English football team.

I'd nodded off again when I felt the sheets tighten around my legs as if someone was sitting on my bed. I didn't know whether this was the end of my last dream or the beginning of my new one until I heard what sounded like a man panting while struggling to take his trousers off. I woke up, switched on my bedside light and saw a Japanese granddad, dressed in a maroon, pale blue and yellow striped dressing gown.

'What the fuck are you doing?' I said. He didn't say anything. He was busy grappling with his pyjama trousers. 'Get the fuck out of here, you fucking weirdo,' I shouted.

He looked at me but didn't say anything. He wasn't scared, surprised or in any way hesitant. His face was a blank canvas. Did jet lag and a blind tasting bring about this dream or was this real? I don't speak Japanese so I pointed at the door like a referee sending a player off.

'Get out now.'

I couldn't get out of my bed as I hadn't got any clothes on and my boxers were draped over a wicker chair. I made a series of hand gestures to get him away from me while being careful not to touch him in case he got belligerent. I'd just woken up, miles away from friends and family, and felt vulnerable. He wouldn't move off the bed. He was sitting extremely close to me. Somebody began to call for him from outside my room. Granddad stood up. He bowed repeatedly and exited my room backwards without saying a word. Was it a dream? And if it had really happened, how could such an elderly man bow so low? He had left my bedroom door open so I put on my boxers as a precaution, and practised my bowing when he left. I was intrigued to see how low I could bow. I was beginning to see it as a privilege to be woken up by a man who could bow so low. It was 5.08 a.m. and I was wide awake so I went to the river to see what may have been dugongs and some bright red-feathered birds.

At breakfast time, Terry and Bendy were sitting at the same table we had used for dinner the previous evening. I joined them while they discussed the sepia photographs on the dining-room walls.

The Japanese granddad and his family were having breakfast. I heard the sound of cutlery being put down, the unmelodic scrape of a chair and the shuffle of feet. The granddad approached my table. I knew I shouldn't have sworn at him but it had happened and that was that. He bowed, and I bowed back. This bowing seemed to continue indefinitely, getting deeper, then gradually smaller and shorter the more times we bowed. It was a kind of a 'Hey, you bowed, I'd better bow again,' to which he responded with a 'Oh no, he bowed again, I'd better bow too,' until the bows got small enough that both sides felt we could stop. This left us staring into each other's eyes which made me even more uncomfortable. I didn't know whether he wanted me to say something or not. Having sworn at him at the top of my voice, I didn't want to be out-bowed by him, especially if the purpose of all this bowing was for me to show respect to him in front of his family.

'Please excuse me for my language when you came into my room. I was half-asleep and didn't know what was going on,' I said.

'Better to beg forgiveness than to ask for permission,' he said. He bowed again and exited backwards as he had done when he left my room.

'These stuffed animals on the walls here, bit of an anachronism, don't you think?' said Terry who was deliberately ignoring the bowathon.

'You're not keen on having pictures of white hunters showing off their trophies?' Bendy said.

'Why are the hunters wearing black armbands and looking so miserable?' I asked.

'They are actually wearing black armbands to mourn the end of big-game hunting. Nobody has shot anything bigger than a sambhur for years,' Terry said.

'Ridiculous.'

'But we've got something better now anyway,' said Bendy.

'What's that?'

'We've got "the little five",' Bendy said. 'Yeah, you know, we've got Ceylon spiny Mouse, Asiatic long-tailed climbing mouse, dusky palm squirrels...'

'Of course you have, I'd forgotten that. I think it's in my book.'

'So are you joining us, Jack?' asked Terry.

'What are you doing?'

'This morning we go on a trail, have a quick bite back here and, this afternoon, horse riding,' said Bendy.

I thought I ought to go just to keep busy. This was what I have been doing since Kay disappeared. When she was around I could opt out but now I didn't have the choice.

By 6.15 a.m. we were off on an adventure. I had already been up an hour earlier than if I had been going to work, except I wasn't going to work since I was supposed to be on holiday. I knew I wasn't at home because at home I didn't have a five-foot bed, lukewarm water, a toilet that smelt of drains and an old, bald, fat, grinning, Japanese granddad as an alarm clock.

Bendy was a knowledgeable guide, pointing out teeth-cleaning trees, stripe-necked mongoose, toilet-paper trees, wild boar, toucans and sloth bears, although he had an unfortunate habit of putting dung in his mouth – I suppose this was to assess how fresh the trail was. I felt fabulous – there was nobody about, I loved the peace and quiet, the sense that the day hadn't woken up yet and the sun on my back and even, and God strike me down, the company. Bendy's gentle enthusiasm made both of us relax. He enjoyed spending time with us because the Japanese had moaned about the lack of Eurasian Thick-Knees.

At lunch, I met my elderly Japanese intruder. He gave no indication that he remembered meeting me at breakfast. The family were noisily pointing out pictures of Eurasian Thick-Knees to Kurt. The Placentian waiter, Caesar, asked me a series of increasingly complicated questions about the precise nature of the finances of the British royal family. I had a choice of a snooze or horse riding; I couldn't brush Caesar's questions off any longer.

Brendan Behan said an Anglo-Irishman is a Protestant with a horse. This makes me Hiberno-English, as I'm a Catholic who loathes horses. It's not so much the horses I hate as the trainers, the bookies and the jockeys. If I went to my room, I wouldn't be able to sleep because all the birds in Placentia had decided to meet up outside my window for a band practice and, besides, I wanted to see if Bendy would put any more dung in his mouth. So I went horse riding on the smallest horse I have ever seen. Bendy had a cowboy hat on. He packed a gun and a machete. He cut the hairs off the back of his hand to demonstrate its sharpness. I wanted to touch the gun but didn't even ask. We saddled up: Bendy the machete-wielding, gun-toting, dung-eating Placentian cowboy, Terry the grey-haired, South African Air Force pilot and me. We weren't offered riding hats, advised how to ride, asked about previous riding experience or requested to fill out insurance claim-waiver forms. What did I need health and safety laws for? I was out horse riding with a gun and a machete and a former member of the South African Air Force. The odds were in our favour.

Our horses – large Shetland ponies really – behaved perfectly. Mine was directed by the availability of food rather than my horsemanship. We stopped for a soft drink on the sandy banks of the Essandoh and didn't say very much. Terry had us both fascinated by some grains of sand that we looked at under his microscope. Perhaps everyone else knew how colourful individual grains of sand are, but I didn't. It was like being a kid again and looking at a kaleidoscope. We had a great ride and saw God knows how many types of deer, Fulvous Whistling Ducks, colourful parrot-like birds, white cattle, cattle egrets and dugongs. I wasn't fussed about remembering different names of species of Crimson-backed Greater something or other; I just enjoyed Bendy's enthusiasm and ability to spot wildlife.

At supper, Terry and I shared a bottle of South African wine.

'Well, if they don't have any proper stuff, I suppose it'll do,' I said.

'South African wine is very good, actually,' said Terry.

'Sorry, remind me where you're from again?'

'Probably not as good as some of your British wines, eh Jack?'

'Very amusing. Now, Terrence, when you're not shooting Angolans and abusing baboons, what do you do for a living?'

'I'm an accountant,' he said.

'Rubbish.' I waited for him to smirk.

'I'm an accountant.' Terry kept looking at his plate.

'Nonsense,' I said.

'What are you talking about?' Terry asked.

'Terry, you used the word anachronism at breakfast today.'

'And what does that prove?'

'It proves you're not an accountant,' I said.

'Why?'

'No accountant could possibly have a word like anachronism in their vocabulary, could they?'

'They might,' he said.

'But they don't, do they? Come on, what do you do? I'm not Secret Service. I'm just interested, that's all.'

'But if I tell you, you mustn't tell anyone,' he said.

'Like who? The elderly Japanese prowler or Kurt?'

'Just don't tell anybody, okay?'

'Promise.' I crossed myself.

'I'm a Catholic priest.'

I waited for Terry to smirk.

'You're joking.'

'No, I'm not.'

'Where?'

'In Cape Town, by Camps Bay,' he said.

'So why the big secret?'

'If I tell anyone, I'll have to answer questions all the time, like, if there's a God in heaven why has my sister just lost a four-year-old to leukaemia? Or how can you believe in a church that has original sin? So I say nothing. And if anybody asks, I say I'm an accountant and nobody asks any questions.'

Terry, or more accurately, Father Terry, called it a day. He called it a day at 9.30 p.m. Once again, I was left to my own devices and asked Caesar the Geezer for another drink. The Japanese had asked him if he could recommend a new guide. Caesar dropped the subject of Her Majesty's funding and chose to discuss how the local lads have beads sewn into their foreskin to maximise pleasure.

It had been a proper day. I had woken up in a place I had absolutely no reason to visit whatsoever, with a bunch of people whom I should have nothing in common with, and enjoyed every minute. Kay would have loved it. Kay preferred animals to anything else. She wasn't a fan of anything flash or gaudy. Now I had one of those *Travel-Makes-You-Truly-Alive* moments. I could smell the jasmine, hear the fan that sounded like an industrial Hoover, see the lime-green geckos on the ceiling and savour the combination of cigarette, espresso and whiskey. This was the reason I travelled, and I loved it. I had no TV, no hot water, and the light made rereading Louis Chagrin's preface to *In Placentia* (1971) impossible. But not as impossible as sleeping on sheets made out of sandpaper and pillows reconditioned from Second World War sandbags.

CHAPTER NINE

Too Hot

I had been too tired or too wired to sleep and was therefore surprised to wake up at 4.30 a.m. I couldn't sleep because it was too quiet, yet at home I can't sleep if I can hear noise. There was a small window of opportunity to sleep, after the tree frogs made a noise like a honeymoon couple testing the mattress for springs, and before the birds got together for a rehearsal just before first light. I had been determined to sleep until my left foot caressed the itch on my right knee. I had been bitten. I scratched myself and found another bite on the back of my neck. My throat felt sore, and I decided to get up.

It was five o'clock in the morning, and it was rush hour. A gang of horses was running around like a group of youths rampaging on the Tube, the wild boars were looking sly and I was worried my travel insurance might not cover culpable homicide involving an irritatingly cheerful and unrepentant Japanese granddad. It looked like, through no fault of my own, I would be joining in this morning's activities. As I walked about the eco-lodge, I saw the two black-mopped Japanese kids switching labels around on the food laid out by Caesar for breakfast. Power ballads spewed forth from a tinny radio. The granddad and the lads' father had showered and were jabbing fingers at their bird book. They took it in turns to stand up and use the binoculars.

Caesar was telling Terry about how a Loris, I assume it was a *Loris* and not *lorries*, defends itself by standing still. It was just after five, and it was too hot. You know what happens with us Brits, Hiberno-English and Plastic Paddies; we go away in November because we want some sun and then we say:

'It's hot.'

'Certainly is.'

'Yes, but it's too hot.'

Terry was shaved and dressed in what looked like freshly pressed clothes. His wet hair suggested he had already showered.

'Hello, how are you this morning?' Caesar asked me.

'Couldn't sleep, bitten to buggery, sore throat and it's too hot,' I said.

'Tea or coffee?'

'Tea please.' Bendy pulled up a chair and nodded. I nodded back. I slurped my drink and called Caesar back to the table.

'If this is tea, I'll have coffee, and if it's coffee, I'll have tea,' I said.

Caesar brought me a tea bag and some hot water.

'Christ, I didn't know I'd have to build the tea myself. Sorry Terry,' I said.

'Help yourself to food,' said Caesar.

'What do you want to do this morning?' asked Terry.

'What are you doing this morning?'

'Bendy and I are going canoeing, if you'd like to come with us.'

'You not going with the twitchers?' asked Bendy.

'The Japanese granddad, are you kidding me?'

'I wouldn't worry about him; he sleepwalks sometimes and so does his son. They've been coming here for years, they like it here because there are no stairs. He doesn't remember anything about it. He's a great guy, clever too, one of the biggest poultry farmers in Japan. So, Jack, are you coming?' asked Bendy.

'What time?' I asked.

'We leave in about ten, fifteen minutes,' said Terry.

'Christ, sorry Terry, I'd better nip back to the room.'

I had to shower, shave, do my teeth, pack my bag, put on sun cream and treat my bites in less than fifteen minutes. There was no hot water, and Kurt had not given me a plug for the basin. However, there had been a concomitant relaxation of personal hygiene standards. I welcomed the prospect of putting sun cream on as much as I did covering myself with Deet anti-mozzie spray. Nothing gets me up for the day more than rubbing lotion over fresh bites immediately after breakfast.

We saw nobody whatsoever on our three-hour canoe ride. That's not entirely true: we saw the Japanese family on the shore. The father walked in front, with his birding book and the binoculars tied around his neck, while Granddad dawdled behind him. Father alternated between looking through his binoculars and shouting at his two boys, who were kicking dirt at each other. Terry talked cricket while I talked football, and both of us waved at the two old boys chatting along the riverbank who were having a beer with their lunch. I didn't enjoy the canoeing at all. The mozzies took my two hands on the paddles as an opportunity to chew me. This must have been how I got bitten on my finger under my signet ring. I chose to avoid eye contact with Terry and, when he asked if I would like to stop, I said, 'No, thanks,' and Bendy asked if I was all right.

'This is ridiculous; I'm getting bitten to death out here,' I said.

'Okay, we'll go back now. The dugongs must be sleeping,' said Bendy.

We paddled back in silence. I pulled the canoe out of the water and stormed off like a sulky toddler with Terry looking at me while choosing not to say anything.

As soon as I got back to my room, I felt guilty. I'd excused myself on the grounds that I was still getting used to travelling on my own again. I conked out on the bed and only woke up when I heard the gong for lunch. Terry had skipped lunch and was wandering about taking photographs so I ate on my own. I had beans, rice, salad, fried plantain and crème caramel. It may have been the leftovers from the previous evening. The coffee was shocking even though it came from only six kilometres away. But I still drank it for its laxative effect.

Speaking of which, a familiar and welcome stirring took place in my intestine and prodded me into returning to the privacy of my own room. As soon as I evacuated my bowels, my spirits revived. I felt as if I was now on Placentia time at last; it was something about shrugging off the last piece of luggage that I had brought over from England.

Feeling relaxed, I sauntered around the estate and told the chaps I was 'Game on for this afternoon.' I had to leave the next day. I couldn't believe it. I had spent months researching Placentia, I was putting ointment on my first bites, and it was almost time to tick off my ninety-ninth country, Kilrush.

Some travel experiences turn out exactly as you would expect: the smell of incense while waiting in line to hand out alms to Buddhist monks; a lion yawning at dawn in the Serengeti; a jeep safari drive in Placentia just as night falls, sitting silent by the banks of the river while the birds squawk, flap their wings and fly away, the cattle chewing the grass and the chital deer watching us watching them. I had taken hundreds of photographs, and now I could see the animals with my own eyes rather than through a camera lens. Placentia did have a distinctive landscape and eye-wateringly beautiful scenery. Its outcrops of rock and boulders looked like they had been dropped there. But the best thing, the very best thing of all, was the silence.

There were no burglar alarms.

There were no cars, car horns or pumping stereo systems.

There were no pub drunks.

There were no mobile phones.

There was no TV.

There was no radio.

There were no tracker knackers.

There was no celebrity bollocks.

There was just nightfall.

Nobody spoke as we meandered back in the crepuscular light; as we saw less wildlife, we heard more birdlife. It wasn't worth showering or sleeping by the time we got back, besides which I didn't want to change into any new clothes and besides which I really couldn't be bothered and besides which it didn't really matter. It didn't matter to Bendy and it didn't matter to Terry and, if it didn't really matter to them, it definitely didn't matter to me.

What mattered to me was getting the chaps down in good time for a drink before supper on my last night. The Japanese had already gone to bed.

Two-or-three-day-old socks, two-or-three-day-old stubble, walking boots, jeans and my mountain goat fleece, packet of ciggies, lighter and a beer: that was me. The air was warm and, apart from the two new mozzie bites on my collarbone, I was relaxed.

Terry was outside the dining-room-cum-bar-area and setting up a whacking great telescope. By now, nothing Terry did or told me could surprise me. He looked very matter-of-factly through the lens of his huge telescope and offered me a peek.

'You really are totally and utterly barking, aren't you?' I said.

'Are you telling me that you're not interested?'

'Of course I am.' I had my first look through a telescope. 'What's that?'

'Rings of Saturn,' Terry said.

'Amazing. What's that?'

'Jupiter. If you look up there, you can see the moon, over there the Southern Cross and over there what we call the Jewel Box.'

'Amazing. Never heard of either of those two,' I said.

I shook my head in astonishment.

I had to go to Placentia in the Coronation Islands, right in the middle of the Indian Ocean, just to see Jupiter and the Rings of Saturn. I said I could see the other stuff, but to be honest I had no idea where or what Terry was pointing at. But I didn't care. I'd just seen Jupiter and Saturn close-up and only paid for Placentia. I prefer to visit countries where there is little, if any, reason to visit. The smaller the country or the fewer the reasons to visit, the more intriguing the place will be. I don't know whether it is because the people try harder, or less so, but whatever the reason, the result is always the same. There is also a direct relationship between the number of rooms in a hotel and the calibre of its guests. The fewer rooms there are, the more likely you'll talk to someone. And the more interesting will be the people you meet. This is the First Law of Travel.

CHAPTER TEN

Contact

The next morning, I had to catch the helicopter for the short hop to Kilrush. At breakfast, Terry gave me a copy of *Playing Snooker with the Somalis* by Preston Burgess, which liberated me from Louis Chagrin's *In Placentia*. I was really looking forward to cracking on to my ninety-ninth country.

It is a sorry reflection that I can be dribbling with excitement at the prospect of a tarmac landing strip in the middle of the Whatthefeckarewelost Delta, anywhere in the world, and within three days I'm saying, 'Okay, thanks for that, I'll pay my bill now if I may.'

'Did you have any drinks from the mini-bar last night?' asked Kurt.

'No.'

'Any chocolate, peanuts, crisps, Mr Kavanagh?'

I shook my head and patted my jacket to make sure I'd got my wallet.

'Can I ask you to fill out a short customer-satisfaction survey?'

'No thanks, just say cheerio to Terry, Bendy and Caesar for me, will you?'

'We look forward to seeing you again some time. They say if you go to Placentia, you always return some day.'

'Quite possibly. Is Nelson here yet?' I stifled a yawn.

Arrival days plus departure days equals tipping days. However pally you get with someone, if you end up saying goodbye with some notes scrunched up in a knowing handshake then you're never quite sure it is, or was, a genuine relationship. And so, sadly, my last memory of Bendy was some notes scrunched up in a farewell handshake. He probably spent the tip on dental hygiene.

Tips – how do you know the difference between too much and too little? I once spent an evening in a tent, on the last evening of a trek, in three inches of water, counting grubby Nepalese rupee notes while working out tipping differentials between two porters, one cook, three cook's assistants, one sherpa and one sirdar. The notes had been passed around so many times you couldn't identify the value of them by torchlight, let alone after rum and beer.

I settled my bill with Kurt, who scuttled away into the back room. I left quietly and quickly. I had to tip Nelson, the driver, after he dropped me off at the domestic terminal. The Coronation Islands are so skint that they only have water and soap in the toilets of the international terminal. The domestic terminal I used for my flight to Kilrush had neither, just a toilet with a broken seat and a hosepipe.

The airport was full of *mazungos* like me: Westerners dressed in a rash of khaki, outdoor eco-lodge shorts, cameras, walking boots, jungle bushwhacker hats, camouflage jackets with lots of zips on them and ankle-length mountain socks. Why do all eco-tourists dress up like big-game hunters? It made me want to wear a black armband.

It is ghastly when you travel halfway round the world merely to bump into your own reflection. I felt like a gatecrasher at someone's party. A gatecrasher with a sore throat and mosquito bites. And while I try to give strangers a chance, I always avoid anyone who reminds me of myself. These were people who definitely saw themselves as travellers and, like myself, all went to the same tourist hotspots: Machu Picchu, Borneo, Kathmandu, the backwaters of Kerala, the Nile, the Amazon, the Okavango Delta, the Galapagos and a hundred other places. If you travel, all you are aware of is the countries you haven't visited and the places you haven't seen.

My mood was not lifted by the airport's easy-listening repertoire which was limited to an instrumental version of Phil Collins's 1984 classic 'Against All Odds'.

To my eternal shame, I am incapable of leaving any airport in any country in the world, irrespective of my adoration or contempt for the place and its people, without looking in the shops for tourist tat. Placentia was no different. Do people still just buy stuff by dint of the fact it has got the name of a country on it? How many batik clothes do people need? Who buys all that terracotta grot? And is terracotta really the best idea shopkeepers can come up with, when you're just about to get on a plane?

I found I could buy wooden boats, beach towels and even ceramic plates with *Placentia* written on them. What I didn't know was *why*? I thought about buying a terracotta tree frog with Placentia written on it but decided against doing so. Instead I bought a badge for my Tilley hat decorated in the purple, green and white of the Placentian national flag.

One down and two to go. Now all I had to do was to get to Kilrush and then to Fulgary and I could join the Travelers' Century Club. See www.travelerscenturyclub.org for further details.

CHAPTER ELEVEN

Oops Upside Your Head

I loathe sprawling airports and passenger-packed terminals. The smaller countries do it better. Having checked my bags in, I was driven out of the airport on an invalid buggy and taken around the side of the domestic terminal building to a hangar where bored people sat around and smoked.

I was introduced to a Mr Dave Carroll who presented me with his business card, upon which he described himself as an *Expeditor, Aircraft Pilot, Taxi Service, Auto Rental, Purchasing Agent and Real Estate Agent*. According to Dave, I was the only passenger on the short hop over to Kilrush, which, funnily enough, suited me down to the ground. The plane had four seats and I would be sitting next to the pilot. Dave had to hire overnight security to clear rocks off the runway and to look after the plane. Sometimes they mixed up the petrol with something else, and sometimes they didn't put petrol in at all.

He told me about a wealthy American couple who'd once flown with him; she was glamorous and younger than her wan-looking husband. She had insisted on treating Dave like an old retainer when they arrived late from the hotel. She took more hand luggage on board than was legally permissible. Her Louis Vuitton suitcases were hard and not soft. (She'd been given strict instructions not to bring hard suitcases, as it was difficult to squash them into the back of the plane.) Having stuffed a lot more of the wrong type of luggage into the back of the plane, she re-applied her make-up before take-off. She brought on board a sizeable red vanity case, which she rested upon her knees. She had probably been loved too much as a child.

The flight ordinarily consisted of a bit of radio chat, a random flicking up and flicking down of some knobs while trying to find the right one, twisting the occasional dial, slamming the windows shut, flicking the air-con on, having a little look about, a bit of do-you-read-me-Foxtrot-Charlie chat and descending.

However, things didn't go to plan with Mr Wan and Mrs Vuitton. These little planes – it was a Cessna 206 – can get very hot. The only air comes from the pilot's window, which is left open until take-off, much to the chagrin of the coiffured Mrs Vuitton. She was a nervous flyer and had never flown in a small plane before. Dave Carroll had managed to get the old rust bucket up when a vulture crashed through the windscreen, screeching its death rattle and flapping its broken wings. The vulture was still alive when it landed slap bang on Mrs Vuitton's lap, displacing her red vanity case. Mrs Vuitton was splattered with the blood and entrails of a twitching, soon to be twitched, vulture. She began screaming. Dave Carroll first asked and then shouted at her to shut up. Mrs Vuitton did what any sensible woman would do in a time of crisis; she tried to catch her reflection in her compact mirror. Once she saw her face covered in the technicolour guts, gizzards and brains of the vulture convulsing on her lap, she became hysterical. Dave Carroll, who was struggling with the controls having lost the windscreen, turned to Mrs Vuitton. He shouted at her to calm down. She didn't. He shouted at her again to calm down. She didn't. He said if she didn't calm down then he'd have to shut her up. She didn't. He turned around to take a swing at her. Her husband raised his hands to stop him, then proceeded to knock her out cold with one punch. Mrs Vuitton was still out cold, bloodied and covered in guts, feathers and poorly applied make-up when a smiling Mr Wan pushed her and her vanity case in a wheelchair across the tarmac at the airport. Mr. Wan thanked Dave for saving their marriage; he said he hadn't felt so alive since college. He gave Dave a two-hundred-dollar tip for a thirty-five minute flight.

I didn't give Dave a two-hundred-dollar tip. I gave him a twenty-dollar tip and began to worry. Was a twenty-dollar tip insulting to Dave? Did Dave tell me the story about Mr Wan and Mrs Vuitton to loosen up some change? Who was I to criticise? I worked as a trader for a non-ethical hedge fund, not the Salvation Army. I'm a man whose favourite things have always come out of a calculator.

Part Two

I am free of all prejudices. I hate everyone equally.

W. C. FIELDS

CHAPTER TWELVE

Don't Fence Me In

According to Frottager's *Guide to the Coronation Islands* (2009),

Kilrush, the only volcanic island in the Coronation Islands, got its name from the Battle of Kilrush which was fought in April 1642 between an English army under the Earl of Ormonde, and Richard Butler, Third Viscount Mountgarret, who led a horde of Irish rebels raised during the Irish Rebellion of 1641. The government troops were intercepted by Mountgarret's rebel militia at Kilrush, near Athy in County Kildare. The Irish troops were badly equipped and completely untrained, and after a short exchange of fire, many of them fled. Most of the Irish reached the safety of a nearby bog, where the English horses could not follow, but some of them were overtaken and killed. Irish sources claim their casualties were very light, while Ormonde claimed over five hundred of them had been killed. It is probable that losses on both sides were very low.

As everyone knows, Oliver Cromwell took exception to the Irish for having the temerity to complain about being butchered, especially to men who were themselves butchers, and many of those 'rebels' or 'complainers', as Cromwell later described them, were exported as slaves to the British West Indies. White Irishmen were exported like livestock and not just because black Irishmen were thin on the ground. They were treated like slaves long before it became unfashionable. We know about the Battle of Kilrush, we know about Cromwell's lack of affection towards those he slaughtered, but what is unclear is the exact route Wrong Way Kaganagh, a distant relation of mine, took to get to Kilrush.

Very little is known about Wrong Way Kaganagh and what is known is entirely implausible. It is difficult to substantiate the historical facts because a lot of the parish records in Ireland were damaged, lost or burnt by English 'Planters' by both sides during the Irish Civil War of 1922–4, and by the IRA.

What has been passed down is likely to reflect myth rather than fact. I have been at family weddings where *facts* regarding Wrong Way have changed between the drinks waiting for the bride to arrive at the church and the drinks after her arrival at the reception. Whatever the facts of his journey, Wrong Way Kaganagh was shipped out to the West Indies as an indentured Irishman, and yet he arrived in Kilrush, in the Coronation Islands, south of what is now Sri Lanka, formerly Ceylon.

The most likely scenarios are that pirates attacked the ship taking him to the West Indies and he fled or became a pirate himself, or that he fled from captivity in the British West Indies. What we can establish beyond a doubt is that he was not a member of the Royal Geographical Society. Instead of turning left when he came out of the harbour and following the signs to Ireland and the Rest of Europe, he had turned right and followed signs to Angola and Namibia, or whatever these countries were called at the time.

Wrong Way Kaganagh arrived in the Coronation Islands while trying to get to Sri Lanka. Exhausted by his journey and suffering from fever, he rested in Kilrush, then known as Dulali, before becoming the first European to *discover* the island. But when Wrong Way arrived in Dulali, somebody must have been on the island before Wrong Way. It is an unavoidable truth that the islands visited by Marco Polo, Vasco Da Gama, Captain Cook, Sir Walter Raleigh, the French, Dutch, Spanish, Portuguese and the Brits were all settled well before they got their grubby little mitts on them. The locals, who didn't claim to find Kilrush, did find Wrong

Way and were mesmerised by this big lump of an Irishman with his thick red-brown hair, sunburnt face and blue eyes and, as was their custom with strangers, they took turns to nurse him back to a full recovery.

For his part, he won over everybody with his generosity of spirit, farming skills and knowledge of animal husbandry honed in the paddy fields of his paddy farm.

Language was a barrier. Whenever anyone asked him a question, he replied, 'Kilrush'. He automatically assumed the Dulalis were asking him where he was from, as was then the custom in the pubs of Ireland. And so very soon the word Kilrush was used by the Dulalis to describe anything from sand to water, from sky to livestock and from coconuts to palm trees. As soon as Kaganagh made a full recovery, he pined for the porter and poiteen of his native Kildare. He began to teach the Dulalis how to prepare their own palm wine and how to ferment their fruit in order to produce alcohol.

Portuguese sailors, running spices to and from Southern India, began to visit Kilrush. Kilrush began to trade moonshine for the rhubarb from Placentia. The people of Kilrush began to sell rhubarb wine back to the Placentians. Portuguese sailors brought spices from Kerala and traded it for rhubarb wine, which they took back with them to Europe. Kaganagh's commercial awareness, coupled with a seemingly impenetrable distribution monopoly, led to an improvement in the standard of living for the majority of Kilrush's inhabitants.

Wrong Way's experiences in Ireland had made him determined to avoid land confiscation, the slavery of its people and famine. The islanders were encouraged to eat communally and to grow their own produce, which in turn would be traded for cash to invest in the distillation process. At the time, Kilrush's brewing and distillery facilities were considered to be among the best in the world, and, if not among the best in the world, undeniably the only ones in the Coronation Islands.

However, all good things come to an end and the end of Wrong Way was cancer of the pancreas. Our family interests began to wane but not before Wrong Way had put Kilrush on the map. The Irish have never invaded anyone but their influence abroad is tangible, with the shamrock stamped in passports upon arrival in Montserrat, in Bobby Sands Street in Tehran and in Bernardo O'Higgins Avenida in Santiago. Kilrush remains the only Irish protectorate in the world, a protectorate born by invitation and not by invasion.

Frottager's *Guide to the Coronation Islands* (2009), asserts 'the death of such an iconic and populist leader (Wrong Way) created a power vacuum'. Wrong Way's son, Michael, was born as a result of his illicit union with an Englishwoman by the name of Lady Margaret Honoria Twiss, wife of the then Governor General of the British Independent Ocean Territories, Lord Cecil Twiss. It is generally supposed that Wrong Way's illegitimate issue, Michael, was conceived when Lord Cecil Twiss passed out after one of Wrong Way's diplomatic initiatives. Michael never really knew his birth father, but adopted his persona in its entirety. A stage Irishman, he set about identifying with Irish interests, much to the chagrin of his legal father, Lord Cecil Twiss, who is described by his biographer, Sandra Dunning, as 'a man who left the candle unlit at both ends'.

Understandably, his Lordship was a mite reluctant to reveal all in his letters back to London. Embarrassed by his son and ashamed by his errant wife, Lord Cecil chose to do what he always did in times of stress, which was to switch off and hope the problem would go away. He also cut Michael off without a penny until Michael took an oath to renounce Wrong Way and any claim to his estate.

Unfortunately for Lord Cecil, Michael was something of a contrarian. He did what came naturally to him and devoted his life's work to his father Wrong Way. Michael became a rabid Hibernophile and charmed the bejeezus out of anyone foolish enough to listen. Michael, or Mickey, as he preferred to be addressed, 'could bring a tear to a glass eye'. According to Dunning, when Mickey was asked whether he had any sympathy for Lord Cecil's plight, he replied, 'The only place round here anyone will find any sympathy is in the dictionary between shit and syphilis.'

His son, Brendan Twiss, was hewn from a different type of rock altogether. He was notoriously known as 'the man who'd steal the eyes out of your head and come back for your eyebrows'. Brendan lived his life by the maxim: 'If you don't act, you'll be acted upon.'

Kilrush was, and still is, a volcanic island. It is one of only two volcanic islands in the Coronation Islands, of which there are seven, of which only three are inhabited. Kilrush is a small island with the same landmass as Wales. But 60 per cent of its land mass is non-arable because of its volcanic soil, and, of the remaining 40 per cent, half is still used in rhubarb production and the scientific study of rhubarb. This does not leave much land to play with, which for anyone other than Brendan, son of Mickey and grandson of Wrong Way, would have spelt problems. But Brendan saw the scarcity of available arable land as an advantage both to himself and to the inhabitants of Kilrush. Brendan understood a shortage of supply could lead to an increase in price. He knew an economy built on rhubarb was not sustainable. He also foresaw that neither the investment in the distillation and brewing process, nor the exponential demand for its much-loved triple-fermented rhubarb wine products, were likely to continue.

What there was demand for, and more importantly competition for, was religion. 'Religions need flocks like dung beetles need dung,' as Brendan used to say. Visiting Dutch Calvinists wanted to practise their faith, visiting Portuguese Catholics wanted to practise their faith, and with so many people wanting to practise so many faiths and with land at such a premium, what could possibly be an equitable solution?

Brendan set up a census and discovered Kilrush was home to Calvinists, Catholics, Theravada Buddhists, Hindus, Muslims and the Cochin Jews of Kerala among others. If religious facilities were afforded to all these faiths, Kilrush should invite, at an early planning stage, suggestions from the interested parties as to where you could go and practise your Zoroastrianism, Jainism, Sikhism and Animism of a weekend. Not to mention the Coptics, the Bahai, Armenians, Greek Orthodox, Russian Orthodox, Sunnis and Shiites.

Brendan was keen to avoid charges of monoculturalism. He was also a pioneer of faith tourism. And so he auctioned off licences for religious premises on fixed twenty-five-year leases, upon cessation of which the ownership of the licence would revert back to the state. There is no evidence to suggest that Brendan trousered these monies himself – although several academics and historians are pursuing these claims. The proliferation of religious establishments gave birth to the so-called licensed and take-home trade. The licensed religions had meeting places: churches, chapels, mosques, synagogues and cathedrals. The take-home trade was first used to describe those religions that did not own a place of worship.

Every religion was keen to be represented on the ground in what Dunning describes as 'a sort of Gold, Frankincense and Myrrh rush'. The opportunities afforded to the native Kilrushi were significant, with the construction and lodging sectors being the obvious beneficiaries. Kilrush rejoices in its title 'the Jerusalem of the Indian Ocean'.

Brendan passed away peacefully in Kilrush, a lover of all things Irish, just three months before he was to visit his 'native' Ireland for the first time. News of his antics had reached Ireland some time before his death, and Kilrush was beginning to attract some of Ireland's biggest messers to seek their fortunes in a sunnier climate.

The success of the ecclesiastical sale and lease-back schemes left Kilrush thirsty for new sources of income. The enthusiasm for the granting of ecclesiastical licences grew exponentially following a bidding war between the Vatican and some Saudis; neither party, and least of all the Senate (the governing body of Kilrush), emerged with any credit in what was to become an international scandal.

Given the relatively small amount of land available for building places of worship, suitable sites became scarcer. The fewer sites available, the more demand rose for those sites; the more demand rose, the higher the price Kilrush could charge for the twenty-five-year fixed-term ecclesiastical lease.

To open up new sources of income and to grow revenue, the Senate looked at various strategic alternatives. Could Kilrush merge with or acquire another country? If Kilrush could not diversify geographically, then could Kilrush diversify through internal diversification, that is, by issuing licences for other non-ecclesiastical premises or functions?

In the *Kilrush Chronicle*, there are pull-out sections on travel, business, sport, entertainment, property, money, religion and licences. There has always been money to be made in trading licences because Kilrush has more places of worship per square metre than anywhere else in the world. The new mosque on Worship Street started off as a place of worship for the French Huguenots, became a Methodist chapel, an Anglican church and was latterly used as a synagogue. The government has granted licences for most commercial activities ranging from car dealerships to tuk-tuk drivers, from hotel owners to sadhus and from licensed pet providers to family members. If you live in a flat and are out working all day then on a Sunday you can ring an authorised dealer and rent a dog for a couple of hours. Alternatively, if you are unmarried or divorced, and you want to talk to someone about family matters, you can rent someone to talk to, go to a party with or attend an interview for a school nursery with a member of the opposite sex. The biggest growth is in the demand for father or mother figures. If, for example, your mother or father has died, or lives many miles away, or you simply have a bad relationship, then you can hire a mother or father figure to ask advice from or to escort you to, say, a graduation ceremony. For every commercial enterprise, you need a licence.

Different religions, however, have different boiling points — drugs, drink, sodomy, gambling, prostitution and animal welfare

– all of which elicit varying responses. What all religions have in common is the collective need to save, redeem or rescue their flock from temptation. A bad poet borrows, a good poet steals, as they say, and the Senate found the perfect business model in the British East India Company's licensed opium dens in China. Licences were granted to nationals and 'blow-ins' alike in order to avoid accusations of protectionism and to foster Kilrush's image as an equal-opportunity employer. Licences were granted permitting the use of opium, prostitution, gambling and alcohol alongside the licensed ecclesiastical trade.

There was a furore in the paper regarding the renaming of the airport. The Vatican have the concession for the airport, thus enabling the Catholic Church to sponsor it, hence St Patrick's International Airport. But with the end of the concession looming, tempers were running high in the local press. Brian McDaid was the minister whose brief it was to persuade the electorate of the far-ranging benefits of changing the name of the airport. With Wii the likely frontrunner, it was proving a difficult sell; the Kilrushi financial community thought The Wii International Airport belittled their reputation for offshore banking, especially back-office and hedge-fund administration. The privately owned confectionery group Mars and Jupiter Fund Managers were also on the shortlist according to the *Kilrush Chronicle*, now sponsored by Hyundai automobiles.

The security at St Pat's was a trifle lax: we had to go out of one door, take our shoes off and then re-enter the terminal through another door while carrying our shoes, carry-on luggage and passports. The flight arrived just ten minutes after they had shut the Forex bureau. This enabled the porters and the taxi drivers to be paid in US dollars rather than Kilrushi punts.

According to Frottager,

The Kilrush national flag is the same emerald green and white as the Irish tricolour but with black rather than orange. Kilrush suffered its last major earthquake in 1759.

As most of the landscape is inhospitable and non-arable, most of its inhabitants live in the only major conurbation, Vilanculos, some 20 kilometres from St Pat's airport. In recent years the government has made efforts to move away from ecclesiastical leases and moved into mainstream back-office and hedge-fund administration.

Frottager continues:

Kilrush was declared a tax-free haven as early as the 1970s and provided refuge for ex-pats fleeing from punitive taxation policies. The commercialisation of the country, which is very much in-sync with its commercially viable religious roots, is encapsulated in its slogan, 'What goes Off-Shore, stays Off-Shore.'

I met up with my guide, Sean Devine, at St. Pat's. There had been a small delay while I chased around the airport looking for my latest must-have – a new badge for my Tilley hat, this time in the green, white and black of my ninety-ninth country, Kilrush. But there were no badges to be had. I found Sean outside the terminal using the card with my name on it to fan himself. He was wearing a bright red T-shirt emblazoned with the Kiltours company logo. He insisted I sat up front with him. Sean took my luggage, threw it on the back seat and turned the ignition key several times before he could get the engine to bite. He pulled out of the car park and seemed to clip an elderly lady pushing a trolley.

'Good man yourself, Jack is it?' Sean drove too fast.

I nodded while adjusting the sun visor.

'Thanks for being on time,' I said.

Sean looked into his driver's mirror to find the trolley had spilt its contents.

'Don't suppose you know any football results?' I asked.

'Now they should be in the paper. Who is your team?'

'Wycombe,' I said.

'Wycombe is it? My brother-in-law played for Brentford,' he said.

'What was his name?'

'Des.'

'I mean his surname,' I said.

'McCarthy.' Sean sent a text as we drove around a sharp bend in the road.

'That's right. McCarthy. I remember him,' I said.

'Okay so, welcome to St Pat's International airport, Mr Cagney. We at Kiltours hope you will love our island and now, if you have all your bags, we'll go on our famous Temple Tour. So please, Jack, sit back and enjoy the tour. No need for seat belts unless you so wish. Kilrush has a population according to the government census, last published in 2006, of 287,000. We have nine autonomous, self-governing, administrative districts of which St Pat's is only one. And now we go to Vilanculos, only twenty minutes actually; the town is handy enough now, and it's also the biggest by population but only the seventh biggest in terms of geographical area. Actually, you might not realise this but Kilrush is the size of Wales. Did you know that we only have one lift on the island, and we'll see it on our tour today? You might be interested to know our history also; we ourselves now were discovered by us and by the indentured Irish labourers and before that...'

'Sorry, did you say the Temple Tour? Do you have my schedule with you?'

'So you don't want to see temples?' Sean looked puzzled.

'Yes, I would like to see the temples. That's why I have booked a Temple Tour with Kiltours for tomorrow,' I said.

'Okay, that's grand, so we'll just go to the hotel anyhow.'

'Actually, I have to change some money,' I said.

'You don't want to change your money at the airport?'

'No, because I was scheduled to arrive at ten minutes past four and the foreign-exchange bureau closes at four o'clock,' I said.

'You have Kilrush punts?' Sean scratched his forearm and kept looking at me when he asked a question rather than the road and the oncoming traffic.

'No, that is why I need to go to the bank,' I said.

'You want to go to the bank? I think it closes soon enough.'

'Yes, please,' I said.

'Okay, so we'll go to the bank now and leave the Temple Tour until tomorrow. I think that would be the better plan. You'll get your head down and feel grand in the morning,' he said.

'Perfect. Thank you, Sean.'

'Not a problem. Relax. Are you on your own, then?'

'Looks like it,' I said.

'Sad, isn't it? Must be terrible being on your own, is it?'

I didn't look at Sean as I wanted him to concentrate on his driving.

'Can we change my hotel? I don't like Hotel Fenix. I had asked for the Hotel Wellington,' I said.

'Would you want the Golden Temple hotel?'

'Not really. People get bad stomachs there. Even my agent knows that.'

'In Kilrush, everybody gets bad stomachs. We have a saying; it's the stomachs that are bad, but not the hotels,' he said. While he attempted to engage my eyes, we had a near-death experience with a packed bus.

'Okay, anywhere – but not the Golden Temple. Okay?' I said.

'Okay.'

'Thank you Sean for all your help.'

'Not a bother. The Hotel Fenix is brutal. Who booked your trip? We'll change that for you soon enough,' Sean said.

We drove down James Connolly Avenue, left along Casement Drive, past St Stanislaus the Splenetic and turned right on Pearse Street until we pulled up at a branch of Ecclesiastical First Union Bank. The road had more hairpins than a BBC costume drama. Sean drove as if he was being chased and seemed to enjoy taking unnecessary risks with his life, which I didn't mind, and my life, which I did. It was like a scene out of *Wacky Races*. But I was too happy to be visiting my ninety-ninth country, just one short, to be fussed.

I left Sean on his mobile phone ringing centrally located hotels. I gave him strict instructions to secure a large, quiet en-suite room with a double bed in a quiet street.

I was the only person in the bank, but I had to get a ticket and sit down until a red light came on with my number on. The branch had white walls, black chairs and wooden high-gloss tables. Three cashiers looked up at the light to see whether the number coincided with the one in front of them. It was only marginally less exciting than watching the National Lottery numbers because now I had two minutes left before EFU Bank shut. And for an offshore financial centre, indeed even for an on-shore financial centre, the precision with which they prepared to shut up shop was impressive. A light flashed before me; a buzzer buzzed. I presented my dollar bills at the counter. The cashier didn't smile to greet me. The cashier unravelled my notes and held them up towards a light designed for this purpose. Several one- and five-dollar bills were rejected because of wear and tear. A ten dollar bill was rejected on the grounds of having an overly sharp fold. I was about to remonstrate when I looked up. Three fatigue-wearing military types were pointing guns at my head. I nodded respectfully to acknowledge their presence, neglected to count my money, or check the rate, and left. They kept the guns trained at my head. Kay would have freaked out altogether. I jumped in next to Sean.

'Not great news now, Jack. The Golden Temple is full. I have had to book you into La Hermita,' Sean said.

'Is that good?'

'Very good, the best craic after the Robert Emmet,' he said.

'And the Robert Emmet?'

'I don't know, I didn't try the Robert Emmet,' he said.

As long as I wasn't staying in the toilet I was initially booked into, I was relaxed. I don't know why but I was tired. It was only a short hop from Placentia but I was shattered. I had done nothing except go to a small airport, look around at some batik and terracotta grot, get on a helicopter and change some money from dollars into punts. I had already had enough of this travelling malarkey for one day.

Soldiers are supposed to march on their stomachs; this sounds painful and would explain why wars always last longer than expected. And that is with God on their side. Imagine how long it would take to fight a war without God on your side. I had three nights in Kilrush and decided to march on my stomach in three different ways: namely, one indigenous meal, a fine-dining option and some street food.

La Hermita ticked all the boxes. The brochure promised, without a hint of hyperbole,

a handpicked, intimate boutique hotel in Vilanculos Old Town, in a perfect setting for your fairy-tale visit within easy (25 Minute) walk of all the major Cathedrals, Mosques and Synagogues. La Hermita combines an enchanting blend of contemporary luxury, comfort, fine dining and outstanding personal service. It is a wonderful, historic, private family house, where guests are very welcome and no effort is spared to make them feel at home.

CHAPTER THIRTEEN

Space Cowboy

I was not disappointed when I saw the hotel. It looked like one of the Maharajahs' palaces you see advertised in the travel brochures. Having stayed in somewhat functional accommodation in Placentia, I was ready to step up a gear.

I was salivating by the time I had read the tribute to La Hermita written by its owners, Orla and Brigid Bosomworth, and I was baffled why it wasn't fully booked.

'Okay, so I'll be in the foyer at 8 a.m. tomorrow,' Sean said.

'And I'll be down at 9.30 or 10 as per my itinerary.'

'Okay, thanks a million. You have the hang of it anyhow. Enjoy your evening, Jack.'

There didn't appear to be any bellboys or receptionists at La Hermita. There didn't seem to be any guests either. Having looked around for five minutes, I banged the standard-issue bell you always spot on hotel reception desks. Nothing happened. I looked behind the counter to see if I could use an internal telephone. I found a young man, with a mouth like a Kermit the Frog hand-puppet, hiding behind the counter. His cap proclaimed *Jesus Is My Boss*. He had an Adam's apple like a jockey's bollocks and was reading Erich von Däniken's 1968 classic, *Chariots of the Gods: Was God an Astronaut?* He didn't look up and continued to read. Perhaps he hoped I would go away. Was hiding behind the reception of a hotel the best way to do this? It was one of those moments when you take stock of your life and make snap judgements based on very little information. What had I learnt? Firstly, I had learnt God was more likely to have been an astronaut than *Jesus Is My Boss* was a receptionist. Secondly, *Jesus Is My Boss* had not been trained to the same exacting standards as one might have expected having read La Hermita's flyer. I also learnt I had better control over my temper than I had when I was about the same age as the dimlo who was cowering behind the counter. This refers to a time so long ago I still had cheekbones.

I brought the bell over to where the receptionist was hiding in his bunker and banged it again, while this time leaning over and looking at him. After some time had passed, he looked up but didn't say anything so I rang the bell again.

'Yes?'

'Yes. Please,' I said. He looked at me again.

'Do you work here?'

He nodded.

'Do you work here now?' I asked.

'Yes.' He squinted at me.

'Great. Sorry to bother you, but are you on duty today? Could you get the receptionist for me?' I asked.

'Name?'

'Of the receptionist?' I asked.

'Of the guest?'

'Kaganagh, Jack Kaganagh,' I said.

'Nobody here staying called Jack Kaganagh.'

'No, that's because I'm yet to check in.'

'Fill in registration form.' He picked up his book.

'Great,' I said.

'You want to pay now?'

'What do you think?' I stared at him until he blinked. He continued to read his book and managed to avoid looking at me. I continued to scribble over my client-registration form and signed in as Bette Davis, gave my address as Kamsusan Palace of the Sun, Pyongyang and my occupation as Psycho-geographer. The gentleman meeter and greeter, who still offered the punter the most generous odds in the Employee-of-the-Month competition, ignored anything remotely relevant to my request for a quiet double en-suite room facing away from the street, slapped a key on the counter and went back to mulling over whether his boss was an astronaut or not. I don't know the answer either, but as a space cadet had checked me in, I supposed anything was possible.

I was pleased I wasn't offered any help with my bags. Actually, that is not true. I was quite pissed off, but at least I didn't have to tip the maddening half-wit. The key to the room was big and clunky with tassels. The room was huge with an enormous bath with Victorian plumbing, what the travel magazines describe as 'shabby chic'. Or, as we travellers call it – overpriced.

I put on my white towelling robe, flicked through the services directory in the hotel guide and plumped for the Signature La Hermita top-to-bottom massage lasting ninety minutes and costing eighty dollars. I dialled the room-service number and was relieved to have avoided the twerp downstairs.

'Hello, do you speak English?'

'Yes,' she said.

'Do you do laundry?' I asked.

'Yes.'

'I need to get it back tomorrow.'

'Tomorrow?'

'I need it back tomorrow, okay?' I said.

'Okay,' she said.

'Will someone come to my room?'

'Yes,' she said.

I had a coughing fit and struggled to clear my throat.

'Will they come now?'

'Now?'

'Yes, please,' I said.

'Yes, please.'

'Are you the person to book the massage with?'

'Massage?' she said.

'Do I book the massages with you?'

'I don't massage. I ring.'

'Yes, please. The signature La Hermita massage ninety minutes costing eighty dollars.'

'Okay.' And with that she clicked off.

While I was waiting for the laundry man to arrive, I flicked through the hotel's guide to Vilanculos only to discover the town was 'inundated in mythological times by a sacred lagoon; today it is mercilessly eaten away by a cement stain.'

CHAPTER FOURTEEN

Accidents Will Happen

I was sitting on the toilet, about to study my complementary hotel copy of *250 Hotel Rooms to die for: Before you die*, when I heard a knock on the door. Nothing happens until you find yourself doing something else. I opened the door. A uniformed woman in her mid-50s, Myla according to her nametag, grinned at me with short, multicoloured teeth. I handed over my hotel laundry bag.

'Leave it outside room,' Myla said.

'Don't you want it?'

'You want room service come in middle of massage?'

'Oh sorry, I thought you were...'

'No problem. You lie on bed. But please you open window in bathroom.'

'Of course, I am sorry.'

'Take off your clothes,' Myla said.

'Aren't you supposed to buy me a drink first?'

'You want to drink something?'

'Don't worry,' I said.

I lay on my stomach with my head hanging over the bed. This caused my nose to drip. Myla was immensely strong and combined pressure-point Shiatsu with traditional Thai massage. Myla put her feet under my back while trying to turn me into the shape of a crab. I could feel her feet move up and down my spinal cord, liberating every vertebra. She tried to rock my pelvis into place by pushing my knees as flat as possible to the bed while lifting up my torso. She kneaded my groin area. I'm not giving too much away by saying when you are travelling on your own, and it's been quite a while anyway, and a female is kneading your groin area, your mind wanders to happier times. I screwed my eyes shut.

'Sleepy dickey?' Myla asked.

'Dickey not sleepy, dickey dead,' I said.

I kept my eyes closed until the door banged shut. If Kay hadn't disappeared in the way she did I wouldn't have been in this situation in the first place. And now I felt like I'd cheated on Kay when it was she that had left me.

I decided to go out for a walk, only to find most of the shops and cafés were shut. For some reason, Belgian fusion was the cuisine of choice for a big night out in Vilanculos. As it was my first night, I fancied native Kilrushi cooking and, as the hotel restaurant was well regarded, and as nowhere else seemed open, I thought I'd stay in and eat in the hotel.

Eating on my own in a large restaurant is one of my pet hates. The key is to look like you are eating alone by design and not out of a lack of options. You should also remember to cultivate an air of mystery. It is important for diners to feel you are there on business and not just a sad, lonely guy who can't persuade, or who simply doesn't have, any friends to have supper with him. Writing notes at the table creates the impression of activity. If you don't take notes at the table, the other diners have more time to analyse your combined facial expressions of despair and loneliness. Perhaps you think taking a book to read might serve as an alternative deception? Please be aware that lighting in restaurants is often not good enough to read by. Imagine the scenario when you've taken a book down – say, *From Murmansk to Magaluf by Moped* or *Talking Shiite with the Sunnis* – only to find you can't read it due to poor light. What do you do? Do you carry on, straining your eyes and looking like someone who may be visually impaired, or just give up and look around at the other gormless guests for a couple of hours? My advice would be to go for the pen-and-notepad scam every time. You have to remember the person dining alone is the sole topic of conversation for most married couples.

I looked at the menu to use up some time before I could flee to my room. I ordered vegetable soup, or to give it its full title, Lukewarm Vegetable Soup, followed by Liver and Goat's Lungs and Chewy Meat in Aspic. The restaurant was confident enough to tell people about Liver and Goat's Lungs but not where the meat came from, which was a worry. The food tasted exactly as you'd imagine, and I decided to become a vegetarian. The soundtrack to the meal was provided by a morose harpist, who appeared to be missing half a thumb and whose remarkably small repertoire revolved around 'A Nation Once Again', 'Yes Sir, I Can Boogie' and 'Girl from Ipanema' to a hitherto unknown musical arrangement. I drew strength from the fact the harpist was having a more miserable evening than myself. I decided to do what I always did when I didn't appear to be getting the rub of the green; I sought solace in alcohol. Douglas, the American barman, suggested a local rice wine like an arak. I knew when I saw the bottle's label, 'Not to be taken internally', that I had to be resilient. One rice wine led to another, until it had surgically removed the revolting taste of my meal.

Douglas was a short, squat and moustachioed older man who looked you in the eye when he spoke to you. Before polishing off my second nip of local rice wine and after Douglas had started to polish the bar glasses, he showed me the regimental dagger he kept behind the bar counter in case, in his words, 'any rascals showed up'. I admit to having been suitably impressed when he also flashed his pump-action sawn-off shotgun at me. He was comfortable handling weapons. Douglas had been in the bar one night when a large gentleman came in holding a machete and said to him: 'I'm going to kick your ass.' Douglas had been tipped off by one of his customers that this might happen. I think they had fallen out over some money. The large gentleman ambled up to the bar while Doug was stacking glasses behind the bar just where he stored his gun. Douglas asked him what he thought he was doing but the big lump wasn't inclined towards civility so

Douglas did what came naturally and shot him in the knee. The large man didn't seem to connect the noise of the pump-action sawn-off shotgun and the burning pain in his leg. He dropped his machete onto the floor of the bar and tried to hop on his one good leg. It took him quite a while to reach the door. The other regulars in the bar said everything seemed to take place in slow motion and talked about how they were only scared after it happened, and not before. Douglas called the cops, to be told if we need you, we'll call you. They never called. You've got to be able to handle yourself if you've got a moustache.

Douglas had served in Vietnam and had been stationed in Cambodia at the very time Nixon went on television to deny there were any US troops in Cambodia. Douglas had been recruiting Thais into Cambodia to train them to fight in Vietnam. He told me about the industrial quantities of speed, Dexedrine and methamphetamine he ingested courtesy of Uncle Sam. When they say War against Drugs what they really mean is War against Drugs unless it is *actually* a war, in which case it reverts to a War with Drugs.

Douglas attended the famous West Point Academy; he was able to muse upon this as he collected the ears of his victims/opponents/ guys who were trying to kill him. He was a mine of information. He told me about when he used to go out fragging. Please excuse me if you know all about this, but 'fragging' comes from fragmentation of, say, a grenade. Fragging is the act of intentionally killing or wounding one's superior officer and is a term and activity, which is very common, especially with hand grenades. It was a sneaky war – Doug also told me the Americans would put big-tit posters up on the trees (the idea being large-breasted women were rare in Vietnam) with unintelligible print thus encouraging people to walk towards the tree. As they approached, the ground they walked on would detonate the toe-popper mines. Thank goodness all that torture stuff has been consigned to history; I was one drink away from blowing myself up.

CHAPTER FIFTEEN

Ask

If I have a criticism of the large, quiet, double-bedded en-suite room facing away from the street, it would be it didn't face away from the street. I know this because every time I got up to get some headache tablets or water, I heard water coolers being delivered or workmen banging hammers against the front of the hotel. In my en suite bathroom, the attachment in the shower unit almost reached the sink and there was no soap. Guests were advised to put used toilet paper in the bin provided. They also ran the scam about saving the world's oceans by not washing your towels during your stay. I don't know whose idea it was, but I suspect he or she had an accounting qualification but hadn't worked for Greenpeace. I tried to ring reception but the phone didn't work. It hadn't worked since I was called at about 2 a.m. 'Jack Kavanagh?' 'Yes? Who's calling?' The phone receiver was clicked off.

Having spent the night dreaming of severed ears, big tits and toe-popper mines, and having not been able to shave or call reception, I had no option but to go downstairs. It was breakfast time and I wanted to play fragging with the receptionist who had checked me in. I was going to bite him if he as much as looked at me.

Tragically, my chum was unavailable and another life was saved. Perhaps he was interviewing for a position as a life-skills coach or attending a seminar on 'How to make friends and influence people without lifting your head up.'

I was disappointed to find an attractive, attentive and professional female receptionist had replaced my old adversary.

'Hi there, I booked a room facing away from the street?' I said.

'Which room please?' asked the young receptionist.

'I am in the Dundalk room.'

'But Dundalk faces street.' She frowned as she looked at her computer.

'I know that now, but I requested a room facing away from the street.'

'The Dundalk room faces street, I'm so sorry Mr Kavanagh,' she said.

'Can I move to a quieter room please?'

'Of course,' she said.

'Thank you.'

'Don't mention it.'

'And can I have a room where the phone works?'

'Of course,' she said.

'Thank you.'

'Don't mention it,' she said.

'Can I have a quiet room facing away from the main street, where the phone works, with hot water and things like that?' I asked.

'Not a bother. We'll move your luggage over. Don't worry about it; we will take care of it for you.' She rang a bell and smiled at me.

'Thank you very much, that's very kind, thank you,' I said.

'Don't mention it. And by the way, your guide is waiting for you outside. He's just finishing his cigarette,' she said.

'It's only just gone eight o'clock.'

'Sean is taking you on Temple Tour?'

'Yes.'

'One of the best guides on the island. Are you doing the Tenements Tour?'

'What's the Tenements Tour?' I asked.

'It is what we market as a Poorism Tour – which is new and very popular – to show tourists how people actually live,' she said.

'Okay, well, that sounds very interesting. Thank you for all your help.'

'Don't mention it. And Sean, what shall I say?' she asked.

'Can you tell him that I will be here at exactly half-past nine as we agreed yesterday? And thanks,' I said.

'Don't mention it. You didn't like your massage yesterday?'

'She said that?'

'You want maybe I call Myla and you try again?' She suppressed a smirk.

'It was fine, thank you.' I lied.

'Perhaps yesterday you felt stressed, no?'

'We'll leave it for today.' I may well have been blushing by this point.

'It happens to a lot of men,' she said.

'Great.' I began to chew my bottom lip.

'Would you mind filling out a short survey?'

'Not right now. Maybe later,' I said.

Sean was still waiting in reception at 9.30 when I came downstairs. The temperature in the hotel foyer was typical of countries where air-conditioning is used. There is a reason why everyone has a cold and suffers from respiratory problems – and it's called air-conditioning. The cold countries' air-con is always set on *too hot* in any hotel foyer and, conversely, any foyer in a hot country is left on *freezing*. I have a family member whose hotel room in Dubai was so cold only Inuit chambermaids were prepared to tidy it.

When the receptionist saw me, she mumbled something to Sean, and he grinned. I am sure I would have laughed too but my cold had made me feel lousy. Sean chipped his cigarette and walked towards his car.

''Tis himself,' said Sean who was wearing his red Kiltours T-shirt.

'How are you?' I asked.

'I'm grand. So are you ready for the Temples Tour?' Sean and I started walking towards his car, a slate-grey people-carrier. 'We're just waiting for one more couple,' Sean said.

'Where are they from?' I asked.

'They're English. They're from your hotel.'

'And is that it?' I had hoped to be on my own.

'Yep, for today,' he said. 'So you happy with the hotel?' Sean drummed his fingers on his steering wheel. He smelt of cigarettes.

'It's okay,' I said.

'Did you get your head down?'

'I did but the sheets are made out of pumice stone and the pillows are made from the recycled inner wrappers of cereal packets,' I said.

'Should have tried the Robert Emmet, best on the island,' he said.

'You're right.'

'You didn't like the massage then?' he asked.

'How do you know about the massage?' I asked this a little too quickly.

'I've known Myla all my life. She's great – she's like family,' Sean said.

'The massage was fine.' I wanted to finish the conversation before the others got on board but I was too late. The English couple opened the car door and threw their backpacks in.

'Yes, you were probably just a little stressed with the travelling and all.'

'Do you mind if I sit up front? It's much more better. Is that all right?' said a middle-aged Englishman as he began to clamber up into the vehicle. He seemed to want to sit down where I was without letting me get out first while his wife got into the back and fidgeted with her seat belt.

'Not at all,' I said. I got out and sat in the back next to his wife. They were dressed from head to toe in matching tropical suits and open-toed ethnic sandals.

'I am Richard, and this is my current wife, Lesley,' Richard laughed.

'So where are you from?' I asked.

'Saddleworth. You know it?' Richard asked.

'Nope, afraid not. Where's that?'

'Dobcross?' said his wife, still struggling with her seat belt.

'Sorry. Still don't know it,' I said.

'Dobcross. Near Saddleworth?' Richard said. I was baffling him. I looked quizzically at Lesley.

'Tell him, Richard,' she said.

'Doesn't know Saddleworth? It's near Oldham,' Richard said.

All the car stickers carried the same messages: 'Undertakers love overtakers' and 'Better to be a minute late in this life than a lifetime early in the next.' There seemed to be a causal relationship between belief in the afterlife and the frequency of suicidal car manoeuvres. There were many different offerings to the gods manifest in the form of lit candles, brightly coloured petals, rosaries and prayer beads. They were all swinging around so much they filled entire windscreens. Besides which, drivers in Kilrush don't use their eyes. Why use your eyes when you can rely on your horn? I am not a nervous passenger, nor a religious man, but the only thing I said on this journey was 'Jesus' and 'Christ, that was close'. In desperation, I turned to Sean for guidance.

'Jesus Christ, well done for avoiding him. What's wrong with people?'

'They drive mad over here, and that's the truth,' said Sean.

'If you think this is bad, you should go to India or Vietnam,' said Richard.

Lesley nodded her head.

'Why do they have lettering all over their car doors? Why is that?' I asked.

'They have to by law; every driver has to have his blood group on the car door.' Sean stared at his cigarette packet on the dashboard. 'Driving over here is mad expensive, car insurance in Kilrush is 20 per cent of the price of the car,' he said.

'How do they get their driving licence, they can't drive?' asked Richard.

'There is a saying in Kilrush; you only need three things to get your driving licence: a good horn, good brakes and good luck,' said Sean.

As soon as I knew that driving standards were a national joke and that I hadn't been singled out for personal attention, I began to relax. The tooting of the car horn in Vilanculos was used in a different manner to home. In Kilrush you toot in an assisting fashion, for example:

1) You toot to tell the lorry that you want to go faster.
2) He (the lorry driver) toots back to say he has heard you.
3) You toot to overtake.
4) You toot to thank him.
5) He toots to reciprocate the thanks.

We drove past the branch of EFU Bank where I had changed my money into Kilrush punts, down Pearse Street, left along Casement, past St Stanislaus the Splenetic and onto Connolly, towards what Frottager called 'the largest concentration of places of worship per capita per square mile in the world'. I had been to a number of countries claiming to have the largest number of churches, Jamaica to name but one.

The main drag was affectionately called Freak Street. Every manner of purple-garbed weirdo was promenading up and down looking for business. Even charismatic religious leaders need to serve their apprenticeship somewhere. Old-age-pensioner travel groups swooped from one side of the piazza to another as they hunted the sadhus down. They moved like a flock of pigeons, all white hair and nodding heads.

'You haven't seen sadhus before, then?' asked Richard.

'Not here, I haven't,' I said while I looked out of the window to avoid conversation with the pair of them.

'You're kidding me, right?' Richard said.

I shrugged my shoulders and looked out the window.

'We've seen loads. We've been all over. We've done Machu Picchu, India, North Dakota. Lesley went to a dental spa in, where was it, love, Doncaster or Sheffield?' Richard said.

Lesley rubbed her feet where her sandals had rubbed against her, and applied some ointment. 'Doncaster,' she said but didn't look up.

'That's right. Lesley went to some fancy dental spa in Doncaster to get her porcelain veneers done and got talking to her dental therapist who did all this type of destress, detox, chakra journeys and whatever. Said she loved it. So for her birthday we went off and booked into an ashram for a spiritual journey.' Richard turned round in order to engage me.

'Are you on a spiritual journey on this trip?' I asked.

'No, it's just a holiday this one,' said Lesley still rubbing her feet.

I looked away from Richard who was scratching his nose.

'You want to try it. Opens your mind, it does,' said Lesley.

'Really,' I said.

'You could sense the aura of Anandamayi Ma just by walking about,' she said. Sean was trying to clear his throat unsuccessfully.

'Aura of who? Where?' I asked.

'I don't rightly remember. You know, like a mystic or whatever,' she said.

'And did you?' I asked.

'No, we couldn't, but I think we were just unlucky with the room,' she said as she re-applied some ointment to her feet.

Sean bought the tickets for the three of us for one of the main temples; I think it was Tanna, where I had to take off anything that was made of leather – belt, and shoes, even my water carrier. I was blessed with saffron and pestered for a donation. A crowd gathered around me, including the guy who I had to pay to look after my water bottle. I gave him a five Kilrushi-punt note; he held up the note like a bank cashier and looked devastated. As I walked away, his friend offered me some kind of musical instrument for sixty punts. I said 'No thanks,' so he pulled his sad face. By the time I opened the car door, he had reduced the price to ten. I didn't know whether it was funny or not. I suppose it was no more preposterous than my job. Thinking about having to go back to work made me fretful.

Sadhus have always fascinated me. Anybody who is supposed to ferret around in the River Ganges to get their hands upon a human skull so that they might clean it up and use it as a bowl for food and begging gets my respect. I am sure many of them are deeply religious, selfless, altruistic, philanthropic ascetics; it's just the ones I've met are always holding their hand out. Freak Street was choked with them. Sadhus outnumbered tourist photographers by about ten to one. It was like wading through Lyle's Golden Syrup. It was only when the coaches spat out their contents that you saw anybody *not* dressed in purple, palm-outstretched, with silly string and stuff tied to their matted hair. They carried off this look while trying to appear as stoned as roadies at a Wailers reunion gig. It was Sadhu Central as they moved down Freak Street, hoovering up any gestures of goodwill they could along the way, like a swarm of locusts chomping their way across a field. Standard tourist fare in Kilrush meant getting your picture taken with the maddest, purple-clad fruit bat you could find. The ones who performed mutilating acts on their manhood were the highest paid. You didn't need to look for them, they came looking for you and signalled their availability by tugging your forearm. This happened if you turned your head to avoid eye contact.

I eventually caved in to a particularly persistent wild-eyed individual who charged me twenty-five punts for a single photograph. He had harassed me for ten minutes before I bought him off. He was tallish with a greying beard that reached his chest. He wore a purple and white striped woollen hat, was dressed in orange robes, had eight necklaces of varying length and a walking stick shaped like a snake, which was covered in purple cord. He wore new Oakley sandals. He posed by the entrance to the main temple and walked off halfway through having his photograph taken. I asked Sean to retake it, the sadhu asked for more money and I offered to forget it. This was not an option according to my new mystical mate. I had been unlucky to end up with the only sadhu who had served as an intern at the World Bank.

I wanted to walk around Freak Street without Richard and Lesley. As soon as I heard Sean say 'here we have the Coronation Islands Calcium Carbide factory believed to be the seventh largest in the world,' I felt restless. I left after Richard from Saddleworth tried to name the other six. I travel around the world trying to make sense of it all, but, as soon as I catch someone trying to teach me something, I turn off. But at least I found out about St Stanislaus the Splenetic: Padua in Italy, I am told, has the tongue of St Antony, and Drogheda in Ireland has the charred head of St Oliver Plunkett; Kilrush has the spleen of St Stanislaus.

Freak Street was full of advertising hoardings: promoting Ryan's skin-whitening products for Asians, Nolan's hair straighteners for blacks and Kehoe's sun cream for whiteys like myself. There was a steakhouse that sold nothing but fish and a tyre shop called *Friends Don't Matter*. This year's big sellers were the snake foetuses in glass bottles. I didn't see anyone selling metal pin badges for my Tilley hat. Groups of beautiful Asian girls tripped over pavements while checking their reflections in shop windows. They rode side saddle on bicycles; families of four rode on a single moped, while all around echoed the sound of tooting horns and expectorating tourist guides. Up the hill, on Nuts and Bolts Road away from Freak Street, and in the main ecclesiastical quarter, there were two cathedrals facing one another. Both had been built and extended many times, both were called St Pat's and both looked down the hill towards Freak Street. The Catholic branch was stuffed full of statues of the Virgin Mary while the Anglican one was decorated with burnt, ripped or disfigured Union Jack flags brought back from former military campaigns. I entered the cathedral, genuflected, lit a candle, said a prayer and sat in the front row. The cathedral had a soaring nave and a huge pipe organ. I was looking up and admiring the Gothic revival architecture when a fella approached me to see if I could spare some change. I gave him some and left.

The only discernible difference between the two cathedrals was the number of drunks, with the Catholics beating their Anglican rivals by five to two. I made sure I put the same amount of change in the Anglican box. Both sets of supporters hid behind the back of the church and away from the punters entering from the front. It was called the Nuts and Bolts Road not because of the attempts by successive architects to make St Pat's Catholic Cathedral look more imposing than St Pat's Anglican Cathedral or vice-versa, but because both churches were built on the same road as the main psychiatric hospital, St Ruth's, and the prison, Long Mesh.

About 5 per cent of all Kilrushi become monks and go and meditate for three years, three months, three weeks and three days in splendid isolation up in the mountains somewhere. They get about thirty punts per week from the government, which is enough for a daily meal of rice, oil and chillies. But if a monk gets married and is caught, he has to either pay back the equivalent price of twenty-five pounds sterling, or, alternatively, cajole every monk (there can be up to a hundred monks in any one community) to lash him with a leather whip and spit on his back. It sounded like a soft lad's version of my Jesuit prep school.

I decided to do some more scribbling upstairs in a café overlooking the main piazza on Freak Street. You had to walk up two flights of stairs, with a wonky, wooden banister rail. The walls were daubed in orange paint. Few of the light bulbs worked. Frottager had talked it up and, as a result, it was stuffed with eco-worriers, brat-packers and tourist guides showing a glimpse of the real Kilrush. I needed a coffee and sat down only to be told it would take twenty minutes to prepare. I couldn't help but be impressed by how much care and dedication the café was willing to put into my coffee. The waiter was brusque when he realised I wasn't going to order food until I had drunk a coffee so I left.

I heard and smelt a group of prostrating pilgrims before I could see them. They were the out-of-towners who Sean (you see how I missed him) said have a festival once a year where they bathe in the waters in Sneem, which is famous for its spiritual and medicinal powers. The travel-stained pilgrims made a noise like a swarm of bees.

As I was waiting for my 'Turkish' coffee, I read Frottager's: 'Education was introduced into Kilrush in 1976 but there were no teachers to teach and no books.' I was mystified as to why the ecclesiastical capital of the world had not introduced education earlier. I thought about the effect compulsory education had on my life. The best I could come up with was education means you think Laurel and Hardy is based on Cervantes' *Don Quixote*. This would be *Don Quixote* translated from Spanish into English because, unlike Sean, I can only speak English. The thing with languages is you can spread yourself a bit thin. I concentrate on speaking one language as well as I can rather than a whole load of them badly. Did I tell you I was lazy too? Perhaps if I had needed to speak another language, I would have learnt one. I did Latin, French and Russian at school, which was great if you wanted to talk to a really old Roman, make an enquiry about where you could get a *plume de ma tante* or hail a cab in Paris. The only Russian phrase I can remember is 'Can I have a vodka please?' and the last time I used it I had to be carried upstairs to the sixth floor of the Hotel Arktika in Murmansk. If I had to master another language, I am sure I could. It's a lack of necessity rather than anything else.

Further along Freak Street was a yellow-painted café-cum-restaurant with a MasterCard canopy hanging outside it. The waitress approached my table, which was the only occupied table at lunchtime. She wore a cap with a MasterCard logo.

'Do you take MasterCard?' I asked.

'No take MasterCard.'

'But your cap has MasterCard on it, as does your awning,' I said as I pointed to the awning and then to her cap.

'No take MasterCard,' she said.

'Ever wonder why you no take customers?'

'No take cards only cash.'

'No take my cash only take my cards,' I said.

I walked along to a crêperie I had spotted earlier but it was closed. I went to a place called Art Sushi; it was open for art but closed for sushi. I went to a place I had rejected earlier due to its appearance and unappetising menu. I thought 'go local' and had a cheese-and-ham toasted sandwich served in a see-through microwavable wrapper. I washed it down with a bottle of fizzy water to get rid of the after-burn.

I went back to the hotel to see if they had changed my room. My least favourite but eminently slappable receptionist at La Hermita was holding the fort. I knew that because I had the foresight to peer behind the counter to discover him reading Dan Brown's *The Da Vinci Code*. 'Hello?' I said. He looked up but did not acknowledge me. We looked at each other. And then we looked at each other for a bit longer. I hadn't played a game of blink for years.

'So?' I asked.

'So?' he repeated.

'So today have you changed my room to what I asked you for yesterday when I checked in?' I asked.

'Sorry?'

'I expect so; I would be; apology accepted. Have you changed my room?'

'Let me check.' He fiddled about with some papers while avoiding eye contact. 'Yes. Your bags have already been moved for you,' he said.

'Thank you. Please thank the professional receptionist who worked here this morning. She was very good, very helpful,' I said.

'You want massage today?'

'No, thank you,' I said.

'You don't want to try again?'

'No, thank you. But can you send a doctor up to my room? Thank you.'

My chum smiled as he dialled a doctor right away. But then he knew I wasn't going up to my room until he did.

CHAPTER SIXTEEN

Down At The Doctor's

The new room looked similar to the old one except it was not as nice. It was dark and had a smaller bathroom but it didn't face the street. What it did have was a Kilrushi version of a Golden Labrador, who was feeding her puppies, sprawled out on her back under a red sap tree in the courtyard. Feeding time took place immediately below my bedroom window.

After twenty minutes or so, I answered my door to meet a grand old chap who was a Tibetan doctor. I liked him immediately I saw him. He said I had smiling eyes. His medical shtick consisted of checking my pulse while getting me to stick my tongue out. He took my pulse in ten different ways while nodding each time and muttering when he saw the state of my tongue. If I'd known, I would have scraped it clean after my toastie. He asked me if I had been having headaches (yes), mild stomach cramps (yes), sinusitis pains and problems with my lower back (all yes). He diagnosed a mild form of respiratory malfunction (a cold) and stomach problems but added I had a good constitution.

He proceeded to measure out any number of medicines (gunshot-like pellets) that all essentially looked the same, and put them into assorted see-through plastic bags. He gave me herbal pellets for headaches (three per night for three days), round tablets for my stomach (two to be taken with every meal three times a day), little brown balls for my sinusitis (one every day after breakfast) and slightly larger tablets for my lower back (three a day before breakfast for two months). He seemed less of a witch doctor than my GP in England, who answered any question with 'I just don't have any time today. You'll have to make another appointment.'

Having changed room and met my local doctor, I was feeling a bit jet lagged. I fretted that if I fell asleep I might not wake up and end up sleeping all day. I felt I should be doing or seeing more of the town, and when the dogs below my window started to bark, I had no option but to make myself head out for the afternoon.

Having taken the Temple Tour, I was toying with the idea of taking the Tenement Tour the next day. I was nervous about making a booking in case I bumped into the couple from Saddleworth. It had been mentioned in my guidebook, and there were flyers in the cafés. The idea behind the tour was most visitors went to the temples, photographed sadhus on Freak Street, got the obligatory picture of them outside Tanna Temple and then, having *done* the temples, left Kilrush never to return. The idea behind the Tenement Tour was to see how and where people actually lived, or, as it said in the brochure, 'to get a taste of poverty behind closed doors'. It sounded a delicious way of whiling away a few hours.

Liberated by not having to rank, in descending order, the world's leading calcium carbide producers, I decided to visit the mystical waters in the district of Sneem, which was within easy walking distance of the hotel; that is, you come out of the hotel turn right until the road forks and keep going on the left and follow the crowds. These waters are imbued with medicinal and mystical powers. I splash on Holy Water when I go to Mass so it all made sense to me.

The noise of the tuk-tuks and the car horns, and the waft of fried food from the street vendors, mingled with the smell of decomposed rubbish under every footstep. Black ink squirted from the exhaust pipes of the multicoloured lorries. This made me feel abroad. In England, you don't find lorries carrying bricks with a hand-painted picture of a lotus; nor with *Horn Please* stencilled in orange and white lettering on a garish pink background on the back of the wagon.

Sneem is, in essence, a stretch of river whose waters have been credited with spiritual and health properties. Followers of various religious sects want to be cremated on the riverbanks at Sneem. The only thing they want more is to live, but that's not always an option, if only for health and legal reasons. There were many bands of free-range pilgrims prostrating themselves along the road to Sneem. This made it a perfect place to sit down and people watch. Kay would have loved Frottager's description of Sneem as 'a cornucopia of organic architecture in celebration of one of nature's most alluring settings'. I missed the voice that Kay used to put on. According to Frottager, holy men believe you needed to wash in the waters at least once in your lifetime. Many people believe, myself included, you should bathe every day irrespective of whether you enjoy easy access to Sneem or not. Even though the temperature was at least thirty degrees centigrade, the pilgrims, wrapped in what looked like sleeping bags around their waists, prostrated themselves, put their hands together in prayer, kissed the ground, took their shoes off, prostrated themselves, put their hands together in prayer, kissed the ground and repeated the process until they got inside the temple. People as devout as this are beyond mockery. I just hope they're right for their sake.

I knew as soon as I saw and smelt the pilgrims I was going in the right direction. The more I saw and smelt them, the more I became concerned the pilgrims were going in the wrong direction, noticeably with regard to personal hygiene. You wouldn't want to cremate a loved one and be downwind from one of these little stinkers.

I took a left turn at one of Kilrush's most celebrated tourist attractions, which, as everyone knows, is the hand-painted roundabout. This is the only roundabout on the entire island. A smartly dressed gentleman, in black boots, white belt and a dark blue beret, blue shirt and matching trousers, blew his whistle and waved his white-gloved right hand like an extra in a Michael Jackson video. It was like having to shepherd a flock of mosquitoes. The Kilrushi driving community preferred to rely upon their tried-and-tested, honk-and-holler approach. Whenever a driver saw the traffic cop waving at them, whistle in mouth, they would reciprocate accordingly by tooting him back in acknowledgement. This meant you couldn't actually hear the whistle, which must have been frustrating for the gentleman entrusted with the job of blowing it. It couldn't have been noisier if it had taken place under a tin-roofed shelter for parakeets during the mating season.

Every time I tried to cross the road, a family of four on a moped would swoop past, clip me and toot. Someone who was hauling fresh fruit to the market pulled his load over my feet, and I almost got knocked over by a lad with a chest of drawers strapped to his scooter. It was fabulous. I hadn't been as excited since I tried to cross the road in Hanoi.

Some auld fella took my arm and helped me across the road, like a lollipop man for the nerve-shredded and needy. No words were spoken, just an exchange of smiles, a nod of the head and then he disappeared over to the other side of the road and carried on along the way. I felt humbled by this random act of kindness. There's nothing more difficult to fight against than a stranger's kindness.

It was marginally less busy on the − not really a road, not really a path − route to the magical waters. You could tell the Irish influence everywhere by the road signs pertaining to Sneem's final standing in the bi-annual Tidy Towns competition. Sneem had finished Best Runners-Up.

The walk down to the waters took me past the street vendors selling spices, mainly different shades of red but also yellow, ochre, cerise, fuchsia pink, orange, purple, black, powder blue, cornflower blue and dark navy, lime green, mid-green and dark green. They sold king-size Rizlas in blue and red, quite a bit of hippy beadery and metal pots for the candles that family and friends placed in the water alongside the burning ghat.

The houses were decorated with yellow, green and red chillies that dried upon the corrugated iron roofs, the primary colours contrasting with the dirt, the peeling paintwork and the decay of the timeworn buildings.

There was no hassle by the waters, which made a change from Freak Street. My technique is to buy some old tat so when a hustler tries to sell his tat to me, I can whip out my tat and try to sell that tat to the guy who is trying to sell his tat to me. I'll give you an example: a vendor tries to sell me, say, a hippy necklace for forty Kilrushi punts. I then produce a wooden pop-up frog, which is priced to go for one hundred Kilrushi punts. The vendor forgets where he is with his sales pitch and finds himself disgusted by my ridiculous price. Within a minute or two, his brain feels it cannot compute the information and he decides to give me the slip. This allows me to go about my business without being hassled. He tells his mates, 'Watch him, he's a nutter,' and they avoid me. I meander about without any trouble. Job done.

The whole place was full of flaky buildings and unfinished pavements, streams of God-knows-what, yet everyone I saw seemed spotless. Bala Ram and Ranesh offered me a guided tour in French, Spanish or English. I chose the tour in perfect English. They told me they didn't beg. They were only about twelve or thirteen years old. I cannot remember whether they were brothers or friends. Bala Ram was taller than Ranesh and was trying to cultivate a moustache. He was dressed in a stripy smart-casual shirt worn outside his slacks. Ranesh, who was the less formal of the two, wore a T-shirt advertising an insurance company. He stuffed the T-shirt into his jeans, which I thought was a curious sartorial move to make. We talked football, the West, prices, Hinduism and, of course, the ancient river of Sneem. Neither of them could understand why I was travelling on my own.

CHAPTER SEVENTEEN

Spoonful

I was beginning to feel homesick for Turtle Bay, for a place that wasn't home, where I'd only stayed a couple of days and had got sick. I missed my little chats with Caesar about foreskin embroidery and bowing at elderly Japanese gentlemen. I decided to do what I always did in that situation and went out for a drink. It dawned on me I couldn't remember whether I had seen a turtle in Turtle Bay or not. I walked around Vilanculos for a while unable to decide where to go. I began to think I didn't have time for a drink before supper. I didn't want to be too late back to the hotel in case I wanted to book the Tenement Tour. I decided to go to the nearest place Frottager could recommend. It was then I realised I couldn't read the section on Vilanculos restaurant tips in the dark and the best place for light was a bar. By now, I didn't have time for a drink. Besides which, I didn't like getting my guidebook out in public places because I didn't want to look like a tourist. The implication being, if it weren't for the third edition of Frottager's *Guide to the Coronation Islands* (2009), everyone would assume I was local.

I panicked into the first place I came to, a place called Mavzoley Lenina. I knew before I sat down I had made a mistake. I've always believed you should judge a book by its cover. You couldn't see the inside of the eatery from outside. By the time I went inside, it would be rude to turn on my heels and run for the hills. Perhaps I was too hasty in judging a Lenin mausoleum-themed diner. It was a cavernous place and the tables were set as if they were expecting a sudden onslaught of coach parties. How disappointing it must have been for the proprietors to only have a handful of the local depressives scattered around their dimly lit restaurant. This was the sort of place where lights are turned down low not because of the ambience of mood lighting but to keep the costs down. Waiters eyed me suspiciously as I repeatedly changed tables. I change restaurant tables like a Vegas card shark asks for a new deck to change his luck. It doesn't.

After a while, a waiter swooped from out of the gloom, cleaned the plastic-coated tablecloth with a piece of rag and asked if he could take my order from a menu only slightly longer than the US President's Christmas card list.

'What can I get you from the carvery tonight?'

'An à la carte menu, please,' I said.

'As you like.' He wiped the menu with a deft swipe of his soiled rag.

'Do you do beef stroganoff?' I asked.

'We are known for our lamb shashlik,' he said.

'Do you have any stroganoff?'

'Hold on please.' Five minutes passed, there was shouting in the kitchens. 'I'm afraid we cannot do tonight.'

'Okay, can you do a chicken Kiev?' I asked.

'We do the best lamb shashlik in Vilanculos.' He looked up at the ceiling.

'Can you do chicken Kiev?'

'One moment please,' he said. Five minutes passed, there was shouting in the kitchens. 'I'm afraid we cannot do tonight. The lamb is good.'

'Can you do a chicken shashlik?' I asked.

'We do best lamb shashlik in all Coronation Islands,' he said.

'Lamb shashlik would be great. Thanks.' Another five minutes passed, more shouting in the kitchens.

'I'm sorry, not have lamb, chicken is all right?'

'I'll have a starter and see what I fancy,' I said.

'Starter?' He looked at the ceiling again.

'What do you have? Sorry, I meant what do you recommend?' I asked.

'Hot, sweet and sour soup.'

'That'd be lovely.' After what seemed long enough for a scrap involving most of the kitchen staff, my hot, sweet and sour soup arrived. I put the spoon down after one mouthful.

'You finished?' he asked.

'Yes, thank you. Lovely,' I said.

'You no like?'

'No, no, really, it's fine,' I said.

'You no like?'

'Well no, not really,' I said.

'Why you no like?'

'Because it's not hot, it's not sweet and it's not sour,' I said.

'You like to see our main course, our specials?'

'No, thanks. I'm fine.'

'And our ice creams?' he asked.

'Sure, what have you got?'

'Today we have avocado, sardines with brandy or gherkin,' he picked up his pen to write the order down.

'I'll just have the bill. Thanks.'

'As you like,' he said while removing the menu from my hands. I felt liberated as soon as I left the gastro-mausoleum. This condition can affect the single traveller. The trick is to call the bill over and to repeat this request to anyone walking past your table. It is quicker to splash the cash, but you might have to spend more time with guns pointing at you in a Forex bureau while having to explain why one of your notes has been folded. If you really want to leave the place, and you've asked for the bill but it still hasn't materialised, just go and hover by the till. This signals to the other diners you have to wait a long time to settle the bill. This conveys the impression of poor service, which will influence customers' tips, which in turn produces instantaneous results.

I didn't have much time in Kilrush. I had eaten a cheese and ham toastie for lunch and eaten supper at a Lenin mausoleum-themed restaurant. It dawned on me that apart from my natter with Bala Ram and Ranesh, I hadn't really got to know the land of my forefathers, so when I got back to the hotel I booked the Tenement Tour with Rushtours for the following morning.

I nipped in for a nightcap, which I hoped would help to deaden the noise of the dogs underneath my bedroom window during Happy Howling Hour. Douglas was behind the bar, the couple from Saddleworth were drinking and were, as they say, full of rubber. A couple that looked Indian or Pakistani, but could have been Bangladeshi or Sri Lankan, walked in, dressed in salwar kameez and sat down.

Douglas was telling me a story about when he arrived back in the USA after a tour of duty in Vietnam. All-conquering military heroes were not the flavour of the month at this time. Thousands of anti-Vietnam protestors went to demonstrate at the airport. Douglas and his pal were walking along just outside the airport terminal, while protestors screamed abuse at them. They were still wearing their military uniforms when some student screamed 'You murderous bastard' and spat throatily in Douglas's face. A policeman deliberately turned around to avoid watching Douglas's mate punching the phlegmatic student. He then turned back and said to both of them, 'Welcome back to the USA.' I asked Douglas what was it like killing all those women and children in Vietnam? Douglas said no one went out to kill women or children; it's just the men could run faster.

The couple from Saddleworth were drunk. He wore a baseball cap to cover his thinning pate. I watched him engage the Asian couple in conversation.

'So how long have you worked here then?' Richard asked. He looked at the Asian man and pointed at him for clarity.

'We don't work here. We're guests,' the Asian man answered.

'You speak very good English,' said Richard.

'Thank you,' said the Asian man. Richard offered to buy the couple a drink but they declined.

'And your wife, does she speak English?' Richard spoke to the Asian gentleman while Lesley hoovered up the bar snacks.

'Yes, I do,' said the Asian lady.

The Brit from Saddleworth didn't look at her and continued to speak to the Asian gentleman. He was smiling but quite drunk.

'You, your English is very good,' Richard pointed at the Asian man's wife.

'Thank you,' she said.

'And your wife, her English very good,' Richard said again, pointing at her.

'Thank you,' the Asian man nodded politely.

'And you, where did you learn English?' Richard asked.

'At Oxford,' said the Asian man.

'Oh, at Oxford. In England? I know Oxford. I'm in haulage, you know, fixtures and fittings for the aeronautical industry. Yeah, got my own business. Yeah, not doing too badly at all, as it goes,' Richard said.

'Oh,' said the Asian gentleman, barely suppressing a yawn.

'So, Oxford, where do you work? At Cowley, the big BMW plant where they make all the Minis?' Richard asked.

'No, at Oxford when we were students. My wife and I did the same course at university,' said the Asian man.

'Oh, right,' said Richard. He gulped down the rest of his lager. 'Fuckin' Paki snobs, the two of them,' he said.

CHAPTER EIGHTEEN

Paradise City

I ate in my room to avoid looking at a balding middle-aged man from Saddleworth wearing a baseball cap at breakfast.

My new gnat bite was on the side of my left palm. It puzzled me that in the twenty-first century, when you stayed in a boutique hotel in a town famous for its temples, you still had to put toilet paper in a bin because of the plumbing. If man could erect temples centuries ago, surely man could rid himself of human waste.

I flicked through the *Kilrush Chronicle*, which was full of price information about ecclesiastical licences, letters to the editor moaning about the mooted change of the name of the airport and vacuous pictures of regional sales executives from CIA at a reception to celebrate the opening of the new St Kitt's–St Pat's route.

At ten o'clock I went downstairs and waited for my tour guide to pick me up from the hotel before going on the Tenement Tour. After five minutes or so, I recognised Sean ambling through reception. We walked along to his jeep. Sean was wearing his favourite red Kiltours T-shirt.

'How are you, Jack?' Sean said.

'Very well, thank you.'

'You happy with the hotel?'

'It's okay,' I said.

'So, are you ready for the Temples Tour?' Sean asked.

'The Temples Tour? We did that yesterday, didn't we?'

'Jesus, Mary and Joseph,' Sean cussed while he struggled out of his red Kiltours T-shirt and pulled out a dark blue T-shirt with a Rushtours company logo from behind the jeep's sun visor. 'Right, sorry for that. Now we're set,' he said.

The continuous drone of the traffic was punctuated by the shrill tooting of horns. We picked up socially aware but uncommunicative punters from other guesthouses and hotels while I sat in the back of the open jeep. A Korean gentleman snapped away at his fellow passengers as they climbed aboard. The outside of the jeep was covered in rope and painted in camouflage colours. Everybody spoke in a hushed whisper with a minimum of acknowledgement.

We drove past Long Mesh prison, past St Ruth's Psychiatric Hospital and stopped in Freak Street where Sean insisted on showing us around the local market. The market looked like every other market in the world. People were selling fruit, vegetables, pug-ugly fish with staring eyes, fly-infested meat, brightly coloured plastic buckets and washing-up bowls. This was, according to Sean, where the locals bought all their produce. There was no evidence of any locals buying any produce whatsoever. There was, however, evidence of locals selling produce to tat-happy tourists who were stretching their legs during a comfort break in Freak Street, before visiting the seventh largest calcium carbide plant in the world.

Having been estranged from yet more Kilrushi punts, we spent most of the trip shuffling around the market playing a game of hide and seek with Hans the German. I have no idea what his name was; I just called him Hans the German. Hans, a short man in his late thirties, was dressed in oversized sunglasses, and had black hair and a pockmarked face. He had been picked up at the last hotel, an unprepossessing blue building with security gates. He insisted on giving both the jeepsters and Sean the slip at every opportunity. Sean asked the Korean man to help trace the missing German with his surveillance equipment. I know this because the Korean showed us on the viewfinder of his camcorder. Within seconds, we found the German on the viewfinder. He was caught buying terracotta souvenirs. When we got back to the jeep, Hans the German sat with his back to us.

Was it only twenty-four hours ago that I was trying to do exactly the same thing as my German friend? I had run off into the sanctuary of the Catholic cathedral because I was suffering from calcium carbide information overload. I think Hans the German was just trying to give people the slip, and I could understand why he wanted to do this. There cannot be anything more awkward than being shepherded around a buzzing market. (I am trying to avoid the word *vibrant*.) I insist on travelling independently so being herded together was abhorrent to me.

I outperformed my peer group at shrugging off unwelcome interest from hawkers. It brings out the marble-hearted in me. But there was one question that got me to turn around and respond. And that was the dreaded, 'Where are you from?' I have no idea why but of all the opening conversational gambits from all the traders in all the towns around the world, 'Where are you from?' has always been the most difficult to ignore. I have travelled around hundreds of smelly, busy markets and souks but I have never heard a better opening line. I suppose it's painfully obvious where the lad, sitting on his haunches, is from. 'Where are you from?' metamorphoses into, 'Are you here on holiday?' And the next moment you're waiting for your change while they pop it in another blue plastic bag.

We headed off down Connolly, past Casement, past the spleen of St Stanislaus along Pearse, drove past the EFU Bank branch where I had changed money, and pulled up a couple of doors down.

The Tenement Tour was marketed as an unforgettable experience if you are looking for an insider's point of view. It was also marketed as instructive, educational and safe and less voyeuristic than other *Poorism* tours. Sean dropped us off outside the tenement. Lead us not into tenement and deliver us from Sean. Sean said he wouldn't come inside because he wasn't known to the people in the area, had done the tour a couple of days ago and, besides which, he fancied a Starbucks.

Sean introduced us to Gerardo, from Rio de Janeiro, who had previously owned an upscale favela tour company. He had been a pioneer in the early days of rich pickings. However, the arrival of new market entrants meant cutthroat competition, the slashing of margins and a price war. Gerardo had made a lot of money from the poverty game but had sold out to one of his competitors and was now looking for new business opportunities. He'd only been in Kilrush for about a year and a half but fitted in well and was much liked – even by the thorny young man in the sunglasses and NBA basketball top holding the firearm at the top of the stairs. He didn't look old enough to smoke, let alone carry a gun. The tenement was the only one on the street with barbed wire outside. Graffiti artists must have targeted it too, as it was the only building with murals that I saw in my time on the island. Both of the bottom windows had been boarded up. They had made a neat job.

'All you hear about this area is violence and poverty,' said Gerardo.

I didn't know that; I had no idea at all. It wasn't in Frottager's. Gerardo wore a bandana and smoked Red Marlboro like the original cowboy. The beat box played hip-hop CDs. It was disappointing how all the young lads were aping the gold chains, gold teeth and shades look imported from the States. The people staring at us were evidently upset about something. Perhaps they had shorted the gold price at the same time Gordon Brown had sold Britain's reserves? I could never understand how poverty and jewellery got along so well. These kids were wearing more jewellery than a darts player's wife. At least Gerardo didn't bother talking to us as if he was trying to mix some decks.

'Given the area's bad-ass reputation, this will give you a much better understanding of local society, and the day-by-day life here in this township, favela, slum or tenements, as we call them here in Kilrush. We call them tenements because of our history. And you guys know your history, right? Well, Dublin, which is in Ireland, had some of the worst living conditions in Europe. The people there lived in buildings called tenements.' Gerardo nodded his head for quite a while until we nodded back. He continued: 'After the potato famine, as some of you may know, the Irish fled. The British sent some of the Irish to Kilrush as what you'd call indentured labour. That means slaves, right? Some of the Irish fled to Glasgow in Scotland where they lived in buildings in slums. These buildings were also called tenements. We have pictures on the walls here of those tenements in Dublin and Glasgow. So yeah, take a look. There are prints available so please write down the number on the sticker on the front of the pictures. The turnaround on the pictures is only forty-five minutes. It's done with high-specification laser printing and costs thirty punts. We also have some nice distressed-looking frames available.' Gerardo pulled a wad out of his low-slung back pocket to indicate he could change money. His pitch went on: 'So, what has all this got to do with here? Well, like Dublin and Glasgow, Vilanculos is a city of contradictions. I would like to talk about security, the local infrastructure and other aspects of tenement living. At the top of the stairs in this tenement, there is a local terrace where we can meet Mick, who is a tenement dweller, see his house, you can use the toilet, buy a soft drink, pause for pictures, yes, Kwang-Su... and for camcorders, a breathtaking view over the city. There will be some times when you can video or photograph and some times when you cannot. I will tell you when you can and when you cannot. This includes mobile phones. Then we will walk through the community, where we have an option to stop for a drink, look at a handicraft centre, and we'll finish off by giving you a chance of making a real contribution to our community school. Any questions?' By now, nobody was paying attention to Gerardo as they were focusing on which tenement souvenir to buy for the folks back home.

'What do they have in the handicraft centre?' asked Hans.

'I'll show you later, but don't worry.' Gerardo wasn't comfortable with interactive pitches. I wanted to ask how much we had to pay on top of the tour price for tips and contributions. I noticed all the prints on the walls were of tenement slums in their heyday; pictures of startled kids with food around their mouths and no shoes. Kwang-Su insisted on recording most of the tour and waved his hand violently if anyone spoke. This affected the quality of his camerawork making him even more upset. Meanwhile, the German gave away chipped terracotta souvenirs to bemused passers-by. We left when youths started to throw the terracotta back towards the jeep. We were still only 150 yards away from where yesterday the sadhu had collared me to take his picture. I looked out for him but he was probably working nights. We got back on the jeep after spending a pleasant morning on the urban deprivation tour. Kid Kalashnikov waved at us and said goodbye in French, German and Korean. He was happy with his tip. The ringtone on his mobile was 'If I Were a Rich Man'.

It was awful. I felt ashamed of myself for going on the tour. Would I have been disappointed if I hadn't seen any real poverty? How poor did I want the people to be, for me to think the expense of the trip was worthwhile? Would it have been worth it if babies were dying of malnutrition and their mothers had to sell their bodies to strangers to feed their young? If Kay had been alive, I wouldn't have gone on the tour; she would have refused to go. She would have said it was like feasting on poverty. I felt more sorry for myself than for the people I met in the tenement. And I felt less sorry for the people who lived there than my fellow passengers. At least the tenement dwellers were being resourceful whereas the jeepsters just got off on gawping at them. Like I did.

I was free for the rest of the day and decided to plot up at Sneem. Bala Ram and Ranesh, who were still not at school on yet another weekday, were in the same place where I met them last time. When anyone saw me with these two chaps, they just formed a queue while I doled out the cash. It sounds silly but I'm not as concerned about being tucked up as I am about the manner in which it's done. The Kilrushi street traders had a fantastic way about them. It's like bull fighting in Spain: you know who you want to put your money on, but it's the technique that draws the crowds. The stallholders in Kilrush were charming even though I was being mean. But my studied misanthropy was no match for these boys.

'Where you from?' asked an Arabic gentleman fingering his prayer beads.

'London,' I said.

'Chelski, Tottenham or are you, by the way, a Gooner?' He flashed a smile that could have defrosted an icebox with the fridge door shut.

'I'm a Chairboy. Wycombe Wanderers,' I said.

'Tell me, sir, can you bend it like Beckham?' He'd hooked me. As a courtesy, he just wanted me to splash about for a few more minutes before reeling me in. He knew. I knew. He knew I knew, and I knew he knew. 'Come see. Looks see,' he said.

'Thank you,' I said.

'Looking is for free,' he said.

'Thank you.' I was wondering what was the quickest and cheapest way of escaping.

'You want I show you more?'

'No, no. That's fine,' I said.

'Buy a little something, please my friend,' he said.

'I've got no money left; all your mates have had it.'

'Buy something today or it is very bad luck for me. You are my first customer. I make you special price. Special rate today for Chairboys only,' he said, swishing his prayer beads like a cow's tail.

'How much for these black leather belts?' I asked in a shrill voice.

'Yes, please, best quality.'

'How much did you say?'

'You like the quality, yes?'

'Yes, very good,' I said.

'Two hundred and fifty punts only.' He said.

'Two hundred and fifty punts?' I said.

'Yes, good price,' he said.

'Nah.' I was trying to avoid making eye contact with him.

'Okay, how much you pay?'

'Fifty,' I said.

'Sorry, my friend. One hundred and fifty only. This is good price. You cannot buy this quality at that price,' he sounded serious.

'A hundred,' I was supposed to do this for a job.

'Sorry, my friend. One hundred and twenty-five only. Very good price.'

'A hundred,' I said.

'Okay my friend. You are, what we say, a fussy onion. You buy one like this for a hundred, and you pay no more, yes?'

'Yes. A hundred. Last price,' I said.

'Okay, my friend. You win.' He reached up and pulled out an identical black belt out of another box. He said, 'Okay, you win. A hundred. You want to buy leather hat, wallet, shoes, leather jacket, presents for your family? You like something for your wife, or maybe your mistress? You want I make you good discount? Please looks see. Looking is for free. I make you special price, my friend.'

I had now exhausted my shopping quota for the week and returned to the ghats where Bala Ram and Ranesh were plying their trade with a young female student. I'd only been to Sneem the day before but it felt, without wanting to sound mawkish, like I was going home. Up to now everything I had seen was different to every other day, it was comforting to return to a place I'd been to. I knew the score as to where I could sit and where I was most likely to be left alone. I walked past technicolour spices, the 'Hello, my friend, looks see' stallholders and followed the narrow path down to the water. The buildings were smoke-aged with corrugated tin roofs and hefty, hand-carved wooden doors. I sat down in the same place I had sat down before and stared at the burning ghats. Kleptomaniac monkeys watched people washing their hair in the river. Whenever I saw people washing their hair I always thought of Kay.

The smoke from the ghats was odourless. Apart from the click of the camera shutter or hushed video commentary, Sneem was a tranquil spot, the only place where you could escape the tooting of the horns. People went about their daily business; most of the people attending the cremations sat quietly staring at the flames. Some chatted in an animated fashion. Other visitors were gazing into the distance. I'm embarrassed to admit that the tourists, like me, were lined up on the other side of the water to get a 'good' view of the ghats. The good thing about going more than once was you didn't feel the need to snap away at anything that moved or had recently stopped moving.

It was the best place I'd been to so far on this trip to the Coronation Islands, by a long way. I was happy to while away the hours, jotting notes in my Red and Black notebook. The rest of the time was spent people-watching while keeping an eye out for monkeys trying to nick my pen. These monkeys made my ex-wife look trustworthy. When they weren't thieving from tourists, they hopped about with their young on their backs, preening each other or cooling themselves down from the sun with a swim. I began to think there are worse things in the world than being cremated by the waters in Sneem. As a pink-faced Westerner, my concern was whether I was experiencing a voyeuristic kick out of being in such an outlandish location where bodies burnt. I wasn't used to this. It wasn't our way. Death for me was a man in black sprinkling water onto a damp, freshly dug grave where fellow mourners hang their heads in pseudo-religious piety while snuffling up their tears. The bizarre thing is I don't remember friends and relatives crying by the ghats. I'm not for one moment saying they didn't cry but what I am saying is I don't *remember* people crying. Maybe they shed their tears before the cremation and not during.

I don't know whether travel narrows or broadens the mind in spite of my exhaustive enquiries. In fact, the more I travel, the less certain I become about anything. Did I think, for example, this was hardcore travelling at its very best? Was this vista the reason I bothered my arse in going halfway round the world, frittering away thousands of pounds, just to get a glimpse? Was I only buzzing because I could imagine the pay-off?

'*So where was the best place you went then?*'

'*Well, I can't say the best place. But certainly one of the most amazing places was the burning ghat at Sneem. Where you'd just sit down, chill out, and the monkeys would nick your pen, while women would do all their washing only a few steps away from a burning body.*'

Perhaps I thought burning ghats were cool because I had been there, hung out and could tell people about it? This, in turn, would make me cool for having experienced them. Was I feasting on other people's poverty and the misery of family loss merely to make myself more interesting, and therefore more desirable, at dinner parties? I was anxious about what my motivation was for travel. Was I just another collector? Some men were ground-hoppers, that is, men who liked to tick off as many football grounds as possible. Some men liked to bring back big game and stick body parts up on the wall as a souvenir. I couldn't help but feel that it was something to do with competitiveness. I wanted to go to more countries than other people. But why? And by joining the Travelers' Century Club, what would I prove? And to whom? And wouldn't I know more about a country if I actually spent some time living with a family rather than gadding about from one multinational hotel company to another? Take the Aspire Hotel Group; I have stayed with them in Doha, Qatar, the Maldives and Mauritius. I think I travelled to more countries to make myself more interesting to potential partners. In another era, I would have learnt to play the piano or dance the foxtrot. Perhaps my whole obsession about running around the world was to do with my fear of standing still. Perhaps I was happy to pontificate upon my experiences abroad because it was easier than thinking about my history to date at home. Perhaps I could only understand what home was from the perspective of travelling away. *I know I must be this because I know I'm not that.* I know I'm a Catholic because I know I'm not

Jewish, Muslim or Protestant. Or is it the case that the more you travel, the more you realise that actually we're all the same. We all like giggling babies, fluffy animals and, most of us, like football. Disquieting thoughts are a bit like mosquito bites, they come and go only to be replaced by new ones.

CHAPTER NINETEEN

Sunny Afternoon

When I travel, it is the minutiae that stay with me. I can remember the two guys by the river in Sneem, both dressed in white and wearing flip-flops, smiling and joking as one of them shaved the other one's hair off with a yellow plastic cut-throat razor. I think it was because the lad having his head shaved had just lost his father, but I couldn't swear to it.

When you travel around Europe, you never really see anything, as everything happens behind closed doors; in Kilrush everything happened on the street. I can remember turning a corner by the waters to find a brother and a sister standing under a street sign with a blue background and white lettering. She was about six, and he was about eight. She was holding a lamb in her arms, while he carried his younger brother on his shoulders. None of them wore any shoes. I had spotted the little girl with the fierce eyes and the matted hair earlier. She had been squatting in the street. Her faeces looked like spaghetti.

The street sign said *SAVE OUR SELF-ESTEEM* and, under that, it said *DO NOT ENCOURAGE BEGGING* and, under that, stood the kids. It wasn't the first time that day that I had seen shoeless kids with unwashed faces. Under the street sign, another newer sign said *Champak Restaurant – Inside the Changu Temple*. Bunches of cobs of corn were hanging up to dry and tied next to the sign. It was my last afternoon in Sneem and in Kilrush. Realistically, I would never return. In my heart I wanted to find somewhere that captivated me so much I wouldn't even entertain the idea of going to another place. It would be pointless, as I would know I couldn't possibly enjoy anywhere as much as my 'special' place. There was a part of me that was quite jealous of people who had already found their 'special' place. Could you find a special place without a special one? Another part of me thought they were dumb. And another part of me was jealous at their contentment.

Perhaps it was the thrill of the chase and the lust for the unknown that attracted me. Maybe contentment wasn't to be found in a place after all. Then you start thinking, it isn't the place but the process you enjoy – the self-deceiving thrill of thinking you can go anywhere. But then you can't do that either. Some countries don't like you coming (Turkmenistan), some places you wouldn't like the food (Mongolia) and some places you just don't fancy (Saudi Arabia).

How could I say I was genuinely moved by what I saw in Sneem while knowing I would never return, when, in the next breath, I say how much I was looking forward to Fulgary? I headed back to my hotel. The stallholders were rearranging their merchandise under the harsh strip lights as I moseyed back. It struck me as strange how a place you have only visited a couple of times could feel so familiar.

Mr Personality hid behind reception and looked at me as if he'd never seen me before in his life. I'd never met anyone like him before in my life either. He half-mumbled a semi-sentence, something along the lines of Sean calling me back at six-thirty that evening. It was difficult to hear what he said as he was looking down at his book and trying to communicate without moving his lips. Or at least, he did the first few times when I asked him to repeat what he had said. Returning to La Hermita in Kilrush, to point out Mr Personality, so my pals knew I wasn't just making it up, suddenly seemed like a very good idea.

CHAPTER TWENTY

Out On The Floor

Sean called me promptly at six-thirty. I was hoping he would. I had just showered and was watching CNN and needed some good news. Wycombe's match was over and I couldn't get the score. CNN didn't cover League Division Two.

'Hello, Jack?'

'Hi there, Sean, how are you?'

'Not too shabby. And yourself?'

'Fine thanks,' I said.

'Wycombe Wanderers drew.'

'Brilliant. You don't know who scored?' I asked.

'No, but I can find out if you want,' Sean said.

'Don't worry. Fantastic news.'

'Grand. And what will you be doing tonight?'

'No idea whatsoever but not eating in mausoleum-themed restaurants.'

'And you'll be leaving tomorrow?' he asked.

'Yep,' I said.

'Would you fancy a look round the town, if it's your last night?'

'I'd love to. That's really kind,' I said. I meant it too.

'Not a bother. My wife's away anyhow. Pick you up in an hour.'

'Thanks a million, Sean.' I hadn't known what I was going to do on my last night in Vilanculos, but I knew nothing would be as interesting as a night out with someone who lived there. Tourists create their own trail, and places become tourist hangouts. So when a visitor asks a local where they should go, then the local recommends a place on the tourist map. If only because they know the place is popular with tourists.

I granted myself some new clothes for the occasion. As I said earlier, I had packed my linen Vilebrequin shirt with the navy background and pale blue leaves and the red, orange, yellow and purple hibiscus. A linen shirt can only be worn once before it looks like you are wearing a scrunched-up crisp packet. I wanted to save it for best and anyway I wasn't taken in by the repeated promise the hotel would return my laundry before I left in the morning. (This was the second evening the hotel had promised to return my laundry.)

I now felt awkward about being snotty to Sean about pick-up times. There is nothing more undermining to a man's bolshiness than a stranger going beyond the call of duty. I had misjudged him. Kay used to give people the benefit of the doubt. I took out some extra cash to lavish upon Sean, hopefully over endless rounds of drinks.

He bowled up on time, and we settled the arrangements for my departure in the morning before going out. It was understood by both of us that, if any serious stuff needed to be done, it would be best to get it sorted out early on and before the drink kicked in. He wore a brown bomber jacket, pale blue shirt and purplish slacks. He drank pints of lager and washed them down with rum. He wasn't overly concerned with drink driving as he had his horn if anything untoward happened. I asked him about policemen; he said only jealous men became policemen and you mustn't spend the rest of your life worrying about them.

We went to a roof-terrace bar overlooked by a neon sign advertising Mirnov Vodka. A band played very loud music that sounded like a Bangra-Irish folk fusion. The band consisted of a lead guitarist/vocalist in a rather fetching check shirt and a bass player who faced the vocalist but not the audience. There was a long-haired lad on the smallest Yamaha organ (I'm tempted to say pocket organ), and a bespectacled lady in a flowing green top sat doing nothing. After another round of lager and rum chasers and large gin and tonics, Sean and I bellowed out the chorus.

There were a handful of other lads, but no girls, with us. They danced along to the music while grinning a lot. There was a big sign saying *No Dancing Please*. The security staff took these lads by the arms, in an incredibly polite way, and escorted them off, still smiling, and away from the dance floor. As soon as they were led away by security, they returned still smiling and still dancing. Security proceeded to do the same thing again but with sterner faces. These men were haunted by the fear someone somewhere was having better fun than they were. We laughed our heads off knowing that, according to Sean, more men die of caution than die of excess.

Leading off the roof terrace was a dining room with tables laid and all set up for tour parties. The only thing missing were the tour parties. Sean was an astonishingly good drinker and very amusing in a self-deprecatory way, quite unlike his fact-obsessed tour-guide persona, and after a few shots of arak, washed down by a few more beers, I nearly drank my tears laughing.

We somehow ended up back at his house for a couple of nightcaps. I was flattered to be invited. He drove along unlit roads. I had no idea where I was in relation to either my hotel or to where we'd just been. I was at Sean's mercy.

The outside of the house was painted white. The house was square, with barbed wire and broken glass that ran along the top of the walls. In the basement, as I remember, his beloved dog's room was bigger than the maid's room. I think I had been invited back to see his house because I had told him I loved dogs, he said he had a dog at home and asked if I'd like to see it. I met Sean's gorgeous daughter, Aiofe, who was about seven or eight, I think the dog was an Alsatian, or a similar breed which I don't like, and I don't remember meeting the maid. But if the dog was there and Aiofe was there and his wife, Anne, was away, then his maid must have been there too.

Anne worked as an air-stewardess for CIA and was flying from Frankfurt to London. Sean adored his wife and carried pictures of her in his wallet.

The remarkable thing about visiting this house was how similar it was to Western European ones; intricately woven purple and red carpets, orange curtains, a chest of drawers with bottles of drink on it, sofas with white lacy throws and orangey chairs. The only surprising feature was a mural that took up an entire wall in the lounge. The mural depicted a white wooden bridge over a waterway and thick lush vegetation by the water; it may have been mangrove, and palm trees. The trees were bowed with orange flowers, but they were not orange trees, there were white clouds and above that, a purple-blue sky. I asked Sean if he could take a picture of me standing against the mural. (I didn't take many pictures of myself in the Coronation Islands; there didn't seem any point.) Sean asked me if I had family at home. I told him I had an ex-wife and a daughter in a home that I bought in England but they shared it with my ex-gardener. He asked me if that was why I travelled on my own. I told him about when Kay and I were on holiday and went on a *Jolly Roger* cruise ship and how I was still struggling to get over Kay and how perhaps if I changed jobs, I might be able to meet new people and move on. Sean said I shouldn't feel guilty. I asked him if he would feel guilty if the same thing had happened to Anne but he didn't answer the question, just nodded thoughtfully, hauled himself out of his armchair and went for a piss.

After a couple more last drinks and a couple more last-one cigarettes, Sean dropped me off back at my hotel. I wobbled into the bar but Douglas wasn't on duty, much to the relief of my aching pancreas. I clutched the banisters, hauled myself upstairs and fell asleep.

CHAPTER TWENTY-ONE

I Don't Want To Be Nice

I had a phone call in the middle of the night asking if I was still Jack Kanganey. And when I said, 'Yes,' they hung up. In my drowsiness, I thought Kay might have been trying to contact me. I was waiting for the phone to ring so I couldn't get back to sleep. I was so tired the next morning I put verruca lotion in my eye and not eye drops. I was convinced this would burn a hole in my retina and render me blind. I thought about arriving in the hundredth country on the day I lost my sight in one eye. What was God trying to tell me about my life? What was his message? Could I have done more to help Kay? Perhaps I could write a book about my adventures and the loss of my sight and draw a parable from the two but it dawned on me I wasn't absolutely certain what a parable was. Besides which, it wouldn't sell; people want biographies of famous people, books with at least one death in them or books by famous writers. What the blue blazes does the world want with a book about a parable, written by a bloke who doesn't actually know what a parable is? The numbers didn't add up; it wasn't commercial.

On the plus side, it was likely that if I was going to go blind it would have happened in the time I had spent worrying about my impending blindness and my prospects of publishing a parable about my life and crimes. I had bathed my eye immediately and washed and washed and washed it, and nothing had happened yet. On one hand, I had recovered my sight, but on the other hand, if I hadn't been such a klutz, it wouldn't have happened in the first place. I was paying the price for my chummy euphoria of the previous evening.

I would like to tell you about the excitement, satisfaction and thrill of being on the verge of arriving in my hundredth country, and thus ensuring membership of the Travelers' Century Club, and my enthusiasm and eagerness for the day ahead; I'd like to but I can't. I had a shocking headache, my guts were all over the shop, my eyeballs felt as if someone had been rubbing an etching on them and, worst of all, my hotel room felt far too hot.

I had to pack up my gubbins and check, recheck and check again my hotel safe. I had to ensure all relevant papers (passport, flight tickets, travel vouchers, travel itinerary and cash) were stored away in my hand luggage. I had to sort out which hotel staff would get a tip (and how much) and make sure I had the right change to pay them in punts. I had to work out how much to pay the bellboys and the baggage porters at St Pat's airport. I had to tip Sean. I had to change cash back from Kilrushi punts before I arrived in Fulgary. I had to check and pay my bill. I hoped that Sean wouldn't oversleep and prayed my flight to Fulgary would be on time. And I still hadn't got my laundry back.

'Hi there, some idiot rang me in the middle of the night, asked me my name and hung up. Do you know who it was?' I asked the receptionist.

'I'm sorry Mr Kearney. I only started my shift at breakfast,' she said.

'Please prepare my bill as I'm leaving shortly.'

'Oh, that's a shame; we hope to have you back as our valued guest again some time soon. We hope you've enjoyed your stay as much as we've enjoyed having you here with us.'

'Oh and another thing, I've been asking for my laundry on and off for a couple of days now, any risk I can have it back before I leave?' I said.

'Certainly, Mr Kearney. May I ask if you've already received it?'

'Of course I haven't,' I said.

'Certainly, Mr Kearney. May I ask, by the way, do you know if it is outside your room?'

'Why would it be left there for Christ's sake?' I asked.

'Certainly. Because we didn't want to wake you up. We left it outside. That is maybe why we called you, to check you were in your room,' she said.

'Okay, you win,' I said.

'Very good. Well, have a nice day and we hope to see you again sometime in La Hermita and that you have enjoyed your stay.'

After a busy breakfast served in my room, an overly long tepid shower, two headache tablets and three bottles of fizzy water, I saw some signs of improvement. Things went as well as could be expected allowing for my health. I paid my bill and was disappointed to find they hadn't overcharged me. It is satisfying catching people overcharging you, if only to compensate for all the times you don't. Sean showed up on time and, by now, thinking had taken over from talking. It was now I remembered he told me last night that Mr. Personality, who was employed to hide behind the reception desk, was, in fact, his wife's brother. I couldn't recall whether this had come out before or after I had told him what I thought of him.

Last night, we were two mates, and, today, we had reverted back to guide and client. This suited me, as it required less talking and less thinking.

Sean helped me to get my luggage checked in. We said goodbye, and I pressed the last of my Kilrushi notes into his palm during the farewell handshake. I promised to keep my eyes open for his wife on my flight back from Fulgary to London Heathrow. Sean gave me his business card, and we shook hands again. I felt sad. I was already on my penultimate flight and the last page of my travel itinerary. As something of an added bonus, and because that's what they did for domestic inter-island flights anyway, I was to take a small plane to Fulgary. Connections between the different Coronation Islands were not great and, if I missed my flight, I was stumped. It isn't easy getting in and out of the Coronation Islands; even specialist travel operators advise caution when they make bookings. This remains the single biggest reason why the islands attract such a paltry number of visitors per year and why hardly anybody has ever heard of them. God knows how people get to the more remote outlying islands. And if I did miss my flight from Kilrush to Fulgary, I would spend my birthday, on the 26th, on my own. This was not an option. It was taking the whole solitary traveller shtick a little too far, even for me. Small aeroplanes, which were booked well in advance, compounded the problem. I had to arrive at the airport check-in at least three hours before departure even though it was still classified as a domestic flight. Government officials weren't averse to appropriating the planes for themselves at short notice or abandoning the schedule altogether. And with the stories I'd heard about passengers being double-booked, I arrived three and a half hours before departure. Time dragged by like a drunken tortoise until it was half an hour before our scheduled take-off.

It is always about this time, the imminent must-get-on-first-or they'll-kick-me-off-the-plane time, that I begin to hover by the departure gate. I lurk by the stewardesses and try to eavesdrop on their walkie-talkie conversations. I am, at this critical stage, looking at my watch. I scrutinise the faces of the stewardesses to see if I can pick up any non-verbal clues as to which gate we'll be using and the time of actual rather than projected departure. I revert to tutting mode while turning around to see if I can rally some other tutter's tutting support. On this occasion, and probably just to annoy me, the plane is five minutes late in being called. While admittedly I don't have another appointment for some days, I'm still miffed. Maybe I'm just not cut out for this type of adventure and should just accept it. But I did need to get home before my birthday. The prospect of spending it on my own was too much for me to bear.

Kilrush airport has only one runway, which is, by local by-laws, supposed to be cleared of livestock before any take-off or landing. I could see some goats nibbling grass out of the large window next to the departure gate but I couldn't see a plane. I asked the young lady with the walkie-talkie what time we were likely to leave. She didn't know. I asked her if the plane was in the air or was it still stuck in Placentia. She didn't know. I asked her what the problem was and she said technical difficulties. I asked her to explain what those technical difficulties involved but she didn't seem to know that either. I asked her to find out from the person she was talking to on the walkie-talkie but she turned her back on me and walked away. She must have answered some questions during the interview process to get the job in the first place but showed little interest in answering any more. I sensed my forensic line of enquiry was beginning to be every little bit as irritating for my fellow passengers as the delayed flight, so I moseyed around the shops again. For an hour, if you include a coffee.

The reason why the plane island-hopped to Kilrush was to fly on to Fulgary so passengers could catch the connecting flight back to London Heathrow. I was trying to remember whether I would have to fly back to Placentia and then on to Heathrow, or whether it would be better to fly from Kilrush to Colombo in Sri Lanka, and from Colombo whether to fly back to Heathrow with either Sri Lankan, Qatar or British Airways. We were already seventy minutes late when I heard a muffled message on the bing-bong saying something about the plane soon to depart to Fulgary, and jostled to get in the queue ahead of my fellow travellers.

The domestic fleet of CIA were all twin-propeller aircraft. We boarded the small plane; the twin propellers started up – we were off – and then the propellers stopped. We were asked to disembark by an overly cheerful, helpful, charming and smiley air-stewardess. This was serious. It was obvious, to me, that the 'technical difficulties' that had caused the delayed arrival were now so serious that the plane could not be reasonably expected to depart for Fulgary without causing a significant risk to the safety of passengers – which would leave me stranded in Kilrush. The domestic fleet had the world's second worst safety record, losing only on a points decision given to Air Cubana. The pilot had to ensure the plane would arrive at its destination in daylight.

Some eighty-seven minutes past our scheduled departure time, a lorry came up and plugged itself into our plane. As this was Kilrush, I was able to stand on the runway and light a cigarette ten yards away from the plane and chat with the passengers; all of whom were totally unfazed by what was happening. I tried seven times from the phone box to ring Dave Carroll to ask how much a helicopter would cost from Kilrush to Fulgary but the line was dead. I couldn't think of anything more pitiful than spending my birthday on my own. No doubt the resort would bring me out a cake and horsewhip the staff into singing 'Happy Birthday' but the visual image was too ghastly to contemplate. The wreckage of a previous flight two months ago lay by the runway but, as one of my fellow passengers remarked, at least it wouldn't be the same pilot. I had another cigarette not because I fancied one, or needed one, but because I knew I would never be able to smoke a cigarette ever again, on a runway, while waiting for my plane to be fixed. And, just as I stubbed it out on the tarmac, the still smiley stewardess stood next to the cabin door and ushered her guests onto the plane. We dined on Guinness stir-fry, poiteen-flavoured crisps and chicory coffee, all of which tasted delicious. I was about to land in my one-hundredth country.

Part Three

'Caelum non animus mutant qui trans mare currant,' which, loosely translated, means that no matter how far away you travel, you are always stuck with yourself.

HORACE

Part Three

CHAPTER TWENTY-TWO

Happy Jack

Fulgary's airport was upmarket, clean and new. It was different to Placentia and Kilrush. There weren't any NO SPITTING IN TERMINAL signs, the trolleys worked and I was the third person to get my luggage from the carousel. My idea was to trade up in terms of comfort: from the twitcher's lodgings in Placentia, the boutique city centre hotel of La Hermita to the sun-drenched, fine-dining-ridden, goose-feathered-pillow-infested, rustic luxury of Omanalak; the only resort in the Coronation Islands featuring in the top hundred list in *Living the Dream* magazine. I was fascinated to see whether Fulgary's fantasy island matched up to its website.

'Mr Kaganagh?' said a sour-faced, teenage stick insect, dressed in a burgundy shirt with epaulettes that was two sizes too large.

'Who?' I thought he must have been the resort's meeter and greeter. I pushed the trolley over to him and began to dump my hand luggage on it.

'Mr Jack Kaganagh?'

'Yep, that's me.' I fancied a long, cool drink. Somebody had got my name right. I had arrived in Fulgary – my hundredth country. All I had to do now was to flop onto the pinkish sands of Meelick Beach.

'Please follow me,' He wasn't there to assist me with my luggage. While he pronked off ahead, I had to keep one eye on him while making sure the luggage didn't fall off my trolley. Mr Epaulette opened an unmarked door, walked in and sat down behind a spartan desk made of cheap, utilitarian timber. Meanwhile, I struggled to manoeuvre my heavily-laden trolley into a tight, unergonomic space. There was no place for me to sit, and I hadn't been invited to do so. I was pinned up against the wall by my own trolley.

'Mr Kaganagh?

'That's right again. For the third time,' I said. His mouth was turned down at the sides so I dropped the smart-aleck approach.

'Where do you live?' he asked.

'South Bucks, just outside London.'

'And what do you for a job?'

'Trader at Fundamental Securities. Has something happened?'

'So why do you say you live in Graceland?'

'I don't know what you're talking about,' I said.

'Are you a radio ventriloquist or not?'

'No, sir,' I said. He slid the form I had handed in on arrival in Placentia over the desk. He had trimmed the hair on his knuckles and kept his nails clean.

'Why are you here?'

'Vacation,' I said.

'On your own?' His eyes didn't believe me.

'Yes. I was going to… I had always planned to come with my, my… something else cropped up.' I said. The man with the crew cut and the smeary glasses wrote everything down, looked up at me, stood up, left the room and locked it on the outside as he did so. He then checked the door to make sure the lock was working. What the hell was I going to do now? The room was windowless, airless and consisted of two chairs and a table. The only thing that was missing was a swinging lamp to interrogate me. I hadn't bargained on this reception. I didn't fancy a strip search. He must have to wash his hands regularly if his nails were anything to go by. Over fifteen minutes later, the same official unlocked the door, looked at me and kept his arms folded. He didn't look very jolly for a kid in a big man's shirt.

'You know it is against the law to fraudulently fill out a disembarkation form?' he asked.

'Yes, sir. I am sorry. I was trying to be funny,' I said.

'But it isn't funny, is it? It is illegal and a very serious matter. You are going straight back out the same door you came in,' he said. 'We can't let you in with this disembarkation form, can we?' He waved the form at me.

I bent my upper body at a thirty-degree angle and held my posture for what seemed like ages. I was bending from my waist while keeping my back straight and keeping my hands flat against the side of my thighs like a Japanese senior executive taking a deep bow at a press conference to demonstrate remorse. I did not move or speak. I maintained my posture.

'Get up,' said the official.

'Thank you, sir,' I said.

'You cannot enter Fulgary with this form.'

'I apologise unreservedly to both you and your fellow officers and offer my sincerest apologies and ask that I might be permitted to fill out a fresh disembarkation form. I am very sorry I behaved in this way. Please help me. I'm travelling on my own, and if I don't get into Fulgary then I'll miss my return flight and have to spend my birthday on my own, miles away from friends and family. I am truly sorry. I apologise profusely to you, sir. Please excuse me.'

He moved his right arm in an expansive gesture like a matador, a matador who was about to kill a dumb, defenceless animal. He read me the riot act while I tried to look earnest. Meanwhile I scanned the room for latex gloves, apologised again with what, at least superficially, looked like genuine remorse and promised to show more consideration for public officials, especially airport officials, now they find themselves, as he said, on the frontline in the war against terror. He muttered something under his breath, looked at me without saying anything and told me to get out of his office. He had left the key in the lock. I couldn't turn the key to open the lock, and I had to ask him to help me. I left after bowing repeatedly like the elderly Japanese granddad I'd met in Placentia. I couldn't reverse my trolley out without running over Mr Epaulette's toes. It was like the crowded cabin scene in the Marx Brother's film *A Night At The Opera* (1935). I rubbed the back of my hairline; it was damp and cold.

CHAPTER TWENTY-THREE

Or: So What?

I looked around to see if I could find my driver. I was looking out for someone with my name on a piece of card who would whisk me away. A woman in her late twenties approached me as soon as I got through customs. She led me into a room with a mahogany reception desk, fresh flowers and attentive, smiling people. Guests were enjoying complimentary foot massages while they waited for transport to the hotel.

'If you'd like to follow me. Please leave all your belongings, including passport, hand luggage and anything else here. Everything is secure. We are the only resort on the island, so please relax and enjoy a drink of your choice and cold towel.'

She wore a blue and yellow uniform, a wonderful smile and had great teeth. I looked and smelt like a bagman; I scraped my pinkish face with an ice-cold flannel and sipped what tasted like ginger tea. She insisted I shouldn't carry anything apart from my camera and introduced me to a toothy, smiley driver in another blue and yellow uniform. The interviews for new staff must have been conducted only upon receipt of a set of dental records.

After a fifteen-minute drive up a vertical track, the jeep stopped. I was handed over to a gentleman whose rubbery, lined face Walt Disney would have felt compelled to draw. He shook my hand for too long and handed me a red jumpsuit and a white crash helmet. I'd decided to arrive at Omanalak, on Meelick Beach, by paragliding down and landing on the beach. It was undeniably the most glamorous manner in which to pitch up in my hundredth country. The game was to put all my gear on (which my grinning friend checked twice), making sure my camera was properly tied to my wrist, concentrate on whatever my instructor was saying and run as fast as I could off the mountain, or at least the highest point on the island, until, please God, I was airborne.

I had done this before in Gorenc in Slovenia and Rio in Brazil with Kay and felt it was the answer to the question as to whether it is better to travel than to arrive; as daft a question as nature versus nurture. It depends... I was attached to the flying machine and to the pilot. He ran through the instructions once more then I ran as fast as my fat little legs could carry me. I had just run out of mountain when the wind yanked us up into the air. It's something to do with thermals and how birds fly. Below me I could see birds flapping. All I could hear was the quiet and the wind. I didn't want to land. I wanted to wander about and go wherever the wind took me. I was not in any rush to rejoin the knots of little people on the beach below. We floated around for as long as we possibly could. I looked at the sea, the palm trees and the corrugated roofs. I aimed my camera at nothing in particular. And while a camera could never recapture the sensation, I knew this was one of the highlights of my trip. I felt even more euphoric when I moved the paragliding cords away from my testicles.

I preferred floating around up in the sky to being in a London office from 7.30 a.m. to 5.30 p.m., Monday to Friday. But if I hadn't spent 7.30 a.m. to 5.30 p.m. Monday to Friday in London I wouldn't have been able to afford (don't ask) the fifteen-minute paragliding check-in at the Omanalak. The conversation revolved around my repeated use of the word 'amazing' and how my fellow paraglider thought Norwich City Football Club would bounce back at the first attempt.

We covered a lot of ground in fifteen minutes. Meanwhile the ground itself rushed up to meet us. There are two things you have to remember with paragliding and they are: a) run as fast as a butcher's dog at take-off; and: b) when you are about to land make sure those legs keep running when you hit the deck. Having gone arse over tit in both Gorenc and Rio, I landed perfectly on Meelick

Beach. I forgot my arak-induced hangover. I was surprised to find people clicking away at me with cameras straight out of a 1940s' film noir.

I feel uneasy about having my photograph taken. How anyone could be comfortable in front of a camera is beyond me. Whenever anybody says 'Smile' or 'Cheese', I straighten my back, push my hair around to no effect whatsoever and refuse to adopt any form of facial expression apart from one that says 'Just put the camera down and nobody will get hurt'. But give me a couple of drinks, and I'll pull silly faces for you all night. I looked quizzically at the goons with the cameras until they realised I wasn't a celebrity and didn't like having my photograph taken.

I thanked Walt for getting me down safely to the hotel beach. He flashed a toothless smile (the implications of which only dawned upon me later) and bowed his head. He touched his heart through his tunic and disappeared. It transpired later the launch pad was one of the most difficult places to paraglide from. The problem with Fulgary is it is not quite high enough. The resort management had made a special effort in landscaping terms to build up the highest point. This enabled the paraglider to be able to catch the gust and land safely on the pink sandy beach. My instructor had been one of the stars of the 2009 Mun Gyeong Paragliding World Championships in Korea. It had been a privilege to have my balls bruised by such an expert.

The photographers lolled about outside by the beach, smoking and waiting for the next arrival while I checked in. While the paragliding had been worth the extra expense, I now wanted to go straight to my room to freshen up. Or delouse, in this case. It dawned on me I had no money, passport or luggage. This was something of a departure for me, as I usually like to arrive clutching my valuables. The hotel voucher I had been instructed to hand in at reception upon arrival was in my hand luggage; the hand luggage had been left somewhere on the island with a lady wearing a yellow and blue uniform whose name I had forgotten.

Resorts like the Omanalak on Meelick Beach don't want new arrivals hanging about the front desk, puffing and panting and trying to grab somebody's attention. They know on holiday, as in life, you don't get a second chance to make the first impression. I was greeted by a row of smiling faces and gravitated towards the young lady with the serene face.

'Hello, Mr Kaganagh, won't you please sit down? My name is Celia, Assistant Reception Manager. She touched her heart through her uniform like a football player lining up before the national anthem. Welcome to Omanalak Resort, here on Meelick Beach, in the beautiful Coronation Islands. Please enjoy one of our non-alcoholic refreshing drinks; you must be tired after your journey. I see you decided on our Celebrity Check-in Option,' she said.

'A what?' I asked.

'Our Celebrity Check-in Option,' Celia said.

'What is that? I asked.

'It is when our guests choose to arrive by paragliding onto the beach. And please, Mr Kaganagh, help yourself to another cold towel,' Celia said.

'What's with the blokes with the cameras?' I asked.

'Some of our guests like to feel like a celebrity when they check in so we have our own in-house paparazzi service. We have a lot of honeymoon couples, and they like to compile a DVD of their holiday here to show their friends when they get back home,' she said.

'What about if you have a guest who doesn't want to feel like a celebrity?'

'Then we would look after him too,' Celia said.

'What happens if you have a celebrity staying who doesn't want to be treated like a celebrity?' I asked.

'We would arrange that too. Would you like a personalised DVD?'

'No, thank you. I'm just here to relax,' I said.

Another slim lady, dressed in a neatly pressed yellow and blue uniform, handed me another cold towel with a pair of silver tweezers. She conducted the manoeuvre with the concentration of a heart surgeon during a transplant. When she took the towel away, she put a garland of flowers round my neck. This hadn't happened to me since Yasawa Island, in Fiji, with Kay.

My registration form was served on a silver salver engraved with the logo of the resort. The entire form had been filled in for me. Correctly. The form required only my signature to be complete. From nowhere and out of earshot, another member of staff swooped and presented me with a Mont Blanc silver pen. This happened before I had sent my brain a signal that I needed a pen. Given the merciless heat (heat in these countries is always *merciless*), I could have sat there for a couple of days. I wanted to steal the Mont Blanc pen. It would have made a great souvenir; I couldn't believe I had forgotten to buy a pin badge of Fulgary for my Tilley hat at the airport.

'Would you like a bag for your shoes, Mr Kaganagh?'

'What for?' I asked.

'Here at Omanalak, our guests tend to put their shoes in a bag. You don't need shoes as we provide you with barefoot luxury. Most of our clients come back every year and find they don't use shoes. We have Arthur who cleans the beach and paths three times a day, seven days a week. Of course, if you want to wear your shoes, it is entirely up to you. No problem, Mr Kaganagh,' she said.

'Okay, brilliant.'

I popped my shoes into the linen bag and scrunched my less than fresh socks into my back pocket to avoid causing offence while another blue-yellow massaged my feet with a hot towel.

'Just to confirm, you are a First Year? Is that correct Mr Kaganagh?

'I'm what... sorry?' I said. So much money spent on my education yet so little to show for it; my inarticulacy was beginning to bore me.

'A First Year, as in – this is your first time with us?' Celia asked.

'Yep, First Year,' I said.

'No problem, Mr Kaganagh. Most of our guests, almost 85 per cent, by the way, are repeat guests, and we like to reward their loyalty with small things, like allowing them free use of bicycles around the island, making sure they are happy with the table they had last time they stayed and, whenever it is possible, fixing them up with the same cabana, house butler and serving staff. So they feel like it is home from home,' Celia said.

'And what if you're not?'

'If you're not what, Mr Kaganagh?'

'What happens if you're not home from home, you've never been here before and you're travelling on your own?' I asked.

'That's not a problem, Mr Kaganagh. We'll take real good care of you with our 'Enrich the Spirit' programme,' Celia said.

'That's lucky. Do you know what's happened to my luggage?'

'And of course, Devon, your house butler, yes, Devon has already put your bags in your room and unpacked them for you, Mr Kaganagh,' she said.

'Thank you.' I hadn't stopped thinking about my friend with the clean nails.

'And you are staying in the Eames Suite, a very good choice. Eames is a super-deluxe sunset-beach over-water cabana. All our rooms are suites and named after famous celebrity designers who have stayed with us, here at the Omanalak.

'Is that what you'd recommend? The Eames Suite?' I asked.

'It is very good. Excellent, in fact. Just one thing, I see you are travelling alone. I would just like to say we have a lot of people like you who come here, Mr Kaganagh, and we take pride in offering all our guests the same level of service. So please don't worry, you'll be sure we'll fix you up to meet some great people.'

'That's okay. Really, I'm fine just reading, snorkelling and getting sunburnt on my own,' I said. Celia was beginning to sound like Kurt from Turtle Bay.

'Please, Mr Kaganagh, you must take care of the sun here and remember to put on plenty of sunscreen,' she said. She didn't look like Kurt.

'Yeah, I know. I was joking,' I said. Celia looked blank.

'But anyway, we look forward to introducing you to everyone. Most of our guests have been here before and will make you most welcome,' she said.

'Perfect, perfect.'

'And Mr Kaganagh, you'll remember to apply the sunscreen?'

'Yes.' I bent down to pick up my hand luggage. I realised I didn't have any.

'So now, Nadine will take you to your suite. And please call reception if there is anything we can help you with, and thank you once again for choosing us here at the Omanalak,' Celia smiled and ushered me towards Nadine.

The Indian Ocean looked a beautiful shade of azure and the waves sounded like a cat lapping water from a bowl. This was a beach where waves hissed rather than crashed, rippled rather than pounded.

My sunglasses had reactolite lenses, which enabled me to ignore Nadine and stare at the guests. Most of the males were men of a certain age dressed in polo shirts with their collars turned up or were lying around in lime green shorts decorated with little camel motifs. The arms of their sunglasses had initials on them, the entry-level Rolexes were Submariner or the GMT-Master. In the pool area, a Biznizman sprayed a dancing lady friend with champagne. This was the first time I clapped my eyes on Oleg and Svetlana. Expensive tropical shirts sprouted white miserable faces while their partners displaced flesh by buying garments two sizes too small. The ladies were reading *Shopaholic* by Sophie Kinsella. The general rule seemed to be: beautiful people lolling about the main thoroughfares or on the beach, less-beautiful people sitting in the shade nearer the bar-cum-restaurant area. Men paced up and down their verandas shouting instructions into their earpieces. I decided not to sit more than five paces away from a bottle of water. It was too hot.

I was agitated about my room; I was anxious about being on my own when everyone else would be part of somebody else; and I was concerned whether I'd enjoy what was supposed to be the highlight of the trip. Omanalak Resort, Meelick Beach, Fulgary – my hundredth country; this would allow me to join the Travelers' Century Club. I knew it was supposed to be the highlight of the trip because the cost per night of the Eames Suite, the super-deluxe sunset-beach over-water cabana, was 137 per cent more expensive than any other room I had ever booked. I recorded a PB and had kept the receipt.

I know you get what you pay for, but the way the accommodation was classified left me feeling whatever I booked I was short-changing myself. There were forty-eight rooms, or 'properties' as the website described them, dotted around several acres of a promontory that jutted out from the northwest tip of the island. There were Pool Villas, Spa Pool Villas, Pool Villa Suites, Spa Pool Villa Suites, Deluxe Pool Villas, Deluxe Spa Pool Villas, Pool Villas (2 Beds), Over-Water Cabanas, Over-Water Cabanas Deluxe, Over-Water Cabanas Deluxe Plus, Over-Water Cabanas Super Deluxe, Private Retreats, Private Reserve, Jungle Reserve, Regal Reserve and Imperial Villas.

This was designed to make you feel cheap, a marketing equivalent of turning wine into water. Only management could design a scenario whereby even though you were throwing hundreds of dollars per night at an Over-Water Cabana Deluxe Plus, you still wouldn't be happy if you didn't spend another seventy-five dollars per night on the Over-Water Cabana Super Deluxe. And what do you get for the extra money? Did I need a bigger fruit bowl when I could eat free fruit all day anyway? And why would I eat fruit all day? If I were going to eat fruit all day, wouldn't I have done it by now? Did the electric fan in the super deluxe have a reverse gear as standard? Did I need to pay an extra seventy-five dollars per night to get a bigger flat screen? No. Did I? Yes. Why did I? Because I didn't want to feel like I was missing out on something and that somebody might be having something *better*? Was I worried that I didn't match up? Why was I concerned about the opinions of people I didn't know and might never meet?

There was a vast price differential between room categories. The net effect of this was to make me feel I didn't have either the funds or the generosity of spirit to stay in a superior room. I was staying in the seventh-cheapest category out of seventeen. To keep things fresh, they even established a price differential between the sunrise and sunset side of the island. I don't wish to portray myself as a skinflint, but it was quite difficult to tell exactly what benefits accrued from the various pricing points.

I was doubly confused when I read the travellers' feedback on www.tripadvisor.com before I left for the Coronation Islands. I was confused by the postings:

> If my husband and I only had three weeks to live, I'd sell one of the twins to go straight back to Omanalak! They've got really neat touches like you put a yellow-painted coconut outside which is like a Do Not Disturb sign. But you must stay in the Private Retreat on the sunrise side. It's AWESOME!!!! Say 'hi' to Arthur. Gary and Arlene, New Jersey. Oct. 2008.

Gary and Arlene gave Omanalak five stars.

Sandy and Tom from Liverpool, England only gave Omanalak two stars out of five:

> We'd read a lot about this resort in *Living the Dream* April issue 2009 and so we booked it for our honeymoon. We couldn't have been more disappointed. The staff were rude, the guests were a bunch of arrogant tossers and the drinks over-priced. And what's worse we both got the squits. I don't expect to pay over $300 per night (yes! Per night!!) only to arrive in the room to find that the previous occupant hadn't even flushed away his yuletide log. I knew we should have gone to Playa de Las Americas in the Canaries when we booked it. If you do have to go, make

sure you stay on the sunset side and take some duty-free with you. Jan. 2009.

Nadine showed me to the Eames Suite, which was quite similar on the outside to all the other rooms I walked past. Nadine confirmed it was a super-deluxe sunset-beach over-water cabana and that my houseboy was Devon. Sweat ran down my face as she proceeded to explain the price – sorry, the facilities.

'So this is your phone,' Nadine said.

'Thank you,' I said while rubbing my shiny forehead.

'This is your outdoor shower,' she said.

'Lovely. No, that's all fine.' I wondered if I had to tip her and if I did, would that set a precedent? Having wiped my forehead, I couldn't shake hands.

'This is your cupboard space.'

'Right.'

'This is your bed,' Nadine said.

'Right, I said.

'This is your veranda.' The waves whispered as they broke, the sea had a sheen-like quality I had never previously seen before.

'Right.' I gave her a tip thinking she might stop showing me things but it didn't work; she had a set patter. So now I felt stupid if I didn't tip her at the end of the demonstration. It was the only time I was likely to be on my own with an attractive female in the room. Let me change that to suite. Let me change that again, it was the only time I was likely to be on my own with any attractive female or indeed any female – even one with a face like a beekeeper's apprentice or a blind cobbler's thumb in a super-deluxe sunset-beach over-water cabana. And I fluffed it.

Nadine did a grand job of explaining which button opens the blinds, which button closes the blinds, which button turns on the television, which button turns off the television, the DVD, the iPod, the whirlpool, the fan and the air-conditioning. I did what I always do when people try to explain things to me; I switched off. I do not understand why, when I stop someone in the street and ask for directions, I can't be arsed to listen to the answer. All I remembered was that you were supposed to put the yellow-painted coconut outside your door if you didn't want to be disturbed by staff and leave it inside if you did. Or vice-versa. I cannot remember which way round it was supposed to be, but it was a nice touch however it worked, if indeed it did.

I felt a complete anti-climax. The same sense of anti-climax I felt as a kid opening my main present on Christmas Day; a room is a room is a room just like a car is a car is a car. (And yet I want to live in a castle with a moat and drive an Aston Martin; the hypocrisy of it all.) I'd spent so much time looking at pictures of my cabana and the 360-degree view, courtesy of the official website, it looked exactly like I knew it would. Well, apart from the bottled Welsh water. Having investigated, researched and deliberated as to what category of room I wanted, now I was standing in it, it felt commonplace. How could I travel to a hundred countries, stay in the best resort in the Coronation Islands, go to my Over-Water Cabana Super-Deluxe and feel it was commonplace?

Why had I been cretinous enough to pay x^n dollars a night when I could stay at home and be miserable? Moreover, it was unbelievably hot; too hot to stay inside and too hot to go outside. The sweat dripped off me even after my shower (but at least I had worked out how to turn it on).

I threw my clothes in a heap in the bathroom. I put the wet towels on the floor so I could get some new ones. I wasn't going to worry about saving them a few quid in laundry bills. After all, they were hardly bending over backwards trying to reduce my bill. Everything on the island was imported, including most of the staff and all of the guests. The cargo comes in by air, but don't worry we'll go green by leaving you with dirty towels.

It was with regret that I failed to turn on either the fan or the air-conditioning. I had to leave the cabana because I was struggling for air. And as for the lighting system – it was more complicated than

Manumission in Ibiza. This was a lighting system that wouldn't turn on lights without the shutters going up and down. I played with the taps for the sunken bath. It would have taken at least forty-five minutes to run it. I couldn't work out whether the plug was in or not, which meant I wouldn't know how to get the plug out if it was in, or in if it was out, even if I figured out whether it was in or out. And if it took me forty-five minutes to run it, how long would it take to drain it?

I walked about, casing the joint like a hungry house burgular. What the blue blazes was I going to do for a week on my own, I wondered. But I know everything appears a little anxiety-inducing when you first arrive, and it's not until you wake up the next morning that you can get the measure of a place so I ambled about looking purposeful. This was my hundredth country, after all.

CHAPTER TWENTY-FOUR

Just Like Heaven

Fulgary Island is a place where the water is turquoise or lapis lazuli, the sky cobalt blue or azure and where jungle is lush or verdant. It is an island of endless vistas where the cabanas have thatched roofs, the beaches are palm-fringed and a clucking bird is always a 'celebrity.' I loved it, and was disturbed by it, and by myself, in equal measure.

To facilitate the observation of my fellow guests, I brought along a copy of Derek Percy-Ffrench's *A Time of Shifts* (1998), a harrowing account of his time working in middle management at the Imperial Group's Coronation Island Hotels in the 1990s. I learnt how you could get seven months in jail for eating during the days of Ramadan. If you were caught with drink you'd be given eight or nine years, and drugs would fetch you twenty-five years or, perhaps, the death penalty. The Coronation Islands have, or had, according to Percy-Ffrench's book, an 80 per cent divorce rate due to so many people being forced to work away from home. *A Time of Shifts* also goes into some detail contrasting the luxurious rooms of the guests with the conditions of the staff who slept twenty people to a dormitory.

Schopenhauer said we love books because we believe we are buying the time to read them. I decided it was time to mug up some more on my Frottager's *Guide to the Coronation Islands* (2009). The foreword consisted of a tribute to Gloria Ballyfermot-Jimenez, penned by Gloria Ballyfermot-Jimenez herself, in which she wrote:

> Given my special talents and powers this makes me even
> more passionate about behaving responsibly. I am passionate

about acting greenly, and eco-consciously too. I feel really troubled about my important role in changing global consumer behaviour and I feel guilty about exposing hidden gems of previously undiscovered islands. But my passion makes me jump up and down about Fulgary, an island of contrasts and the jewel of the Coronation archipelago, a land of tranquillity and calm waters, where tomorrow meets today in unsurpassed exquisiteness. This, as everybody knows, is the Coronation Islands' best-kept secret. The Omanalak is eco-friendly and exclusive, making it an ideal location for the environmentally-conscious traveller. I have a passion for places and Fulgary is an island where the beautiful people have passionately embraced the charm of discreet elegance away from the glare of publicity. This remains a gem of a place to visit, to see and be seen, but still sufficiently secretive to attract the celebrity who is looking for a retreat or a spa for the soul.

I needed to use the toilet. I don't feel at home abroad until I've done two things: walked around feeling lost, and had a sit down. But I couldn't go back to my cabana until somebody had switched on the air-con so I had to walk all the way back to reception where I sauntered up to the lovely Celia.

'Hello, there. I forgot to ask, has a fax arrived for me?' I asked.

There was a part of me that was petrified my company might try to contact me so I took the precaution of giving them the wrong telephone numbers but the correct addresses of where I was staying.

'I'll just check. No, there's nothing here. If anything arrives be sure Devon will tell you straight away, Mr Kaganagh,' Celia said.

'How strange,' I said while tapping my fingers on the counter.

'Is there anything else, Mr Kaganagh?'

'No, I don't think so, thank you, Celia. Actually, you could check my air-conditioning unit; it makes a noise like a one-fingered typist. If someone could look at it and leave it on at seventy degrees exactly, that would be grand,' I said.

'Certainly,' Celia picked up the phone and dialled maintenance.

I had a look at the gym instead. It is entirely within people's rights to exercise on holiday but for me going on holiday meant leaving routine behind. My routine included going to the gym at work. This allowed me to disappear from my desk. Going to the gym also meant I didn't drink with my friends at lunchtime. I was as excited about escaping from my routine as I was about getting away from the office. It meant I wouldn't have to use the gym.

An Asian woman, who appeared to have a personal trainer (for $120 per hour, I'll carry my own water) was holding a towel to her mouth while looking at herself in a full-length mirror. She was moist with self-love. She had strutted in, turned up the volume on two televisions, changed the channels and barked into her mobile phone. Wearing her sunglasses as a hairband, she kept checking her phone for texts. She complained loudly she couldn't hear 'because of the noise' and left without closing the door. But not before re-applying her lipstick.

On my way out, I heard the nanny say to a podgy kid who was tiptoeing on some scales, 'Oh don't worry, honey; I think it's in euros.'

CHAPTER TWENTY-FIVE

Kung-Fu Fighting

My room was a perfect seventy degrees. I liked my cabana more now because it felt like mine. It ticked all the boxes: floor-to-ceiling glass, teak furniture, white Boca Terry monogrammed towelling robe and matching pair of white slippers. I loved the view, sitting on the Egyptian cotton sheets of my queen-size bed looking out over the Indian Ocean. I had a veranda which wasn't overlooked and was just big enough for the Balinese table and chairs and hammock; but best of all, it was only a hop, skip and a jump from the crystal-clear water of the ocean. The room looked like a photo shoot from *How Much?* magazine.

I found Derek Percy-Ffrench's *A Time of Shifts* (1998) impossible to pick up so I cracked on with my Frottager's guide. I read my Percy-Ffrench in public and my Frottager's in private. According to Frottager (2009):

> The population of Fulgary is 73,477 and its geographical area is 192 square kilometres. The national flag is blue and green, divided diagonally by a thin red stripe. Fulgary's only tourist attraction is Lovers' Leap, situated on the west coast of the island, where visitors can see for themselves where the indigenous people leapt to their death rather than surrender to the Portuguese, Dutch, French and British.
>
> Following World War Two, the British ceded control to the islanders and concentrated their resources in granting independence to former Commonwealth states. The Kung-Fu riots of 1982 left several hundred inhabitants dead. Kung Fu had swept all before it when Bruce Lee films reached

the country in the 1970s, spawning numerous clubs, whose members came predominantly from the Highlands. The country's only cinema is based in the capital, Saparmurat, which is the largest settlement in the Highlands. The films were shown every night to packed audiences. To this day, Bruce Lee films and Carl Douglas's 1974 hit single, 'Kung Fu Fighting,' remain banned.

There are two distinct groups in Fulgary, the Highlanders and the Coastal people. Until recently, mixed marriages were frowned upon. Following the Kung-Fu riots in the 1980s, the British Government turned a blind eye to the cultivation of marijuana as long as it was for personal use. Marijuana grows naturally like a weed in the Highlands. It was mooted in diplomatic circles that the widespread use of marijuana might alleviate some of the internecine stress. The Highlanders are descendants of a Leper Colony, established as far back as the twelfth century, by the Order of St Lazarus, named after the patron saint of Lepers. The Highlanders tend to be shorter, squatter and more aggressive. The Highlanders keep themselves to themselves, preferring to concentrate on farming and livestock.

Latterly, the Coastal people gave their consent for the development of the island's first tourist development, the Omanalak resort on Meelick Beach. Vernon and Mardy Cripps, natives of Burbank, California, are the joint owners, although latterly their son, Vincent Cripps, has managed the property. This exclusive hideaway, partly financed by regional aid from the British Government, was finally opened in 1996 to critical acclaim in the tourism industry. The Omanalak Resort won the 1997 Sun-kissed Hideaway award for the Indian Ocean in *How Much?*

Following the tsunami on Boxing Day 2004, the resort, like many of the islanders' homes, was flattened. This time the British Government refused to provide any financial assistance whatsoever. An application was made to the British Government to rebuild Omanalak but this was rejected, as was the right to appeal. When asked to explain, the British Government said financial assistance was 'not in the public interest.' Assistance was provided to many other islands in the archipelago, but no monies were allocated to Fulgary.

The Coastal people see themselves as more progressive, more outward looking and more modern in their ideas. They tend to be lighter skinned and taller. Fishing tends to be more lucrative than farming, or at least historically has been, although this is likely to be affected by dwindling stocks of skipjack tuna, yellow fin tuna, little tuna and frigate mackerel as well as octopus, squid and giant clams. Echinoderms like sea cucumber, and crustaceans such as shrimp, lobster and crabs have brought the Coastal people into contact with a plethora of international trading partners. There is a significant and growing demand for their products in Japan. Since the global credit crisis of 2007, the British Government is rumoured to be in talks to sell commercial fishing licences to the Japanese for the first time.

The economy of the island is broadly broken down as a percentage of GDP according to 2005 official estimates as follows: Fish 49%, Bitter Orange 15%, Palm Oil 13%, Cinnamon 10%, Copra 6% and Sisal 2%. There is no formal monopoly that prevents people applying for commercial fishing licences, but the Coastal people need government approval, and sources close to Sir Rupert Fairholm-Bentinck, the British Consul, indicate they will not get it. Experts suggest it is to punish fishermen for selling Green Turtles, while fishermen claim it is because the British want to re-settle the islanders and sell the island to the United States as a military post. Others suggest offshore possibilities.

Bitter Orange (*Citrus Aurantium*) is used in essential oils and herbal medicine. It is both a stimulant and an appetite suppressant and has replaced the banned stimulant ephedra. It is often used in Tamil cuisine. The possible loss of income from a tailing off or outright banning of Bitter Orange products would have a crippling effect on the Highlanders. There is a saying in the Coronation Islands: 'Placentians sleep all day, the Kilrushi work all night, and the Highlanders complain while the Coastal people catch crabs.'

Following the Global Credit Crunch of 2007, and the so-called War against Financial Laxity (WAFL), the British Government has gone on record and admitted it is conducting a root-and-branch review of all overseas holdings. While the future remains unclear, Fulgary stands at a crossroads. The leper colony is now home to the beautiful people. Having previously thrown themselves to their deaths in order to avoid the colonialists, the best chances of survival for the islanders now lie in the hands of a husband-and-wife team of former corporate lawyers.

Vernon and Mardy Cripps were political activists in California prior to their move to the Coronation Islands. They were perhaps best known for setting up California's first 'Disability Day' whereby people dressed up like the disabled. The British Consul, which claims to be gravely concerned about the safety of the islanders, has made contact through the official channels. Both the Cripps and the British Consul have indicated they will act in the best interests of the islanders.

CHAPTER TWENTY-SIX

I Travel Alone

Reading about Fulgary motivated me to crack on with *A Time of Shifts*. The next thing I knew I woke up in the dark not entirely sure where I was or how to turn on the bedside lights without filling up the jacuzzi. To wake up in the dark feeling totally disorientated is one of the best things about travel. I liked the millisecond between thinking, where am I and have I overslept, and remembering I am on holiday in a flash resort in the Indian Ocean waking up to the rasping of cicadas. Getting up late meant I wouldn't have to hang around too long before supper. Although guests were invited to meet for a drink before supper, I didn't have the front to do this alone on my first night.

I walked along barefoot from my cabana to the restaurant. The paths were well lit and great attention had been paid to the tropical vegetation of purple, orange, red and yellow. It was so darned tasteful.

I took my novel with me, had dressed in my most studiously casual schmutter, sidled up to the bar and ordered a Long Island Iced Tea. I pined for Turtle Bay where I could just roll up and have a natter with whoever was there. Most of my life has been devoted to analysing what is the best value-for-money cocktail and the Long Island Iced Tea wins hands down. It answers many of the I-don't-know-what-to-have questions because most of the drinks that you don't know what to have can be found in it, namely: vodka, gin, tequila and rum. I couldn't bring myself to order cocktails with silly names like Slow Comfortable Screw. I did see one called Parrot's Piss, which I took to be ironic. It'd be interesting to see a drinks list named after the drinkers themselves with names like: Cheap and Nasty, Nouveau Riche, Old and Ugly and my perennial favourite, Mutton dressed as Mutton.

As I've said, there is no fun in eating on your own. You feel everyone in the restaurant is looking at you and thinking – *he's on his own. I wonder why that is?* I can't bear it when the waiter asks, *is that a table for one?* You try to answer in a clear and confident manner but your voice croaks. As you walk to the table, you hear the murmur: yeah, he's on his own.

Banning smoking from public places was the death knell of the solitary diner-observer. The very act of smoking allowed you to take your time and look around. The great thing about travelling on your own is you can cultivate an image while knowing you'll never have to meet anybody again; you can be whoever you want. This is liberating: you can smoke and swear because it genuinely *does* make you look cool. All of which makes it even weirder that I wanted to be the guy who sits on his own, smashing back Long Island Iced Teas.

The restaurant was outside, on the beach and under the stars; my friends from Placentia could no doubt name them all and the constellations. From where I sat, I could hear waves lapping the beach. Because there is less ambient noise, you can hear waves more at night. The guests were couples ranging between honeymooners and some in their early sixties. The few couples that had brought kids with them had either stumped up for the nanny to come on holiday (so they could have supper on their own) or had hired help from the resort. It was one of the most wonderful places I have ever been to.

I wasn't sure what the protocol was. Do I go up and help myself or do I wait to be served? I sat at a table for two and moved when the Biznizman and woman I'd seen earlier came in and glared at me. I was sitting at a table with a sign saying *Reserved*. I was out of my chair before the waiter started to speak. Sadly, I had to go back to the table because I'd left my Red and Black notebook. I sat as far away from them as possible. I ordered instantaneously from the menu and bolted my food down as soon as it arrived. I wanted to go back to my room.

The restaurant area was set back from the pontoon, and the main bar was further away from the beach towards reception.

Between the restaurant and the bar was an area for lounging about – playing cards or chess, looking at a DVD of the morning's dive played back on the television screen, having a drink, having a sleep, reading a book or relaxing in the shade and away from the sun. There were no floorboards, rugs or carpets. I was amazed you could walk around without any shoes as you'd think the staff and management would be jumping up and down about someone dropping a glass and worrying about everyone walking about on the shards. Perhaps if glasses fell on sand, they didn't break.

I am happy to fly to the other side of the world if it means getting away from the Health-and-Safety militia. We were perfectly content gadding about the world chopping peoples' heads off, but now it takes you ten minutes to read the safety warning on a shopping mall elevator. This didn't mean some of the beautiful people shied away from wearing high heels at breakfast. I used to love watching these incredibly glamorous women, tottering around in stilettos, calculating the calorific implications of a slice of melon and a slice of papaya. Do two slices of mango plus one slice of pineapple equal two slices of melon plus one pineapple slice? It's the eternal question.

Even in the reception area, the guests walked about on sand. (However, the toilets were next to reception, and guests looked decidedly less glamorous walking back through the bar with tissue paper stuck to their feet.) The Biznizman, Oleg was now puffing away in the khazi dressed in a see-through string vest and a pair of casual dark blue pinstripe trousers. When his thighs rubbed together they sounded like sails being put away. I monitored Oleg from the mirror above the urinal as he pissed, preened himself in the mirror, patted his hair down, sucked his teeth and left without washing his hands.

I enjoyed the cool sand underneath my feet as I ate under the stars and listened to the gently crashing waves. It was all very grown up. This island certainly lived up to the slogan from the Coronation Islands tourist office: *Islands adrift in Time and Place*. I decided not to hang out in the bar afterwards on my first evening.

CHAPTER TWENTY-SEVEN

She's Not There

It would be easy to get used to this lifestyle: breakfasting on Eggs Benedict served al fresco by my breakfast waiter, Shaggy, a leisurely walk along the beach looking for spider crabs, sunbathing in a hammock, which was damned uncomfortable by the way, and a snorkel marvelling at the underwater treasure of the crystal-clear waters of the Indian Ocean, followed by more lying down in the sun until my face felt tight. I was trying to work out whether it was too hot to read, in which case I didn't need to go back to pick up my book, when I heard someone singing. One of the staff was singing away on a deserted beach, brushing up palm fronds and sweeping towards me. My first reaction was – why, on an empty beach, does the man have to come up and clean right next to me? My second reaction was – I must move to avoid striking up a conversation before he gets much closer. My third reaction was – if I get up and move – will I cause offence? I was paralysed by awkwardness so I pretended to doze. The closer he came towards me, the more I wondered whether I should put my shirt back on or not. I had a lot of questions but no answers. After about thirty-five minutes of relaxing, under the blinding sun, the groom with the broom approached. He said something, but for the life of me I couldn't tell you what it was.

'What a great place. Wonderful,' I said.

'I'm fine. Thank you,' he said.

'You must get very hot doing that.'

'Arthur. My name is Arthur. I clean the beach three times a day, and I take care of all the paths too,' he said. Arthur said something else, which I couldn't catch, guffawed, pointed at me and guffawed again while he swept away the palm fronds.

I went back to my cabana to check my face in the mirror for squamous cell carcinomas and to pick up my book and Tilley hat. I could tell by the trolley of linen and cleaning products that my room was being cleaned. Devon had taken his chance to inconvenience me. He hadn't been able to wake me up but he could prevent me from doing my ablutions, for ablutions read bathroom and for bathroom, read Devon mopping the marble floor.

'Mr Kaganagh, sir. You are having nice time?'

'Very nice time. Thank you, Devon.'

'You like Omanalak?' Devon had a wide, open face that he used for chuckling with at the end of every sentence.

'I like it very much,' I said.

'Oh good, that is good.' Devon waited for me to speak.

'You worked here long?' I asked. Devon laughed at this but didn't answer at first.

'You know how long?' he asked.

'Absolutely no idea.'

'No idea at all?' Devon asked.

'Nope,' I said. Devon chortled some more. 'I was your houseboy in the Aspire in Mauritius.'

'Oh my God, I'm sorry. Of course, you were. Unbelievable, I'm sorry,' I said. I wished I was anywhere but the Omanalak and wondered, if I changed rooms on some nonsensical ruse, whether I could give Devon the slip.

'Yes, with a very pretty girl. Brown hair, brown eyes, big smile,' he said.

'Small world, isn't it?' I said. Devon nodded.

'Do you still see her? Is she with you?' Devon said.

'No, she's not I'm afraid. Drifted apart you might say,' I said.

'Oh, well. Perhaps next time you come back with someone new.'

'Yes. I'd love to, but I can't think it's very likely, I'm afraid.'

'Good to see you.'

'Good to see you, Devon. I didn't recognise you. You've, you've...'

I made a series of futile hand gestures to explain in what way Devon had changed but I gave up halfway through this set of meaningless exercises. Devon picked up the mop and the rest of his cleaning equipment. He walked towards the door humming tunelessly.

'I see you tomorrow,' Devon said.

'Look forward to it. Thank you, Devon.'

This was not to my liking. I would never have booked the same hotel group if I had, for one minute, even dreamt there was the faintest possibility of bumping into anybody who knew me or Kay. I didn't know what to do. I couldn't complain. I didn't want to slag off Devon to his employer or kick up a fuss and, equally, I didn't want to worry about bumping into Devon every time I was in my cabana.

After lunch, I hung out by the pool for a change of view. The best-positioned sun loungers had towels on them but no people. They were either in their rooms or having lunch. This time I was ready: sun block bought from the boutique shop, Tilley hat, camera, cigarettes, novel and bottle of mineral water. It was very hot. If I sat up with my hat on, I showed off my man boobs, but if I assumed the horizontal position then the sun would scorch my tingling face. The other possibility would be to lie down, thus flattening out my body, the downside being I'd have to put my Tilley hat on my face to prevent any further melanomas. I was keen not to fritter away hundreds of dollars per night on a super-deluxe over-water cabana just to spend my days lying by a pool with a hat over my face.

Relaxing on a beach was like starting a romantic relationship: it just needed time. The try-to-relax mantra makes people check their watches while spending the day by the pool. This wouldn't have concerned me if I hadn't left my watch in my personal safety-deposit box. At least, I hoped I'd left it in the personal safety-deposit box because, if it wasn't there, it was either on my bedside table, by the sink or I had lost it. If I had left it lying around then the quicker I went back, the less chance there was of someone pinching it. Equally, if I couldn't find my watch, it would ruin my holiday. You only realise how much you look at your watch when you don't have it on. And by a pool, with nothing to do for a week, I can't think of anything else apart from – what time is it?

Meanwhile Oleg, who liked to spray champagne but not wash his hands after a pee, had stepped up his game, which now involved ordering a bottle of champagne, spraying his girlfriend, Svetlana, and clicking his fingers at staff to order another bottle. As if this wasn't funny enough, when the waiter approached, Oleg would take the bottle and glasses, put them on a table by the pool, make as if he was signing the bar bill and then push the waiter fully clothed into the pool. It was so funny Oleg did it again and again.

Guests slipped away from the pool area. The pool attendants picked up the towels from the same sun loungers the guests had reserved to stop anyone else from having them. Couples giggled into each other's ears and slunk off while I retired to my room alone. My watch was exactly where I'd left it by the sink.

Someone had popped an invitation under the door to the Manager's Weekly Drinks Party tomorrow night. I'd read about this in the marketing blurb: every Tuesday night, the guests would be ferried out onto a spit of white sand for canapés and free champagne. I didn't know whether I wanted to go or not. If you're a couple and it's a stomach-churningly hideous experience, at least you can laugh about it with your partner. But if you are on your own, you can't even do that. Equally, I might as well go along. I might end up meeting someone. I had already seen one or two women who I'd love to meet. It was unlikely I'd meet anyone who was travelling with a partner on a fly and flop.

I started to read about the services the resort offered in one of those leather-bound brochures they always have – the ones with the writing paper with the address of the resort printed on it, along with a list of business services, the room-service menu, the pamphlet on international dialling codes, the list of DVDs and the spa directory. At the very good places, the manager writes you a letter welcoming you to the resort and signs it personally.

As Celia had mentioned, 85 per cent of people who go to the Coronation Islands return, which I don't believe unless it includes journeys made by locals and not just tourists. Ninety-five per cent of people who stay at the Omanalak for the first time do not leave the hotel; the percentage for people who return to the resort goes up to 98 per cent. I found this staggering and decided to do four things: to enjoy a drink at sunset, get someone to take a picture of me at sunset, go to the Manager's Weekly Drinks Party and get out of the resort.

My face was already pink when I scraped the razor over my stubble. Before I went out for supper, I had to slap after-sun grease on my charred neck and stomach. There was an outline of my book on my stomach. The white line of my shorts revealed the sand-fly bites I had acquired while lying on the beach. It required self-discipline to stop myself from scratching them, which I enjoyed, in a Catholic sort of way. My white Boca Terry towelling robe chafed against mosquito bites.

I thought I'd celebrate the end of my first full day by going down to the Dhow Bar and drinking a Long Island Iced Tea at sunset.

The hotel had four or five different spots to take a drink; the Dhow Bar was built in the shape of an old wooden dhow that had been cut in half. The seating was arranged in such a way you could sit in the dhow and watch the sunset.

Sunset is an important time of the day for honeymooners and romantic couples. People like to photograph it particularly at the beginning or end of their holidays. I know we used to.

I carried my book with me to avoid looking like a voyeur. On the beach, and to the right-hand side of half a dhow was a bath, with a shower fitment attached at the tap end, for people who wanted to sit in the bath with a drink and look out towards the ocean. But more importantly this was where you could be seen having a drink looking out to sea; it was for this purpose it was most commonly used.

I took my seat, but kept jumping up as I was being bitten by something. Some couples, having identified me as either a loose cannon, a solitary prowler or a disturbance, finished off their drinks and left; others looked at me in a way that suggested they could see me but I couldn't see them. They turned away whenever I looked up. Some asked me to take pictures of them at sunset. I didn't use my camera, as I felt stupid.

The Asian woman, whom I'd seen earlier in the gym, was sitting in the bar with her boyfriend. He wore a red Ralph Lauren polo shirt with the collar turned up. She made herself busy by waving a Dolce & Gabbana handbag about. She kept picking it up while checking her phone, then put it down on different parts of the bar in case anybody mistook it for somebody else's.

Her boyfriend, a peacock-like multi-tasker, studied a map of the grounds of the hotel while barking dealing instructions into a mobile phone. He plodded around the bar, while clearing his throat, in a pair of azure Gucci loafers, as if he was wearing someone else's shoes. She furtively picked her nose and, following close inspection, sought to dislodge her nasal detritus by stroking his soot-black hair with her hand. I coughed loudly to signal I'd seen her do it. She looked at me as if I had done something wrong. She wasn't going to swallow men finding fault with her, and certainly not a grinning idiot with a pink face. I made a mental note not to shake hands with her if introduced.

I was trying to remember the statistic I'd read for the average number of traces of urine on peanuts served in a public bar, when out of the corner of my eye I saw a lizard about three-foot long. It slunk over the sand and dashed into the undergrowth.

'What the hell is that?' I bawled at the bartender.

'It's a teju,' he said. I've forgotten the bartender's name, which amazes me.

'A what?'

'A teju,' he said.

'Sorry mate you're going to have to be a bit more vague. What's a teju?'

'A teju is like a lizard,' he said.

'What's it doing here?' I asked.

'Vernon and Mardy introduced the teju onto the island to control the population of palm squirrels. Unfortunately, these palm squirrels, or rats, are nocturnal and the tejus, the lizards, come out at daytime. And they come out in the daytime because that is when they find it easier to eat the seabirds' eggs. It is also when Arthur feeds them. That is, when he's not singing to them,' the barman said.

Nightfall fell, tree frogs croaked and cicadas rasped. I didn't want to sit at the wrong table again so I ate snacks at the bar nearest reception. I feigned interest in a week-old version of *USA Today* and watched couples slip off to their rooms. I gave up at 9.43 p.m.

CHAPTER TWENTY-EIGHT

Superfly

The quell birds, also called the uh-ho birds because of the uh-ho
call they make, wake up very early in the archipelago. I know this
because they woke me up every morning. I decided to breakfast
so I wouldn't have to make small talk with Devon about Kay. I
couldn't sleep anyway because the sand-flies had chewed lumps
out of my buttocks. I had to sleep on my front, which meant I had
to keep re-applying after-sun to my chest and face.

I ordered Eggs Benedict from Shaggy, my breakfast server for
the week. It was too hot and too early, and I felt murderous – so I
wore black shorts, a black wife-beater vest and black sunglasses,
like a flabby Irish version of Mike Tyson. After watching
Shaggy tortuously spoon my guava jam into a smaller pot, Oleg
approached me.

'Are you finish?' When he bent down I thought he might hit me.

'I'm sorry?' I said.

'You are sorry.'

'Yes.'

'Sorry? Okay. But are you Finnish?' Oleg asked.

'No, I'm sort of half-English and half-Irish, conceived over
there and hatched over here, that sort of thing.'

Oleg was dressed in a Haile Selassie T-shirt, flip-flops in the
national colours of Jamaica and a Rastafarian belt. He had a face
like a photofit ID and was sitting with a personal fantasy of mine.
Svetlana moved around as if to dance – that is when she wasn't
sneaking a look at herself in her compact mirror. They took turns
in snogging and texting. It was unlikely she would die lonely.
Svetlana's T-shirt read *The camera loves me*. Oleg picked up the

small pot of guava jam and strutted back to his table. I'd been trapped in a conversational cul-de-sac. I responded to this invasion of my personal defensible space by putting sachets of Tibetan medicine on my breakfast table to ward off passers-by.

I was sunburnt, had the imprint of a novel on my chest and had been gang-raped by sand-flies. Sunbathing was out of the question so I thought I'd have a spot of Beginners' Scuba at 10 a.m. down by the pontoon. Scuba is for extreme-sports enthusiasts only, who, like snappy dressers, tend to be the dullest people often to be found in the dullest places like New Zealand or Slovenia. But I thought I'd give it a go because a) I couldn't lie down, b) I couldn't sunbathe, c) I might meet people ahead of the Manager's Weekly Drinks Party and d) girls like scuba diving.

People lolled about by the pontoon, continuously looking over their shoulders, as if they were waiting for someone to arrive. I'd tried an introductory dive in the Seychelles but gave it up as it required too much time holding hands underwater with a Frenchman. I thought I'd give it another go, though I never liked the palaver of diving, the culture of divers and the whole bureaucratisation of a pastime. Besides, I wasn't very good at it; I didn't like taking orders from tough, mid-thirties, blonde diving instructresses like Alejandra. She had a boxer's nose – as in the noble art, not as in puppy. I found her attractive, all beach blonde and perfect skin.

'I'm Alejandra, I'll be your diving instructor today for the Beginners Scuba course. So, where are you all from?' she asked.

Nobody could be that friendly, surely? Alejandra had ball-bearing hips, blue eyes and tiny, leprechaun ears. She was about five-eight, trim, wore a piercing in her tummy button and I'm pleased to report, no visible tramp stamps.

'I'm Lilibet from Paris,' said a plump lady in a garish, red bikini. Alejandra looked at Lilibet just long enough to acknowledge her before turning her head slowly and smiling at the lady sitting next to her.

'Hi, Lilibet. Actually, I was born in France, in the Dordogne,' Alejandra said while scrunching up her hair and fidgeting with the strap on her diving mask. Then she grinned, patted the French lady's thigh and nodded. The next person was Mike from Vancouver. I wasn't interested in Mike; he looked as if he couldn't crack a smile. Shortly after introducing himself, Mike looked at Alejandra for approval. 'Really?' Alejandra said, 'I'm Canadian myself. On my mother's side.'

Mike from Vancouver wouldn't have been any happier if he'd got married and found out he'd won the lottery rollover all on the same day.

'My name is Barbara and I'm from St Pete's in Florida.' Barbara smiled at Alejandra and waited for validation.

'Great, actually, I've got a condo just outside Clearwater,' Alejandra said.

You could sense the relief in Barbara's face. It was like playing pass the parcel. Nobody wanted to be the one who dropped the baton of Alejandra's goodwill.

'Jack from London,' I said.

'Do you know Cornwall? Do you surf?' she asked.

'No and no. I can't bear cold water and it takes hours to get there,' I said.

Alejandra had been everywhere but didn't know where she was from, which is why she spent so much time looking for clues underwater. As they say in politics, it's what's on the surface that's important not what's underneath. To me, a sport is not a sport unless it's got strict crowd segregation and a heavy police presence.

While watching Alejandra test Mike's regulator, I decided that passing my PADI (Professional Association of Diving Instructors) exam on holiday would give me a sense of purpose. I would meet other like-minded guests with whom I could watch the DVDs being played back in reception every night. And, more importantly, I could hang out with Alejandra. And the Coronation Islands have a world-class reputation for diving. But I kind of already knew this wasn't going to happen as I soon as I sat next to her in the boat.

We pootled off and started by putting the kit on in about five to ten feet of water, doing some breathing exercises and elementary hand signals. Everything was fine and dandy until Alejandra asked me to take my mask off underwater. I thought this was a poor idea and explained that I wanted to learn how to scuba with my mask on. But she wouldn't have any of it. And she wasn't a lady people could say 'no' to. I took my mask off, panicked and if it wasn't for Alejandra holding my hand and calming me down, I don't know what would have happened. But I do know I must have made quite a chump of myself. Alejandra only made it worse by being sympathetic and explaining how difficult she had found it. I didn't know whether 'it' referred to taking her mask off underwater or having to hold my hand. The others by this time were engaged in some kind of underwater synchronised dance routine, swimming in a way that made dolphins look graceless. I tried to slink away. Alejandra asked if I wanted to try again, which I didn't. She shrugged her shoulders as if to say, 'Well, what else do you expect me to do, if you won't even try?'

It was now or never between scuba and me so I decided to give scuba up and keep trying to get me right. If at first you don't succeed, give up, as my careers teacher used to tell me. Besides which, I didn't know where to put my glasses when I put my mask on.

The saltwater dried on my sunburnt shoulders and made me want to scratch my sand-fly bites as I schlepped around the resort, carrying fins, towel, mask, camera, sunscreen, Tilley hat, book, sunglasses, anti-mozzie spray and anything else I could manage. It still wasn't midday, but it was skin-rippingly hot. After carting stuff about, washing this off and re-applying that, it was almost time for lunch. I walked past the pool where Oleg, my fellow guava jam fan, videoed Svetlana. They had to grab the moment before the next bottle of champagne arrived.

The people who were stuck in the middle of their vacation looked glum while the people who had stayed at the resort before were sprawled comatose. They had learnt to surrender to relaxation and not fight the need to do something, which kept gnawing away at new arrivals like myself. You don't have to do something to be happy – just sit and stare out to sea, or collapse in a heap by the pool. I wondered whether big-game fishing might be an option.

I didn't want to stuff my face if I was going to the spa later so I had a fresh stir-fry and went back to my cabana to look for some shade. I was tired and I hadn't impressed at my scuba class. I had to ring reception for a wake-up call to go to the spa. My treatment, designed to relax me, cost $120 plus taxes for ninety minutes. The spa was in the 'enrich-the-spirit' business which meant form-filling, signing insurance waivers and an obligatory and expensive introductory consultation with the Spa Director, Dr Vijay, who claimed to be an Ayurvedic doctor.

For many people, the spa is the be-all and end-all of hideaway resort vacations. The reason they may be skulking away in the Ayurvedic treatment room undergrowth is that they, and by they, I mean the ladies, were recovering from extensive cosmetic surgery. They hid in the dark recesses like aye-aye, wrapped in expensive white initialled towelling robes, reading *What For?* and sipping freshly made ginger tea brought to them by bowing oriental ladies with whom they pretended to have a relationship.

The spa's manager was a gay Thai guy who was straight out of Central Casting. He introduced me to Dr Vijay, who bored me with loads of questions, made me stick out my tongue and got me to lie about my lifestyle. I rushed through the interview so more of my money could go on massage and less on form-filling. To shut him up, I agreed to Thai massages, ashtanga Yoga and emetic vomiting.

The spa was full of miserable whiteys who were having their corns done by sweet brown people because either:

1) They were too fat to touch their toes. (Check.)

2) They couldn't get anyone to sleep with them so at least this way they'd experience physical friction. (Check.)

3) They couldn't stay outside or they'd burn. (Check.)

4) The only conversation they could get was if they paid someone to talk to them. (Check.)

The Thai massage was great, as was the masseuse, but I lost about twenty to twenty-five minutes answering questions relating to subjects ranging from bowel movements to sleep patterns, from alcohol consumption to hereditary medical history. I told Dr Vijay if he was concerned, he could ring my GP, who is also from Sri Lanka; they might find they have mutual friends.

I spent the entire massage trying to work out whether the time for the massage (ninety minutes) included the time for the consultation or not. If it didn't, would I have enough time to catch the boat that took guests to the white spit of land for the manager's drinks? It was very stressful, and now I was running late.

I had to run back to my cabana, wash my hair, shave, apply after-sun and anti-mozzie spray, get dressed and catch the boat from the pontoon in just under eighteen minutes. Two minutes were spent dropping bottles of shampoo and conditioner in the outdoor shower for reasons I cannot explain. I cut my lip shaving and was bleeding and sweating when I slapped after-sun on my burnt flesh while applying anti-mozzie spray to my bites. I remembered I'd left my personal safety box in my cabana unlocked; I ran back to lock it up, which was good because I'd forgotten to put my watch on. I sprinted down to the pontoon barefoot and sweating as if I'd just been chased out of a Turkish hammam. I legged it down to the pontoon only to find everything was running a little late anyway.

My fellow guests had saved their best outfits for that evening. The women looked beautiful, and the men looked dashing. They looked like extras from an exclusive photo shoot from one of the off-the-beaten-track Caribbean, Polynesian or Maldivian Islands. I had had to stick toilet paper on my top lip to stem flow from the nick from my razor. The paper came off when I ran to the pontoon. My expensive pale blue shirt shipped water under the arms, which left a salty tidemark. Thank God I hadn't launched my new Vilebrequin shirt with the hibiscus flowers.

It was not an occasion to which I could bring my book so I concentrated on looking as relaxed and as intriguing as my unctuous sunburnt face would allow. It could have been worse; I could have been teetotal.

The speedboat went to and fro picking up punters from the pontoon. Every time the boat came back to pick up passengers, an ungodly scramble to board took place. Never in the course of my travels had I seen so many, who were spending so much per head per night, pursue free champagne so energetically. I hung out at the back of the stampede; it wasn't as if I was keeping anyone waiting.

It was the last boat that took me. Mr Polo Shirt and Mrs Nasal Detritus shouted at us to wait. He was on the phone and wore a set of keys on the outside of his belt while she checked her phone for texts. I nodded in acknowledgement as they clambered aboard, holding my arm out to help them, but they ignored me.

The staff, in white liveried uniforms, poured champagne or carried trays of canapés; couples shared private, romantic moments; and groups of friends chortled. The staff nodded and smiled; guests wrinkled their noses and picked away at silver trays while prodding the canapés.

Nothing grew on this little stretch of pristine white sand. I stood and stared at the empty horizon while clutching a glass. I was courteous to the queue of people waiting to top up my glass and force-feed me like a pelican. I saw Oleg and Svetlana, who had a private dining set-up for the evening. She held her cutlery like a pen; he chewed his food as if it was too hot. Oleg wore a tropical shirt and wore an expression that suggested the last number in the lottery hadn't come up. They stopped snogging to take bones out of their mouth or to answer their phones.

The return guests were telling the First Years like myself how to do it, how to *do* Omanalak. They knew the Christian names of all the staff and stayed on the sunrise side of the island as they found the cabanas on the sunset side too hot and overpriced. The old guests loved Meelick Beach, received Christmas Cards from Vern and Mardy themselves and came the same two weeks every year. They were still in touch with people they met three years ago; they said it was more like a private club in those days. They used to have more to do with Vern and Mardy in the old days but now it was Vinnie, their son, who was more involved in booking trips and taking care of guests. Frottager said there was nothing to see on the island, apart from Lovers' Leap, that is, if you haven't seen it before, but they wouldn't go to the capital, Saparmurat, if you paid them. They went on about how I may have seen them on their bicycles and did I know they didn't have to pay for them, as they were return guests. They said I wouldn't like the Highlanders; they were nothing like the Coastal people who worked at the resort; it was like chalk and cheese. They recited the same liturgy to everybody; every conversation solicited what sounded like a congregational response at Mass.

If you recognise the faces and the names of all the waiting staff only by their lapel badges, it's time to switch to soft drinks or it's last call for mingling. I spotted Alejandra talking with a group of guests including Mr Polo and Mrs Nasal. She looked so wonderful I thought I'd been premature in rejecting scuba. It dawned on me I was unlikely to be on the island the next time she ran her Beginners' Scuba course, which made me gloomy. I felt sad at what was supposed to be the highlight of the week at Omanalak, on the palm-fringed island of Fulgary, my hundredth country. I was a lot nearer the end of my holiday than the beginning.

I knew what I needed to do; I needed to ask a question to integrate myself into the group. I couldn't launch in with the old, 'Hi, I'm Jack, the guy who flunked Beginners' Scuba, the guy with the sunburn who is travelling on his own.' So I tried, 'Hi Alejandra. Do you, or does anybody else, know anything about the marlin fishing here?' It was a corker of a question, summoning up images of Hemingwayesque men wanting to chance their arm with Nature. Marlin fishing says boats, which says money, which says prestige, which says to the guys, 'Hey, I'm in the same gang.' It also tells ladies I'm the mysterious, laconic loner-hunter, which, again, pushes a lot of buttons. All I needed was a beard. The men voiced opinions, none of which seemed to answer the question, but it did give me an in. Alejandra said she'd talk to Vinnie and ask him to contact me.

I was introduced to the old timers, Alan and his nubile wife, or girlfriend, Fuchsia. Alan was something to do with bulbs in Lincolnshire. He was in his sixties with dyed black hair and wore a tropical shirt over a pair of skimpy Speedos. He doddered about on spindly legs that were close to giving way after years of supporting an enormous paunch. I'd clocked Fuchsia in reception when I checked in. She wore plaster-sized pieces of fabric, barely concealing her reproductive organ and her erogenous zones; in some outfits she had to choose which erogenous zones would remain covered due to a shortage of fabric. She had long black hair the colour of 1940s Bakelite phones, a trout pout and cosmetically engineered breasts. She looked like she might be in her late thirties but you'd need to carbon date her. Alan and Fuchsia loved to talk; the only rule being they never asked anyone about themselves.

They took me under their patronage and introduced me to Bernd Poric, the pasty-faced Swiss-German manager, who, in a bizarre twist, didn't have a sense of humour. Mrs Nasal Detritus had two lines running from the bridge of her nose like a pair of exclamation marks. She gave a consumptive snort as soon as I joined the group and left to air-kiss strangers while Mr Polo scuttled after her with her glass.

Between them, Alan, Fuchsia and Alejandra knew every guest on the island. I told them my 'Are you Finnish?' story about Oleg to establish my comedy credentials. I displayed self-deprecation with my description of how inept my performance was at my scuba class. I'd played my way in like an opening batsman at Lord's who had made seventy runs before lunch.

The conversation got round to the owners, Vernon and Mardy. Alan and Fuchsia knew everything about them, due, in part, to the leather-bound folder, which lay unread on the desk in my cabana. They had given intimate details of their life together in order to be able to share them with the guests. I was a little disappointed at not having met the owners upon arrival, but Alejandra assured me again Vinnie would talk to me about marlin fishing. Alan and Fuchsia teased Alejandra about Vinnie. Alejandra blushed and rubbed her nose, which gave me the queasy impression they were an item. I hoped it was just teasing.

After sunset, the speedboat started taking guests back to the beach. Everybody was jollier on the way back, making wisecracks and being indiscreet about other guests. I hoped we might go on and have supper together. However, as I was keen not to implore anyone to do so I made sure I diverted my spaniel's eyes. Bernd, the manager, had things to attend to so I hoped Alejandra, Spindly Legs, Plastic Tits and I might make up a foursome. We sat down and had a drink together at the Dhow Bar. I had to resist my urge to talk knowing that if I wanted to appear interesting, I had to remain relatively quiet and ask people questions about themselves. It was difficult to know how I could look at Alejandra without being caught. I should have worn sunglasses but after dark it isn't a good look. I managed to sneak a look at Alejandra every time I scratched a gnat bite on the back of my head.

'Do you have any spray?' Alejandra asked.

'I do thanks but nothing works I'm afraid,' I said.

'Have you tried Vitamin B6?'

'Nah, I don't go in for all that homopathy,' I said.

'It's hom-e-o-pathy not homo-pathy,' she said.

'I am sure you're right but it isn't the bites on the back of my head that are driving me mad so much as the ones on my arse. Have you been bitten by sand-flies?' I asked.

'No,' said Alejandra. She stretched her legs as if holding a yogic posture.

'No sand-flies here, and I should know,' said Spindly Legs.

'Why do you think they are sand-fly bites?' asked Alejandra.

'Well, what do you think these are?' I lowered my linen trousers carefully just to illustrate my point while Plastic Tits hoovered up Spindly's glass of wine.

'Look like zits to me,' said Alejandra.

'If I had zits on my bum, do you honestly think I would show them to you?' I asked. This conversation was beginning to go as well as my scuba class.

'I don't know. Who knows what you might want to show me? You can do what you like. You are on holiday you know,' Alejandra said.

'If you have any ideas, will you call me?' I made a big show of plucking a business card out of my wallet and presented it to Alejandra Japanese-style with my head bowed. They all laughed, even Plastic Tits, who was quite sozzled. I caught Alejandra laughing along with the rest of them. When she laughed she opened her mouth wide and her shoulders shook. When I looked at her, she stopped laughing and put her beach-blonde hair behind her pointy little leprechaun ears.

Perhaps if I hadn't gone into detail about my arse being invaded by sand-flies then Spindle and Plastic wouldn't have gone back to their room to freshen up. If they hadn't gone back to their room perhaps Alejandra wouldn't have felt compelled to ring her mother before supper.

And so I was left on my lonesome, another conversational winner from the Jack Kaganagh stable. Rule One in Know-the-Game Luxury-Resort Conversation: if you strike up a conversation with a MILF, her ageing wallet and a mermaid called Alejandra, sitting in a Dhow Bar, overlooking the Indian Ocean, don't mention they are sitting on the exact bar stools where sand-flies ripped your arse off the previous evening. It simply doesn't do.

Having consumed my fair share, it was time for dinner. But first I had to stand around by a lectern and wait for someone to seat me. Every night I had to confirm 'Yes, a table for one, please.' Then the other diners would break into laughter and song while screeching and making defamatory hand gestures. It felt like it anyway.

The waiters made light of their appalling sleeping conditions and bad pay by having a game of asking if everything was okay with the food every time I took a mouthful. By the time I spat most of it onto the tablecloth, they had disappeared. I was about to light another ciggie when a man with a salt and pepper ponytail sat down at my table. He was with a lady with a big red flower in her frizzy hair. She wore a batik-type wrap and chunky, ethnic, wooden jewellery.

My welcome visitors were Vern and Mardy. I spotted them at the champagne reception but thought they must have been new arrivals. They were dressed casually in an 'I'm living the dream' kind of way. Vern was in his sixties and did most of the talking while looking round the room; Mardy had a fixed smile but was clearly bored. They didn't want to talk to me but felt they had to because of what Alejandra had said. After an anodyne exchange of pleasantries, Vern asked me if I wanted his son Vinnie to organise some fishing and asked me to wait a while until he could fix me up.

Vinnie bowled up towards the end of my last drink. He was tall, lean, tanned, looked good in shorts and had a curious way of speaking to me with his eyes shut, only opening them when he wanted me to answer. He had a tone to his voice that could grate cheese. I was biased but he wasn't what you'd call a people person.

'Alejandra tells me you want to catch yourself a big fish,' Vinnie said.

'Well obviously, I wouldn't say no,' I said.

'So what are we after? We got shortbill, spearfish, sailfish, skipjack, yellowfin, mahi mahi, barracuda, we've got trevallies...' he said.

'I'm only really interested in marlin. Do you catch those here?' I said.

'Yeah, sure we've got striped and if you're lucky, black,' Vinnie said.

'What about the boat, bait, price, that sort of stuff?'

'I'm no expert but I'll get Shorty from the Marlin Club to come and see you. And we'll fix you up, relax about the rest of the stuff, we'll take care of you real good. Do you want to go tomorrow?' Vinnie asked.

'What do you think?' I asked.

'Well, some guests went out today and Shorty says the water looked like you might get deep blue for tomorrow but after that we might have some clouds coming in. How long you got here?'

'Not that long, a few days, no more,' I said.

'You best take it because if the weather changes, you've missed your chance. Unless, of course, you come out and stay with us again some time.'

'Okay, tell Shorty I'll take it,' I said.

'Fine, you're in the Eames Suite right?'

'Yes.'

'Shorty from the Marlin Club will call you to tell you whether or not he can organise it for tomorrow. Anyway, tight lines,' Vinny stood up to leave.

'Tight lines. And thank you, Vinnie.'

Vinnie opened his eyes now the conversation was over and wandered off without saying goodnight. He looked like the guy who I used to box when I was at school, the guy who beat me up every day in front of the juniors. If I could have swapped his looks for mine, I would have done so however arrogant he was. And wow, was he arrogant.

CHAPTER TWENTY-NINE

Sweet Leaf

I grabbed the phone to stop it ringing.

'You changed your mind Mr Kaganagh?'

'Sorry, who is this?' I said.

'My name is Shorty, Mister Vincent asked me to call you,' he said.

'What time is it?'

'It's nine forty-five,' he said.

'I thought you were getting me a wake-up call?'

'I thought you were organising it,' said Shorty.

'Is it too late to go now?'

'Up to you. A Russian guest wants the boat right away,' he said.

'But I've got it today. We agreed last night,' I said.

'Okay, Mr Kaganagh. We'll pick you up in thirty minutes,' Shorty said.

I decided to skip breakfast. I didn't want to bump into any of my new buddies who'd blown me out for dinner, watch Shaggy scrape guava jam off a spoon for half an hour or run the risk of fresh fruit if I was going to be out on a boat for most of the day.

Even I knew that to stand a chance of catching marlin you needed to be up early to get out into the deep blue water before the fish knocked off for lunch. The more serious the captain was about catching marlin, the earlier you'd have to get up. You seldom caught anything in the middle of the day. I didn't know how much it was going to cost me. But I did know if I could tag and release a marlin, it would be worth every penny. I have fished all over the world and caught every type of fish except for marlin.

Everton, the Captain's mate, picked me up at 10.15 and whisked me off to Bootless Bay. At least I got out of the resort and saw a bit of the island. Fulgary looked a bit like a cross between the palm-tree strewn idylls of the Maldives crossed with a sort of rural Vietnamese vibe. The journey from Omanalak to the harbour took twenty-five minutes. It was about a quarter to eleven when I arrived. I was guaranteed to be out on the reef during the hottest part of the day. Everton, who wore a T-shirt with *Child Legend* emblazoned upon it, was short and squat, professional but not friendly. He introduced me to Captain Shorty, who was about six foot three and built like a pipe cleaner. He dismissed me as a serious fisherman, as I'd rolled up nearer lunchtime than breakfast. He told me the Russian had offered twice the asking price to go out for the day. He told me a story about four biznizmen and twelve prostitutes. They had chartered a boat and partied hard but had fallen out with the girls so they dumped them in the sea ten kilometres from shore. It was Everton and Shorty who had to pick them up. I promised I wouldn't say anything at the hotel. It wasn't something anyone wanted to talk about.

The boat was called *Sea Gypsy*. Judging by the number of rascals in sunglasses whizzing about on James Bond speedboats, we weren't the only buccaneers on the waterways. The harbour was stuffed full of the braying gin-and-tonic drinking, golf-playing buffoons you find in any harbour in the world. I'm sure some genuinely liked boats; like I'm sure some made money legitimately. It's just names of boats can be misleading: *Isle Survive*, *Poppy Palace*, *Alimony*, *Falcon Maid* and *Flash Kant*.

I stopped looking at the boats when I realised I was waving. Why do people wave when they are on a boat? Perhaps they are imbued with a sense of well-being. This would explain why I couldn't understand why people do it. It must be a terrible bore if you capsize and people just wave back.

'Where are all those speedboats going?' I asked.

'Just shipping stuff around the island,' Everton said.

'Just shipping stuff… good stuff or bad stuff?' I giggled.

'Mainly good stuff. Ain't any bad stuff in Fulgary,' Everton guffawed.

'That can't be bad. What about customs and police?' I said.

'They have to buy their own like anybody else,' Shorty said.

'The dope here has an excellent reputation in England,' I said.

'You wanna try some?' Everton asked.

'I'll buy enough for a couple of joints but I don't want to take stuff home or anything like that,' I said.

'Just chill,' Shorty said.

Shorty gave a piercing whistle as if it was a sheep-dog trial. One of the James Bond boats circled and came up to ours. I felt nervous. Shorty and Everton spoke to the Bond boat operative; they slapped hands together for a considerable time and Mr Bond sped off. Shorty opened his palm to show me the dope. It smelt sweet, was full of seeds and stalks and sticky to the touch.

'You want to try some?' Shorty said.

'It'd be rude not to,' I said.

After a bit of fiddling about Everton passed the joint to me to light. I've always been drunk when I've tried it before but this time it felt very strong, even allowing for the regrettable fact I was sober. We passed the joint around and began to relax with one another. We had something in common; the trick is to find how to connect. It was a little less client-and-crew and a little more me-and-you.

I don't remember Everton skinning up the second joint but it can't have been very long after he flicked the first butt overboard. I looked up to find we were about to crash into another boat, a very large one that was moored in the harbour. Everton had to clamber over me, knocking my Tilley hat off my head, to prevent us from hitting it. Shorty had forgotten to put down the anchor after meeting his mate with the James Bond boat, which struck me as strange.

'Sorry, chaps, here we are in a huge harbour and yet we almost smash into another boat, and neither of you even saw it coming…'

They were both stoned; they had bloodshot eyes, which they were pushing back into their sockets, and yelping as if they were struggling to breathe. I was beginning to enjoy the first boat I had been on since the last time with Kay.

'What time is it?' asked Shorty.

'You tell me… aren't you boys supposed to tell the time by the position of the sun in the sky, and the tides and all that sort of shit?' We creased up again.

'Did you have breakfast?' asked Shorty.

'No. Did you?' I asked.

'Just some banana cake and some coffee,' said Shorty.

'I could do some banana cake,' I said.

'You hungry?'

'Bloody starving,' I said. Everton was sorting out the lures.

'You want pizza first?' said Shorty.

'Sorry is that a question? I could murder a pizza. How are you going to get pizza? We're on a boat,' I said.

'Just ring up and order in the harbour, they bring it to you,' said Everton.

'Amazing,' I said. Shorty spoke into his telephone or receiver or whatever they call those things on boats.

'What do you want?' asked Shorty.

'What have they got?'

'Sausage, ground beef, pepperoni, chorizo, black olives, ham, green peppers, pineapple, sweetcorn, onions, tomatoes, anchovies, smoky bacon, jalapeño peppers, mushrooms, tandoori chicken, tuna, thin crust, deep pan, small, medium or large,' said Shorty.

'Sorry what was the first one again?' I asked. Everton laughed so much he farted which made us laugh even more; Shorty was coughing into the receiver quite unable to catch his breath.

'Sorry Shorty, I didn't realise you were so stoned; you'll have to come in for this one,' said the voice over the tannoy. We trudged off the boat, feeling quite embarrassed, and climbed up to a hillside restaurant. There were no tourists apart from me. I was invited to sit down at a table, away from the crew, by a waiter. He was employed to point but not to speak to me under any circumstances. There was more hand slapping between Everton, Shorty and his mates. The hand slapping did not involve me; this suited me, as I cannot get the hang of it whatsoever. The pizza was delicious. Everton and Shorty sat on a separate table with their friends. I looked out towards the bay feeling very stoned and quite paranoid.

I thought about the *Jolly Roger* booze cruise in Mauritius on our last holiday and how Kay didn't want to go, how if I had been talking to Kay and not to a bunch of frat-pack drunks she might be alive today and I wouldn't feel like crying every time I woke up. But she was my responsibility and nobody else's. Everybody apart from Kay just went to have a good time.

The idea of catching fish left me cold. But we went out and everyone fell silent. I followed the rituals that were supposed to bring good luck; I tossed a coin into the ocean and sprinkled the tobacco from a cigarette as gifts to the fishing gods. Shorty and Everton started acting like professional fishermen. I stared fixedly at the horizon. I didn't want to get seasick. We trawled for about two or three hours. Needless to say, we never had the problem of how to tag and release a marlin or any other type of pelagic fish. We didn't have a bite. We saw some decent-sized flying fish off the side of the boat, the smallest of which was washed onto the gunwale, so at least I had caught something. (I keep the baby flying fish in a matchbox in the top right-hand drawer of my desk.)

The sea was not deep blue but more of a spinach-green and getting choppier. This made staring at the horizon more difficult. The smell of diesel, as we drifted about looking for sea birds to guide us, made me nauseous. The conversation had stopped since we set off, and none of our hearts was in it. Shorty and Everton nodded at me as if to ask permission to return to the bay. I nodded and smiled back as if I didn't know what they wanted. After three hours of catching nothing more than a flying fish so small you could keep it in a matchbox, I surrendered. Everton reeled in the lures while we sped back to the harbour.

I gave Shorty 435 dollars in cash, which generously included thirty-five dollars for a pizza, one glass of Diet Coke and an espresso, and Everton drove me back to the resort. I had to pay in cash because Vinnie from the Omanalak wouldn't pay for Everton or Shorty to use a credit-card machine or, more accurately, Vinnie had wanted them to pay for the machine and the phone line out of their cut and not his. I asked Everton all the questions after the fishing trip I should have asked Vinnie when he discussed fishing with me the night before. He told me they hadn't caught a marlin, striped or black, for two years. I found this disappointing to hear from an employee of the Marlin Club. There had been reports of someone in Fulgary catching a marlin last year but neither Shorty nor Everton knew the people involved. Vinnie brought in most of the business but his 25 per cent cut of the gross was so punitive they had decided it was going to be their last year.

If I had done my research, for 435 dollars, inclusive of lunch and taxes, I could have ordered the deep pan with everything on it. It shows that just because you can, it doesn't mean you should; white women braiding their hair are but one example.

I felt knackered by the time I got back to the hotel. Maybe it was because I hadn't caught a marlin (again) or maybe it was because I wasn't going to catch one. I was more likely to go back to my room and find Kay washing her hair. I was pissed off to be back in the hotel because they played Kenny G all afternoon. Kenny G plays smooth jazz on a soprano saxophone making Joy Division sound like Freddy and the Dreamers. Kenny G is played in every resort I have ever had the misfortune to stay in. You cannot be happy anywhere Kenny G's music can be heard. Kenny G is the reason why men check their watches by the pool on holiday; Kenny G sounds like the soundtrack for your granny's homemade porn movie she made with her fat next-door neighbour who suffers from angina; Kenny G is the reason why people are friendly to waiters at the beginning of their holiday but not at the end. Kenny G was why the white folks wearing the bright colours by the pool looked so miserable.

CHAPTER THIRTY

Excitable Boy

My Russian friend, Oleg – he may, of course, have been Tajik, Uzbek, Turkmen, Kazakh, Chechen, Georgian, Kirghiz or whatever – read every word of his book out loud while his Svetlana dissolved into shrieks of laughter. She lay facing the sun with her leg cocked like the girl in the Nivea sun-cream advert. Svetlana positioned herself by the side of the pool thus blocking access to the steps. Oleg wore his Omanalak baseball cap back to front. He was in his forties and looked like he lifted weights. Dead weights. This would explain why he had to go up to the breakfast buffet five times a day. Oleg had no discernible neck but a very broad back. Svetlana wore bikini bottoms that said *Slippery When Wet*. She was cute, but not as cute as she thought. She pointed her body towards the sun at all times like a sundial. They were the sort of couple who, when you walked past them, could be overheard saying something like 'a headshot would have been fine'.

When Oleg wasn't reading out loud (perhaps he had a test when he got back), he relaxed by chewing gum with his mouth open and bouncing it about on his back molars. When he read he moved his head from left to right. Oleg was proof that money is no guarantor of manners. I remembered Bernd's story at the Manager's Weekly Drinks Party, about the Saudi party of twenty who spent 30,000 dollars in one night. When they rang to arrange another visit, they were not allowed to return for fear of upsetting any more staff and guests. I've always thought there must be money to be made in introducing old money to new money but have yet to work out how.

It was too hot, the salt of sea spray had burnt my cheek, the sand-flies had chewed my other cheeks and my arms itched all over with plankton rash.

After lunch, screwed up beach towels and detritus surrounded the pool. The unread novels and sunglasses hadn't been left because people were coming back for a dip but to stop passers-by nabbing *their* spot.

Most people used the pool in the morning so they could ring people they hadn't spoken to for ages to tell them they're on holiday. People used their phones when they were in the infinity pool and glared at the luddites who still used a pool to swim up and down.

I decided to leave the pool when the attendants started an impromptu chair-dragging competition, which superseded the random workmen's hammering competition, both of which drowned out Kenny G.

Arthur was prodding a hole in the sand with a stick while making sure he didn't cast a shadow. I've never seen a man concentrate more.

'I think it's terrible people reserving loungers all day,' I said.

'Always happen,' Arthur said. He crouched down to look into the hole.

'I think if they're not there, clear all their stuff away.'

'They're probably having a sleep or snorkelling,' Arthur said.

'Yeah, probably.' I sighed.

'You been snorkelling yet?' Arthur brushed the sand off his shorts.

'I think it's the water that's giving me a rash,' I showed Arthur my arm.

'I swim every day before and after work.'

'What do you think I should do today? Any bright ideas, Arthur?'

'You want to think less and feel more,' Arthur said.

'Right. So nothing springs to mind?' I said.

'Try and be in the here and now. Nature is all around,' he said.

'So where are the tejus, then? I haven't seen one in a while.'

'When the weather is about to change they leave the beach for higher ground,' Arthur said. 'And today Vernon had to ask me to help get their cat down off the roof. And if you look, you don't see any spider crabs either.' Arthur pointed to the hole with his stick. It was like being back in a classroom.

'Yeah right, anyway, Arthur, best crack on, I've got to rush to yoga or I'll be late. And I hate being late for anything.' As I dawdled down to the spa, I couldn't believe I'd been crowbarred into taking the ashtanga yoga class by Dr Vijay. I approached the spa with a heavy heart. My spirits revived after a chat with the gay Thai guy on reception and a splosh of ginger tea.

I met a consumptive snorter from the United States. She was one of those people who lurk around in the shadows of the spa while recovering from cosmetic surgery – who make a point of being on first-name terms with every member of staff. She used employees' names in every sentence, 'Why thank you so much, Gretchen. What time do you finish today, Pei-Hsuan? Are you working tomorrow, Carly?' But God forbid if a mere guest spoke to her – all hell would break loose and her face would distort with disgust. I made the faux pas of being dumb enough and rude enough to ask, 'Excuse me, is this seat taken?' She hadn't got to where she was today by having to deal directly with the public. She waved her long, bony fingers at me like she was trying to flick snot off.

It was, therefore, not a surprise to find her in my ashtanga yoga class with old bushy moustache himself, Dr Vijay. Mrs Flicky Fingers was better at yoga than the rest of the class. Yoga is not known for its competitive nature, yet it was this that had attracted her. She had better kit, she held her postures for longer, breathed deeper and sat closer to Dr Vijay. When he wasn't helping her, she asked questions to eliminate the risk of him communicating with anyone else. I tried not to break wind while keeping my posture. This meant I only had my emetic vomiting and a Thai massage left before the end of the holiday.

I had a lie-down when I got back but couldn't sleep because of the sound of the crickets changing key as if they were being conducted. It sounded like crackling electricity – either that or it was the sound of my freckles popping from the sunburn like popcorn in a pan. I went to the bar with only a week-old newspaper for company, and after another evening of sitting alone I went back to my room.

CHAPTER THIRTY-ONE

Wunderbar

The next day was a washout; it felt like a non-holiday day. It reminded me of the Maldives during the tsunami when Italian guests summoned the manager to their villa to complain the tsunami had ruined their holiday and what was he going to do about it. He did what he could. He got them off the island before he chinned them.

The sky was grey, the sandy beach looked like freshly mixed concrete and the sea was choppy and brown. Walking along barefoot in garish shorts and a loud shirt to breakfast on an overcast beach felt like a cruel joke. Hardly anybody was about, and those who were looked wretched.

I had no idea how long the bad weather was going to last. Was this the beginning of something or just a blip? Whiteys are perfectly happy to go swanning off to tropical islands with thick, lush vegetation but we get very unhappy very quickly if the thick, lush vegetation takes a shower.

What was I going to do, on my own, in a barefoot luxury resort in the rain? Even the daily copy of the *Omanalak Times* couldn't help me. There was a trip around the kitchen garden where they grow vegetables, and I didn't fancy the all-day snorkelling tour where you visited another island in the rain for eighty-five dollars, lunch not included, plus taxes.

Perhaps it wasn't so bad I was nearer the end of the holiday than the beginning. It was a shame the Marlin Club found it easier to locate weather fronts than shoals of pelagic fish. I had packed away the matchbox with my flying fish in my luggage, just in case Devon decided it was empty and threw it away. The matchbox was a 435 dollars keepsake.

I decided to go into Saparmurat and buy a Fulgary pin badge for my Tilley hat and take in the sights of Lovers' Leap. Frottager advised on what to wear: 'Women who go out on to the street wearing low-cut dresses, sleeveless tops, short pedal-pushers, or do not wear pantyhose are open to criticism.' They added that 'Men must avoid wearing sneakers unless absolutely necessary.'

Reception waffled on about how it would be better to use the resort's driver to show me the island and how Royston, the resort's driver, came recommended by Vinnie himself. Alan and Fuchsia had been told about unrest in the capital and how tourists some while back got badly beaten up by Highlanders. They said I was mad to go into town without Royston. I walked out of the gates of the hotel, turned right and grabbed a taxi. I couldn't afford another one of Vinnie's ideas.

Before I entered Saparmurat, I passed a sign that read, *You are in the embrace of history*. We stopped by a tired park, overlooked by the governmental building, which had the national flag of Fulgary fluttering on the end of a flaky white pole. I asked the driver where I could buy a pin badge for my Tilley hat and took it off to show him. He said the place for souvenirs was Main Street.

I was looking forward to meeting my first Highlanders but I found myself clutching my bag tighter than if I hadn't heard of their reputation from the Coastal people. Because of the weather, for the first time since I arrived, I had to wear a pair of shoes, which felt uncomfortable and alien. I walked past several signs: *No riding on the sidewalk*, *This way to John the baker man*, *No bare-back persons allowed* and *Give way to landing and departing aircraft*.

The shops on Main Street sold the same batik and terracotta pots, which were ideal for taking on as hand luggage or throwing into the hold of a plane. They also sold snakes, lizards and rodents preserved in alcohol in bottles. The Coronation Islands seemed to lead the world in the pickled-small-animal market. What is it with tourists and shopping? You see people laden down, bags full of tat, looking knackered from walking all day. Hawkers chivvy them every time they stop. And if they do buy something, they end up lugging stuff they neither need nor want. And when they get to rest their creaky bones, their friend says, 'You've done well.' No they haven't, they've wasted a day of their life and spent 250 dollars on junk.

After an hour of looking at items you'd sneer at in shops at home, your mindset changes. For example, Lithuania is known for its amber. I've never felt the need to own anything made from amber. After looking at dozens of stores selling stuff you'd never dream of giving house space to, you get to thinking one amber product is marginally less ugly than the other ten thousand you've seen. There is a thin line between thinking something is the least *ugly* amber product you've seen all day and thinking it is the most *desirable* amber product you've seen all day. I'd use my unwrapped amber cigarette case and lighter I bought with Kay in Vilnius, Lithuania as an example.

I found a pin badge designed in the shape of the island with the colours of Fulgary's national flag. If I'd bought a badge on arrival at the airport I could have saved myself the bother, but then I would have been part of the 95 per cent of tourists who never leave the hotel. I decided buying a bottle with a rodent preserved in alcohol could wait until I returned to the airport.

I made sure the cab driver was still there and went to a bar off Main Street to check out the locals over a drink. The sky was gunmetal grey, and the weather looked unlikely to change for a day or two. I had nothing to do and all day to do it. I had secured my objective in buying a pin badge, which I would attach to my hat when I got back to London. It would be naff to do so before then. People surprise me when they go into a shop and wear T-shirts with the name of the place they are staying in. I was never one for joining in.

There was nobody in the bar apart from the proprietor and me. They kept baby caimans downstairs by the gents' toilets. They both smelt. The caimans were kept in a small wire-mesh pen in fetid water with a handwritten sign that said, *Don't play with them they're much more faster than you* and *Feed fifty cents*. In the toilet was another sign that read *Children, more taken care please*. As I approached the urinal, I felt grateful for my shoes.

I didn't want to drink upstairs in what little natural light there was. The barman and I eyed each other, while both pretending not to see, until he descended upon my table and took my order. I sat outside under a leaky Coca-Cola canopy and watched the rain until my drink arrived.

A small kid about eight years old, possibly older, approached me. He had black hair and an earnest face. He was selling pictures and postcards of Saparmurat and Lovers' Leap.

'Where are you from?' He spoke without smiling.

'Ireland,' I thought this answer would be more problematic for the boy than England.

'Ireland's president is Michael Higgins, the capital is Dublin, population is four and a half million, your prime minister is Enda Kenny and the GDP per capita is 40,000 dollars. Your currency is the euro,' he said.

'How much are your postcards?'

'Five dollars each.' He sifted through them.

'Here, give me three and keep the change,' I said.

'Thank you, sir. Would you like to buy some pictures?'

'No thank you,' I said.

'Have you seen Saparmurat?' The boy asked.

'Yes, thank you,' I drained my drink.

'If you want, I can make special tour?

'No thanks.' I picked up the postcards.

'Have you seen the waterfall?' he asked.

'No.' I put my lighter in my pocket and stubbed out my cigarette.

'Have you seen Lovers' Leap?'

'Not yet,' I said.

'You want I tell you about Lovers' Leap?' he asked.

'No, thank you.'

'I show you shopping district, batik and terracotta pots...'

'No you're fine.' I put my bag on my shoulder.

'You want factory visit where they put animals in bottles?' he asked.

'No, really, that's fine. Thanks for the cards and best of luck,' I said.

I left the bar and shrugged off the kid. He was as bright as an octopus. He would either become president or a high-risk repeat offender. I checked to make sure he wasn't following me and went back to meet my driver.

The houses had corrugated-tin roofs with livestock scrambling about snuffling household waste and building materials left by the side of the unfinished road. The driver pulled into the car park at Lovers' Leap. Coaches disgorged fat tourists dressed in lightweight rain gear with white pumps and rolled-down socks. Cameras banged against hips as they clambered to the summit. Entrance to the park at Lovers' Leap was ten dollars, inclusive of taxes, and the fee included a map.

My driver, who was smoking with his other cab-driving mates, was surprised to see me and stubbed out his cigarette as if caught smoking at school. What was the point of climbing to the top to get a picture of a rock that people jumped off to avoid meeting people like me? Besides, it was raining. I felt as if I had let my driver down. He said he didn't get much business out of Omanalak since Vinnie became involved. I didn't pay my entrance fee to see the attraction so the trip would be shorter which would mean he'd earn less. He asked if I wanted to see the waterfall. Mindful of my missing out on the previous hotspot, I said yes. After a long drive in the opposite direction from the resort, we pulled up outside the other Fulgary national park. He stopped and got out. I followed him and took the protective lens cap off my camera. He pointed to something far away. It was the waterfall. The force of the water was less than the electric shower in my spare bedroom. I asked him if that was it. He nodded and asked if I wanted to take a picture. I shook my head, put the lens cap back on the camera and walked to the car. We drove back in silence as I tried to work out how much I should tip him. He gave me his card and asked me to give it to reception.

After a curt goodbye and a twenty-dollar tip, I was back in time to catch a West Indian steel-drum cover version of Sting's 'Englishman in New York' playing on the hotel's sound system. It made a change from Kenny G. but not enough to make me feel I'd missed the place. The pool was empty apart from the podgy kid sitting with his nanny. They were always together with no parent to be seen. The kid, dressed in Versace pinstriped trunks, was reading a book called *Is Daddy Dead?*

I went to the beach to find Arthur to ask him about his day so I could tell him about mine. To the left of the Dhow Bar, staff had erected a flimsy marquee with a two-step stage, a strip of sandy red carpet, multicoloured bunting and the type of chairs you only find in conference centres. The marquee was flimsy, and a lot of the love-heart decorations had blown away. I saw a few awkward-looking guests milling about, clutching champagne flutes and laughing louder than was strictly necessary. The groom was resplendent in a duck-egg-blue suit and white open-necked shirt, while the bride wore a figure-hugging knee-length teal and aubergine summer dress. They were both barefoot on wet sand. She held her hat on with her right hand to stop it blowing away. I walked towards the happy couple thinking I might bump into some people I knew until I realised the wedding photographer was taking pictures of Oleg and Svetlana. I waved at them but they were too busy concentrating on the photographer to notice me.

It was time for my emetic vomiting session. Dr Vijay preferred his patients to have this treatment in the morning. I told him if it worked I would book more before my return to London. He diagnosed the same type of ailments as the Tibetan doctor who had prescribed the herbal bullet-like pellets. Dr Vijay said I had too much phlegm and some congestion of the lungs as a result of my smoking. He said I suffered from deranged bile, which might explain the headaches. The treatment consisted of a full-body massage using Ayurvedic oils and three or four glasses of what tasted like a mixture of lukewarm salty water and liquorice. It tasted bitter, hot, sharp and dry. It took several attempts to suck the foul liquid through a straw. Then my saliva began to flow, my eyes ran as if I had hay fever, mucus sprang from my nose and I began to chunder. I hadn't vomited like that since a camping holiday in France when I was seventeen. About fifteen or twenty minutes after my purgation had ceased, my neck and my head felt clear and my body felt lighter. Dr Vijay handed me a customer-feedback form, which I left blank. I apologised to him about his shirt and walked gingerly back to my room.

I tried to sleep but the rain made a guttering sound like someone having a piss on the roof. I picked up my umbrella to go down for supper but I changed my mind. I didn't fancy seeing any brooding, cheerless faces. I decided to stay in and dial room service. I ordered a DVD of *The Naked Gun 2½: The Smell of Fear* (1991), a large bottle of fizzy water, a club sandwich and a selection of imported fresh fruit.

CHAPTER THIRTY-TWO

Rise

The uh-ho birds woke me up at the normal time. It was the penultimate full day of my holiday. The stormy weather front had blown over and, apart from the sand feeling wetter and cooler on the feet, there was little evidence of the rain we'd had the previous day. At the risk of sounding happy, I was happy; I'd had a cracking night's sleep. There wasn't any negative reaction to my emetic treatment but I did wonder if the vomiting would counteract the pellets the Tibetan doctor had given me. I felt nice and empty, like after colonic irrigation or food poisoning.

The day before, water had seeped up from the ground, forming pools where previously it was scrub and sand. They disappeared as quickly as they had risen. It was like coming downstairs after a party to find somebody else has cleaned up. I was back in the land of endless vistas, where the sky was made out of lapis lazuli, the sea was turquoise and the island was palm-fringed. The only difference was waves crashed upon the beach whereas before the sea was calm.

I had two and a half days to get a suntan before returning to Heathrow. I couldn't think of anything to say to Shaggy. There is an ebb and flow to my relationships with waiting staff, particularly those who work at breakfast. I start off the holiday being over-excited and chatty, but once I've decided I don't want to chat at mealtimes, I go mute. I just want to be left alone. Heaven knows what it must be like working with people who are on holiday. Shaggy had smiled timidly when at the beginning of the holiday I had said, 'You don't know how lucky you are to be working here' and 'I'd rather have your job than mine. Do you want to swap?'

This is the waiting staff equivalent of saying 'What time are you working till?' to a taxi driver.

The early risers had snapped up the sun loungers by the pool. Judging by the deployment of splayed novels and designer sunglasses, I wouldn't be able to get one until after lunch at the earliest. The guests spoke on their mobiles, managing to look like security guards restricting access to the infinity pool. The man with the polo shirt and the snotty partner practised his golf swing, yawned and checked his watch while awaiting instructions.

I had absolutely nothing to do. Even on holiday you feel, or at least some people feel, obliged to do this and to look at that. But I was free until the Head Chef's Weekly Buffet. I was intrigued to know what the live entertainment was and hoped it wasn't a Kenny G tribute band.

I had no reason to leave the resort until it was time to return to the airport. I had no treatments booked in the spa, and I was not game fishing or sightseeing. I was not going to spend the day in the car retracing ancient suicide rites or inspecting waterfalls whose velocity was markedly less than my guttering. I was going to have to lie down and relax before it was too late. I had a couple of days left and then it would be over. I was running out of time.

I went back to my room and moved stuff around from one bag to another without anything to show for it. I needed sunglasses, my book, which I wanted to finish, camera, anti-mozzie spray, Tilley hat, sunscreen, beach towel, spray for when I had been bitten, my Tibetan medical pellets, postcards and stamps. It would be better to walk on the beach before the morning sun got too hot. It was soon going to be time for a dip.

My sunburn had been greatly helped by the downpour but it made my plankton rash itch even more. Perhaps I could burn it off. I agonised over whether I could get away with wearing my wife-beater vest, and, if not, should I go for a dirty T-shirt or a clean one? What was the point of wearing a clean T-shirt if it was just going to get sweaty and sandy? Equally, with only a couple of days left, why not wear the clothes I'd packed? What was the point in saving my summer clothes for winter in England?

It was mid-morning before I hit the beach. A few minutes of sun on both sides and it would be time for lunch. I saw Alan, the Lincolnshire bulb man, walking about and staring at his feet. Every time I had seen him, apart from mealtimes when he was with the lovely Fuchsia, he was walking around on his own, dressed snugly in his black Speedos, looking down at the ground. But when he finally saw me on the beach, he waved at me and I waved back. The impressive thing about Alan was how little he carried when he went off on one of his jaunts. By now, the Asian woman had found Mr Pink Polo Shirt Collar Turned Up; he kept himself busy by carrying mobile-phone chargers and bags from the boutique shop.

I was keen to finish Derek Percy-Ffrench's *A Time of Shifts* before I got back to the airport. I start off every book in good faith, but my enthusiasm begins to wane, and I trudge through it as if finishing it is an achievement in itself. I wasn't interested whether the architecture he was banging on about was Byzantine or Baroque. His was a world of spandrels and tendrils, post-colonialism and transculturation – a world where things were oleaginous but never greasy. I wasn't judging the book by how many languages the author could read Goethe in, and I didn't understand what a Homeric plot was. But I know a lot of *The Simpsons* writers went to Harvard. I began to turn the pages, looking for an absence of print and for chapter breaks so I could turn over the page without too much effort.

I was tired of holding my book at an angle to keep the sun out of my eyes. I looked at my watch. I had been looking at the same page for five minutes. It would be easier to read while sat at a table.

I had the same stir-fry for lunch every day. But before I ate the same thing, I would walk around and look at what was on offer. Lunch was organised on a national cuisine basis. You'd have Japanese, Indian and Italian for example. I walked around clutching my plate, ogling the dishes, worrying about how sweaty the chefs must be, standing outside by hot grills wearing chef's whites, and about where the sweat went. As soon as anyone got in my line of vision I'd just apologise, smile and move on. There is something embarrassing about walking around gawping at food in a part of the world where there is malnutrition and people dying of malaria because they can't afford medicine. The podgy kid, with the nanny but without the parents, shouted at the pasta chef, 'My mother is Italian and that is *not* penne.'

It is difficult to justify complaining about indigestion having eaten a plate of crème caramel after wolfing down a stir-fry of curry leaves, deep-fried chicken and half a jar of mango and chilli cooked in oil. The food was served under the palm trees so guests could look out over the pontoon and the Indian Ocean. It was faultless, which rebutted my theory that the better the view from a restaurant, the worse the food.

I didn't spend too much time at lunch because I was in a rush to get a suntan. I lay down for the afternoon smothered in suntan lotion. As I perspired it went into my eyes and made my glasses greasy. I lay my Tilley hat on my face to stop my skin from burning. I spent most of the afternoon trying to work out whether I wanted to go for a snorkel and whether it would aggravate my plankton rash and if I should go back to my cabana or not. It was too hot to decide so I closed my eyes and concentrated on the sound of the waves.

I don't know whether I drifted off, but judging by the taste in my mouth I may well have done. It was about three-thirty in the afternoon, and the strength of the sun was waning. I had got up, had breakfast, gone back to the room, picked up my stuff, lay down, had lunch and lay down again. I still hadn't actually done anything. It was time for a swim in the aquamarine waters of the Indian Ocean under a cloudless, sapphire sky. Time to swim off some calories before supper.

When I arrived at Omanalak, the sea was calm and blue, but yesterday the sea had been the colour of brown Windsor soup. Today it was aquamarine. I went for a dip wearing my Tilley hat to protect my face from the sun. The waves seemed moderate from the beach and were hardly colossal even when standing in the water. But the further I moved into the water, the more I could feel my feet being yanked away from under me. I was being pulled out to where the waves broke and was beginning to lose my balance. I needed to swim past the breakers so I could splash about in calmer waters. I am a strong swimmer and can do front crawl or backstroke non-stop for about forty-five minutes. I approached the waves and I tried to jump over them. The swell grabbed me by the ankles and tried to shove me over. I struggled to plant my feet flush against the sandy bottom. The sea tugged me into the breaking waves. I held onto my hat and glasses and used my other hand for balance. They were my favourite glasses with tortoiseshell frames from Roger Pope in New Cavendish Street. They weren't even sunglasses so I shouldn't have had them on in the first place. But I am as blind as a welder's dog and wouldn't have a clue which way I was facing without them. My toes struggled to grip the sand and, in one sudden movement, my feet lost traction, I lost my balance and went under. I knew I couldn't keep hold of everything; I'd have to let my glasses and hat go and hope I could pick them up once I'd got through the waves. I was in a spin-dryer of turbulence and gritty, brown sand. The eddying current slammed me onto my back. I kept my eyes closed underwater, but through my shut eyelids I could sense from the sun where the sky was and, while I waited for the water to drain away, I felt as if my life was going down the plughole. I made a determined effort to regain my balance and came up for air before another wave knocked me down again onto the sea's silted floor. Again my back crashed against the sand and my foot slipped. I felt as if someone was holding me underwater, like a bully in a school swimming class. I needed to stand up and to stay on my two feet. I hadn't swallowed any seawater. I didn't make a conscious decision about this, I just reacted; there was no time to consider options. It was instinct and reflex, nothing else, and I was convinced if it happened again I wouldn't be so lucky. If

I swallowed seawater it would be the end. I have almost drowned on two previous occasions: Collioure in Languedoc-Roussillon and Biarritz, in the Bay of Biscay, where however hard I swam, the tide whipped me out further away from the beach than where I'd started.

I wondered if Kay's lungs had filled up with water or whether she had hit her head when she slipped off the boat.

She had a period coming on and already had too much sun. Kay didn't want to drink alcohol at lunchtime. She wanted to relax by the pool. I felt guilty about going off fishing and leaving Kay with Naz and the boat boys so I insisted she came. We were dropped off by a Toyota Land Cruiser at the bar next to the dock, which was only ten minutes from the 'pirate ship', and they provided us with a rib to get there, which was great unless you don't like bouncing up and down at breakneck speed. When we finally set off, the boat was full and there was nowhere to sit.

The last time I saw Kay she was standing bolt upright, trying to look as awkward as possible. She didn't want to eat anything and she felt sick. She waved her arms around every time I lit a cigarette. She didn't like the ladies' toilets, she didn't enjoy the music and she wanted to go back to the room and to have a lie down. Her neck and chest were red and blotchy. She was driving me nuts with her moaning and was determined not to enjoy herself. She wouldn't even go up to the bar area, where Naz and the boys were serving the drinks, although she got on well with all of them. She said she needed to get out of the sun but I told her if she went below deck that would be the end of her. I thought Kay was being ridiculous so I ignored her and helped myself to a cocktail. If she didn't want to come and hang out with me, Naz, and the rest of the boat boys, that was up to her. I wasn't going to spend my day babysitting a petulant child. I ignored Kay because she was sulking and got into a conversation with some blokes from Rutgers who were polite, chatty and loved hearing all my stories from my travels. I had thought there was nothing to be gained by fussing over her but now I wouldn't have felt any guiltier about her if I had killed her with my own hands. My lifestyle drove her away from me. I always put my job first as I couldn't cope with late nights and early starts. Maybe I was drowning as a punishment for losing my fiancée. I could have surrendered. If I opened my mouth, my lungs would fill up with shitty, silty, salty water and I'd choke and drown. The sea tried to drown my voice to stop me from screaming out. All the times I should have cried out for help and didn't, and now I wanted to cry out, I couldn't.

I was almost drowning because I had set myself the needless task of going to one hundred countries. I couldn't visit my pals in Madrid because I had been there already. We couldn't go to Paris because she used to go out with a Frenchman. I couldn't go to Brazil because I'd been there on a day trip from Iguazu Falls. America was out of the question because we had refuelled at LAX, and I was effectively barred from Continental Europe because I went inter-railing as a student. I had to go somewhere new, somewhere untainted by the past, somewhere that wasn't second hand.

I don't know what happened to the water that must have gone up my nose; I've always hated water up my nose. Was it easier to get it over with or was it easier to fight? I wondered if Kay had fought or did she just give up? Did she, at any point, think trying to live was too difficult, that it just wasn't worth all the bother? Did Kay give up on me, on herself or on both of us? And why wasn't she with me? Why didn't someone stop her? How can somebody disappear from a boat in the middle of the day without anybody seeing *something*?

We had stopped for happy hour just off the beach where we were staying. Some people had swum back but I thought I had better wait for Kay so we could disembark together. What with the sun, a big lunch and a boat trip, I was ready to go back to the room. Naz helped the guests clamber off the boat. I asked him if he had seen Kay. Naz said he hadn't seen her on deck for a while. I looked for her on the dock but she wasn't there. I waited for all the passengers to disembark, but she was nowhere to be seen. I went into the *Jolly Roger* bar – she wasn't there.

I asked a woman to call out her name in the ladies' toilets. She wasn't there. I was pissed off; she was having a hissy fit and had stormed off without telling me. Who the hell did she think she was for Christ's sake? I rehearsed the bollocking I was going to give her when I got back to the room. But Kay wasn't in the reception area of the hotel, or on the beach, or hanging out by the water sports like she always did.

She wasn't swinging in her favourite hammock under a palm tree by the spa. She wasn't in our room and she wasn't in the toilet. *Fine*, I remember thinking, *if she wants to sulk, let her sulk as long as she wants.* I walked about a bit, went into the spa and asked if Kay was having a treatment. They hadn't seen her. I went back to the water sports to ask Naz but he wasn't there. One of the boat boys said he hadn't seen Kay since before lunch when she'd been talking to Naz. She'd asked Naz if he could drop her off back onshore as she didn't feel great which was the last time he'd seen her, and that was what he had put in the police report. When I asked him why he hadn't told me that earlier when I was looking for her, he said he had. I spoke to Naz later and he just repeated the same thing; he said he was very shaken up by it, you could tell, even if he did keep his sunglasses on. Kay didn't come back. I notified the hotel management who notified the police, who, in turn, notified the British Embassy. It may have been a consulate, I cannot remember now. Nobody could have been more considerate really. I had to go into town to a police station. I was interviewed for four hours but I didn't begrudge them this. They checked my story out with the guys from Rutgers and I flew home. I went to my local police station and spoke to my local coroner's office and that was about it. They never found Kay's body; it was never washed up onshore. And without a body, it is difficult to ascertain what happened. Kay was a missing person.

I would never know what had happened to her. But how could I not think about it? How could I not think about the fact that Kay had disappeared on holiday? And it didn't matter whether I thought about it or not; you could see it on everybody else's faces: *oh yeah, so you're the one whose fiancée went missing when you were on holiday, you're the one, I know who you are now.*

But now I had to concentrate on myself. Kay had gone but it didn't mean I had to. I wasn't going to submit. I was going to fight. I wasn't going to make it easy. It dawned on me I'd spent my whole life being pushed, pulled and held down, and I'd had enough. I didn't know how I could get up without being knocked down again; I made one last attempt to retrieve my footing. If I couldn't muster my balance this time then I was unlikely to do so the next. I pumped my legs towards the shore. I started to believe that as long as I kept moving towards the water's edge. Eventually, which in real time meant only a few seconds later, I was free. I'd lost my glasses which meant I couldn't see a thing; my trunks were full of sand and weighing down above my knees; and I'd lost my Tilley hat which I'd worn since we went to Tanzania. But I didn't care. I hadn't drowned, and felt a great sense of achievement in my self-preservation. I also felt embarrassed. I'd been knocked over by what looked, from the shore at least, like perfectly innocuous waves. These were just ordinary, stupid little waves that had sucked me in, knocked me down, turned me over, spun me around and spat me out. I felt impotent, scared, shocked, tearful, relieved, humiliated, embarrassed and lucky to be alive. It didn't matter about my tortoiseshell-framed glasses; I had another pair in my personal security box. I wasn't bothered by the ridiculous spectacle of exposing myself to whomsoever had been sitting on the beach at the time. I didn't have my glasses on so I didn't know who was on the beach anyway. A couple of women helped me clamber out of the water, and one rather thoughtfully hoiked up my sand-filled trunks. They asked if I wanted to retrieve my Tilley hat and glasses. *Thank goodness*, I remember thinking, *it wasn't Alejandra and Vinnie who spotted me*; and, actually, I was relieved I'd lost my Tilley hat. It was ridiculous to try to capture memories of countries through the medium of tacky hatpins. The three of us made a token effort to retrieve my belongings, but I quickly gave up and went back to my room feeling exhausted but exhilarated.

The waves may have snatched her from me but, on this occasion, I had been just a little too much for Mother Nature. I knew she would win the tournament, but I had won the match. And as every Chairboy knows – you have to celebrate your victories. But with whom was I going to celebrate? My imaginary new friends from the Travelers' Century Club?

I thought I would cheer myself up by ringing somebody to tell them I was alive and well, thank God, that I had at least arrived in Fulgary, my one-hundredth country. There's no point achieving a milestone if you don't tell somebody about it, is there? I tried to ring my daughter but Graham, the gardener, picked up so I thought I'd ring Robin Hunt to tell him the good news that I had decided to take up the job offer trading the volatility index. I told the person who answered the phone where I was ringing from to get Robin off the phone. I was left on hold. I clicked off. My life had been put on hold for quite long enough since Kay's death.

CHAPTER THIRTY-THREE

Cinnamon Girl

I relaxed in my cabana by flicking through a big, black, glossy book entitled *Passionate About Travel*, which offered 'tailor-made solutions for the discerning, luxury traveller, a company for those who were because of today's lifestyle, cash-rich and time-poor'. These people were so time-poor they didn't have time to check prices before handing over their card details. *Passionate About Travel* offered aircraft charter, limousine, luxury-car rental, yacht and concierge services to Philippe Starck or Balinese-inspired design hotels with names like the Grand Hotel Majestic or the Imperial Boutique Hotel. There was no better book to read in the bathroom than this catalogue of escapist fantasies.

My air-con made a noise like a car engine left running in winter to defrost the windscreen. I switched it off to put on the fan that sounded like a one-fingered typist. The cicadas began to rasp at the end of another day. I stayed in my cabana so I wouldn't miss Robin when he rang me back. I know it's only in books, or in films, where people have their moment of 'epiphany' but I do concede – I did feel different. The drowning bit, well, whether I was close to drowning or not, I don't know, but it was as close to drowning as I have ever experienced and, secondly, it was as close to drowning as I want to get. We are not talking about the kind of waves that get young men dashing into the big blue with a board under their arm, but the kind of swell that can slap a man of my considerable heft onto his back, at least twice. It could have been the end for me, in six-star paradise, on a beach with palm trees, cabanas and all the other sort of execrable guff that doesn't add up to a crock of shite if you're on your own.

It was the Head Chef's Weekly Buffet with live entertainment to follow. I rummaged through the cupboards to pick out what was left of my best clothes. I wore my Vilebrequin linen shirt with the navy background and pale blue leaves and the red, orange, yellow and purple hibiscus and, having trimmed both nasal and ear hair, and having tried to remove every grain of sand, I was ready to party. I waited and waited to tell Robin the good news but the phone never rang.

There was steel-band music for the guests to enjoy along with a complimentary glass of champagne. I was in the Hylands Hotel in Ballyvaughn, County Clare once when they played the same song eight times in succession, but it wasn't as harrowing as the steel-band's cover version of Bryan Adams's '(Everything I Do) I Do It For You'. For the first time on my holiday, I wanted to go home.

My near-drowning incident justified my first Long Island Iced Tea of the evening; the Bryan Adams cover version and the original version of the Celine Dion drowning song justified my second. Ms Dion is popular among taxi-drivers in Madagascar. This was not in the brochure. You'd be told if there was diphtheria in Madagascar, so why not warn visitors about Ms Dion?

The guests huddled together for a drink in the Dhow Bar before the Head Chef's Weekly Buffet. I had half-expected the crowd to fall silent before I walked in to a standing ovation in celebration of my heroic struggle against the sea. I looked around but nothing happened so I hooked up with Alan and Fuchsia. Every time Alan went to the bathroom, or walked over to talk to yet another guest he'd met on a previous holiday, Fuchsia filled her glass from the bottle or simply drank Alan's.

Alan's bloated stomach was gift-wrapped with a T-shirt that blazoned *Lame in Bed but Rich* while Fuchsia wore a spangly *J'Adore Dior* T-shirt. It was lovely. I couldn't stop staring at it. It was less intimidating than the lady at the car-rental office in Kilrush airport, who had worn a T-shirt with the message *This Bitch Bites*. I wondered if Alan and Fuchsia were the type of couple who hosted parties where friends threw their car keys into the fruit bowl on the dining-room table. I wondered if you could go to swingers' parties on your own and say your partner couldn't make it because she was ill.

Everyone was looking everyone else up and down out of the corner of their eye; the women, dressed up in party frocks, were scrutinising the other women to gauge whether they were beautiful or not, and the men were trying to work out how their Personal Net Asset Value stacked up alongside that of the others in the room. There was a lot of looking and sipping champagne but not a lot of talking. Everybody assessed everybody else; and they all thought they hadn't been seen doing it.

Soon, it was Vinnie's turn to stand up. Vinnie delivered his sales pitch about an all-day excursion to another fantasy island, which was leaving the pontoon at 9.30 a.m., for an all-inclusive price of 110 dollars plus taxes. While Vinnie spoke, Alejandra looked up into his eyes like a presidential candidate's wife. Vinnie stopped halfway through his speech and checked his mobile phone for text messages. He kept his eyes shut while he addressed the room and only opened them to read his texts. So limpet-like was I to Alan and Fuchsia that I was invited to share their table at supper. This made a change from my usual supper-time activity of rereading the week-old copy of *USA Today*.

There is nothing else in the world I detest more than standing around with fellow guests, who are solely motivated by the desire to invade your personal defensible space, holding a plate, waiting for food. I must point out that the difference between barbeques, buffets and carveries is a matter of semantics. I must also point out that to dismiss the head chef's efforts as a buffet is like describing an Aston Martin DB5 as a runabout or Kenny G's music as a tad depressing.

The buffet looked so extraordinary that guests were invited to go up to video it before anyone ate anything. Given every single item had to be imported, it was inconceivable how food could be so beautifully presented and taste so fresh. People scampered up and posed next to giant fins of exotic fish for snaps taken by the hotel paparazzi and eagerly sought photos of themselves taken next to the chefs. It was the most impressive banquet I have ever been to.

Alan approached first while Fuchsia took another slug from his glass. Alejandra joined us to dine at what I expect was the behest of senior management. When Alan came back, I went around with Alejandra to look at the different varieties of salads, curried goat, deep-fried corn cakes, a side of beef, legs of lamb, crab, lobster, a haunch of venison, spit-roast pork, vegan haggis, sweet red bean pie, soba noodle and edamame salad with grilled tofu, calamari, cuts of offal, pasta, pizza, nasi goreng, lamb and mixed fruit pilaff, tajines, kebabs, dried meats, flatbreads, sushi, sashimi, ice carvings of swans, cheeses, pastries, cakes and puddings. I walked behind Alejandra so I could look at her without her seeing me. Standing next to her was even more exciting than the display. I nibbled away so there'd be less on my plate when I sat down; you can't eat an elephant at one sitting. By the time I sat down, I had forgotten what I had eaten and what it was that was left on my plate; a chilli went through my tongue like liquid nitrogen.

There was a famous centre forward, who had played for one of Italy's top four clubs, as well as playing for Italy, who had come down for supper. I had heard from Alejandra that he was staying on the island but it was my first glimpse of him and his wife. He had clearly spent most of his holiday working on his sideburns. He was so emotionally and physically drained by this, he didn't have the energy to carry his own plate. Every time I saw him, his wife was holding it and enquiring as to what he might like. She then carried it over to their table, before coming back to choose her own food.

Fuchsia had polished off most of the wine so I called Vinnie over and asked if I could order a bottle of white Côtes de Nuits. Vinnie bent down, as people are taught to do in the hospitality trade, to establish eye-level contact but not before winking at Alejandra in a very noticeable manner.

'Excellent choice, Mr Kaganagh.' Vinnie's breath was as rancid as yak butter tea, and I recoiled while Alejandra looked doe-eyed up at him. She must really need a job, I thought. Vinnie wandered off clicking his fingers at whatever member of staff was nearest.

'If ever you need my help just call me,' I said.

'Why on earth would I call you?' Alejandra coughed and giggled so much as she said this she almost snorted wine back through her nose.

'Because I think you have a boyfriend problem,' I said.

'What boyfriend problem?' Alejandra wiped her eyes on the napkin.

'Well, he clicks his fingers which is bad enough in itself, and he needs to see a dental hygienist.'

Alan gave his business card to Alejandra and insisted she was to look them up the next time she was at a loose end in Lincolnshire. He became embarrassed at not offering me one and inviting me so he did both. I offered him my business card and fantasised about getting a call from Fuchsia when she was down at their mews in Maida Vale, when he was away in the Hook of Holland on a business trip. I was thinking about this, while making a determined effort to only look at Alan and Alejandra, when Vinnie returned with the wine.

'Would you like to taste this?' Vinnie asked.

'No, of course, I fucking wouldn't.' The words had come out like an involuntary burp. 'Ha-Ha! Only kidding,' I said.

I nudged Vinnie and winked at him. He managed to remember to keep his eyes open while he poured the wine. He fixed me with a stare and chuckled a little too forcibly. I tried to waft my joke away but it hung around anyway. Fuchsia thought it was hysterical, but Fuchsia thought everything anyone said was hysterical. I made every effort to catch Vinnie's eye with a playful wink, or a thumbs-up, to establish chumminess. I started drinking fizzy mineral water and stopped drinking wine.

I was grateful when the after-dinner entertainment bowled up. The first act was a Coronation Islander who danced with candles on her head. I'm sure this is difficult to do. It is, however, pointless and not in the least bit entertaining. The Coronation Islands candle dancer got a round of applause but after the fire-eater's act, nobody clapped. He said, 'Thanks, you've been a great audience,' and left without a murmur.

I feel awkward for any performer, or any band, that leaves a stage without a whiff of appreciation, genuine or otherwise. It must be soul-destroying playing cover versions in an empty room or in front of guests who ignore you while chatting away in the queue for food. As a rule, if a performer opens with 'I hope all you guys are having a wonderful supper tonight,' then their career is not evolving in the way that they hoped.

Elephants die when their sixth set of molars drops out and they can't chew their food. Looking at the age of the guests, I assumed the average guest must have been on their fifth set. Alan must have been on his fifth or six, judging by the way he cut up his food before eating. Fuchsia was on her third or fourth set of molars, about her third or fourth face and at least her second pair of breasts. She held her knife like a jazz drummer held his brushes.

The live band played cover versions of Bob Marley, Celine Dion, Abba and the Spice Girls. When I say a band, what I mean is a woman with blonde hair and a gentleman with a pronounced limp. He wore his hair long in the mid-1980s' style of Michael Bolton. He played synthesiser, she strummed a guitar and they took it in turns to have a go at singing.

Oleg and Svetlana got them to play 'Money, Money, Money' at least three times while leaping around and trying to pull other guests up onto the dance floor. Plastic Tits and Spindly Legs showed us a few moves. I sat and grinned, looking at my watch, while Alejandra and Vinnie danced like a couple of French rock-and-roll dancers. All the more impressive, given how much they'd both drunk.

The Michael Bolton lookalike spent most of his time apologising to the audience for his bad voice, which made a refreshing change from people who couldn't sing but didn't apologise. When he spoke to the audience you could tell he was suffering from a cold. Meanwhile, a host of dancing zombies bent their knees on the sandy dance floor and flung their arms about while locals went about their business and cleared up the mess.

After about thirty minutes, the male singer spluttered into the microphone and told the audience, 'We're going to take a short break.'

'No, no. Take your time,' shouted Oleg.

The band lost confidence after Oleg's interjection, muttered inaudibly into the microphone and began to pack up their equipment, winding the microphone leads around their elbows before leaving in silence.

Alejandra had slipped away and was wrapped round Vinnie, our recalcitrant sommelier, and soon Alan said to Fuchsia, 'Shall we?'

I knew it was the end of the evening as far as I was concerned. I slunk away, like the band, unannounced and unwanted, back to my room. I expected a note from room service about Robin's missed call but there was still no message, which peeved me considerably. As soon as the room stopped spinning, I fell asleep.

It was dark o'clock when I woke up to screaming and crashing. The cabanas were far enough apart for privacy and you seldom heard the other guests. At the most you might hear music coming through in the middle of the day. The rooms weren't soundproofed, but you never heard noise. But what I'd heard was enough to wake me up and make me feel concerned. It was a man and a woman screeching at the top of their voices. I heard shouting and what sounded like breaking glass. Given the escalating intensity of the row, I decided to ring reception and dialled 9.

A receptionist with a high-pitched voice answered. I wasn't convinced she understood but I gave her my details and tried to go back to sleep. The argument got louder. I got up, put my shorts on and took a look for myself. Sound is supposed to carry over water, and I wasn't sure exactly where it was coming from. I walked around the beach to the left and, after about ten minutes, I was standing outside the cabana itself.

I didn't know whether it would be better to arrive when they were arguing or not. If they were still arguing they might not appreciate me turning up, but if they had stopped arguing – how the hell would I find their room and what the hell was I doing there anyway? The woman was screaming when I rang the bell and knocked on the door. Then I heard whispering inside the room and then complete silence. I rang the bell and knocked loudly three times on their door.

Eventually, the door was opened. It was Vinnie, who was very drunk indeed. His eyes said it all: he was not happy to see me, not happy at all, not one little bit. He shook his head and looked at me as if I was the biggest loser he had ever seen. The sad man who has to travel on his own because he couldn't find anyone to go on holiday with him. I hoped he wouldn't hold my comments regarding the pouring of the wine against me. I wondered if Alejandra had told him about me giving her my business card. Perhaps he had found it on her and beaten her up. Perhaps she had taunted him over it. His tanned, lineless face looked careworn and sweaty. His black hair was sticking up erratically and his already fetid breath stank of booze. Alejandra was sitting down in a hotel dressing gown crying and smoking a cigarette. Her make-up needed fixing, and her face showed the early signs of bruising. I had arrived just in time.

'Hi there, could you keep the noise down please? It's very late, and I'm trying to sleep,' I said.

'Okay,' said Vinnie. He yawned as he began to shut the door.

'Is everything okay?'

'Yes.' Vinnie rubbed his nose and checked his palm for blood.

'Are you sure?' I said.

'Yeah, there's nothing to see here I'm afraid, so if you'll just…'

'Hey, look; I only came over because it sounded like someone was getting the granny bashed out of her. I was asleep and the banging woke me up. Okay?' I said this while Vinnie tried to close the door on my foot.

'Okay, so now if you've seen what you want to see, we'll just call it an early night,' Vinnie pushed the door against my shoeless foot again.

'All right, no reason to talk to me like that,' I said.

'I want you to go away. Now,' he said.

'He's only seeing if…' said Alejandra behind the door and out of view.

'Just shut the fuck up, will you? And stub the fucking cigarette out, you look like a fucking tramp.' As Vinnie turned to speak to Alejandra, I thought he was going to hit her.

'Don't talk like that to her, butt breath,' I said. I began to push against the half-closed door of their cabana. I didn't want to leave minus one foot.

'Who are you calling butt breath, you fucking useless, pathetic loser?' He extended his thumb and index finger to create the letter 'L.' 'Look, I don't give one shit what you think, so just fuck off back to your sad, little room and your sad, loser, lonely life and leave the grown-ups to it. Comprennez? Capiche? Geddit?' The cabana door pinched the skin on my unprotected foot.

'Okay, you take that back,' I said as I went towards him and pointed at him.

He grabbed my index finger and twisted it violently. This hurt and I bellowed out loud, which made Vinnie twist it some more. He was grinning at me. Alejandra shouted at him to stop but he ignored her so I pushed my head into his chest and shoved him back. He let go of my index finger, grabbed hold of me by my shirt, and tried to throw me down the steps. And he would have done, if my new Vilebrequin linen shirt, which Kay had given me, hadn't ripped first. I heard it rip. I looked down at it and for the second time that day felt completely calm.

'You've made a big mistake,' I said.

'Go away now or you will get hurt,' Vinnie said.

So I hit him. I didn't think about it. I didn't think how I was going to hit him or whether I'd connect or not. I just hit him. I hit him as hard as I could with my right hand, a short rabbit punch plum to the side of his head, and, as he crouched down, I hit him again with my left hand flush against his left temple. He didn't want to play anymore. Vinnie held the base of his neck with his right hand and held up his left in surrender. Alejandra was screaming and helped Vinnie back into their room.

'If everything is okay, I'll go. And fuckface, you look at her the wrong way, and I'll fucking kill you. All right?' I said this as Vinnie slammed the door shut. Luckily for me, he missed my foot.

CHAPTER THIRTY-FOUR

The Fever

The uh-ho birds woke me in time for me to drink a bottle of fizzy water, take two Nurofen and find my CIA Business-Class ear-plugs and eye-pads before trying to go back to sleep. I could not believe what had happened. Looking back now, it was a concatenation of events that led to the main bout of the evening: almost drowning and being scared I was going to die, the euphoria of feeling so alive, being pissed off that Robin couldn't be arsed to ring me back, drinking more than was wise, fancying Alejandra, thinking Vinnie was a schmuck and then him abusing me so I gave him a smack. I was proud of myself for doing so but worried about the repercussions. I couldn't believe I had hit anyone. I hadn't hit anyone outside of a boxing ring since four boys with stinging nettles chased me when I was eleven. I couldn't snooze because of plankton rash and sand-fly bites, and the sheets rubbed against my back where I had been slam-dunked by the sea. I felt like I had been crucified, brought back to life and then crucified again.

I needed to get out before Devon arrived to clean the cabana. I wasn't in the mood for chitchat. I didn't want to give Devon a post-fight interview so I headed out for breakfast.

What would happen if Vinnie, or any of his mob, had called the police? What would happen if Mr Epaulette on passport control had got to hear of it? I'd end up on those Wanted Dead or Alive posters as I foraged for food in the Highlands. Still, as my Japanese granddad once said, it's better to beg forgiveness than to ask for permission.

I wore a pair of sunglasses and took my unfinished book by Derek Percy-Ffrench, and, while wearing sunglasses at breakfast made me look like a prat, at least they kept a grinning Shaggy at arm's length. It was my last full day, and I had to relax, get fit, get healthy and get a suntan. I had twenty-four hours to get a suntan to cover my blushes and embarrassment, and I was keen to avoid any further confrontation.

I was speed-trialling tea, fruit juice and water for the first hour. There were some people, whom I hadn't seen before, with a teenage girl who breakfasted with her earphones on and a dreadlocked teenage boy who had a tattoo that read *Only God is my Judge*. He was as bright as a ventriloquist's dummy.

Mrs Nasal Detritus and Mr Pink Polo Shirt were saying goodbye to Vernon and Mardy in reception so I hid my face. Their limousine driver wore a white liveried suit that made him look like he worked on a cruise ship. Their departure cheered me up a little so I ate some fresh fruit and moseyed back to my cabana. There was, of course, not a wave to be seen. The sand was dry and hot for the newcomers who had checked into the resort.

The repetitiveness of the days recreates the routine of work. Minute things become important – should I snorkel first then sunbathe or sunbathe first then snorkel? I was walking about, not knowing what to do, apart from not bump into Vinnie, unsure where to go or how to relax, and feeling dehydrated, having been woken up by quell birds at first light. I was suffering with a headache in over thirty-five degrees at ten o'clock in the morning.

I had plankton rash, a badly grazed back, gnat bites and I'd lost the Tilley hat purchased to protect me from the sun. I'd spent my entire holiday thinking I would be able to relax when something else happens or when something else is over. And, having spent my holiday thinking about it, I was unable to relax because it was my last full day and now I was worried about that.

The last full day of the holiday always sends me into a spiral of depression. In the latter days of my stay at Omanalak, I recognised fewer of my fellow guests. It was a bit like a microcosm of life, and it made me focus on what little time I had left. This drove me to snorkel so I could say goodbye to the multicoloured fish and concentrate on my tan.

It is difficult to overestimate the futility of trying to get a suntan if you are a Celt. You can only go as brown as your melanin permits. I had mocked Michael Jackson for trying to look white, and now I was no better than him. I don't believe in any of these magic creams either. Has anybody ever explained, for example, what happens if you put too much age-reversal cream on?

I had burnt off most of the plankton rash from my legs by the time I had my usual stir-fry lunch for the last time. There was no point packing while the sun was out, so the afternoon was spent in miserable contemplation about what emails I'd have waiting for me at home and in the office, and what was I going to do about my job. I resented the everyday world seeping back into my brain when I could be swimming in the sea under cloudless skies and gawping in wonder at palm trees. I remembered how I jumped out of my chair when I saw a teju. And now, I'd be disappointed if I didn't see one clambering about in the undergrowth. I was narked my holiday was almost over and dreaded having to put my shoes on to catch a flight home. Having flown thousands of miles, which cost me thousands of pounds, I had earnt the right to get up at 6.05 a.m. until my next holiday, which would be eight and a half months away. As the sun's powers began to wane, I was conscious of a sense of loss, both of time and opportunity.

Arthur wove his way up the beach making sure all the palm fronds were tidied up before sunset drinks. He was affable enough, but every day he cleaned the same beach and the same paths in the same hotel. I remained unconvinced about the man's ambition. I thought it was depressing for a man to do this for the rest of his life. It meant he missed out on getting up every morning, commuting and sitting in an office until it got dark when, if your boss has left for the day, you got to commute home and do the same thing the next day. Arthur and I had struck up a good working relationship based on a few sketchy facts about Sri Lankan cricket; however, he wouldn't agree that their bowlers were 'chuckers' and not bowlers. While we teased each other, he stopped and leant on his rake as if he was looking over the garden fence.

'I'm off tomorrow, Arthur,' I said.

'It won't be long till you're back,' he said.

'Maybe,' I lied.

'Where you live, London?'

'Near enough. Outside London,' I said.

Arthur nodded. 'Devon says he know you from before.'

'Sort of. But I didn't recognise him. He looks different,' I said.

'Devon says you always like someone who likes someone else,' he said.

'It wasn't anything like that. I was woken up and I thought I heard a woman scream and I went to help,' I said.

Arthur looked at me as if I was talking gibberish. 'Devon says the guy who did it, took pictures of her on his phone.'

'You're telling me Vinnie has pictures from last night on his phone?'

'Who said anything about last night?' Arthur said.

'So what the hell do you think I am talking about?'

'I have no idea,' Arthur said.

I scratched the bite behind my ear.

'You didn't recognise Devon because we all look the same?' Arthur said.

'No, because...'

'Because you had woman with you then?'

'Perhaps,' I said.

'You have no woman now?'

'No. We drifted apart, you might say,' I said.

'Yes, Devon was your houseboy then, too,' Arthur said.

'You seem to know all about it, you and Devon,' I said.

'Nobody's perfect,' Arthur said.

'I know I'm not.' I said.

'Not you, her.' Arthur's face flinched. I looked at him, waiting for him to continue. I scratched until Arthur took my arm and inspected the bites.

'You might want to get a banana,' he said.

'Do I look as if I haven't eaten?'

'You rub the inside of a banana skin on your bites.'

'Thanks, Arthur, I'll try it.'

'Or chew some tobacco and mix it with spit,' he said.

'Good tip.' I stared at my feet while Arthur made a loud clicking noise.

'So you go back to your big house?' Arthur asked.

'Not big,' I said.

'Yes, come on. Big house?'

'You'll have to see the house for yourself when you come over for the cricket, if Sri Lanka still thinks it's worth playing against us,' I said.

'Big garden? Big house, land, I bet.' Arthur prodded me with his rake.

'What about you? You got much land where you live?' I asked.

'It depends on whether the tide is in or out,' he said. We shook hands with lots of awkward pushing thumbs together, which I can never get right, and said goodbye. I knew I'd never see Arthur again, but hoped I might be wrong. I hoped I'd never see Vinnie again and knew I had to find Devon to find out what the hell Arthur was talking about.

CHAPTER THIRTY-FIVE

Don't Explain

I wanted the sensation of dried salty water on my skin to last as long as possible to remind me I was on holiday. I made time for one last swim, in the infinity pool, leaving me enough time to dry off before my last treatment in the spa. It was my last swim. I swam perfect breaststroke, making sure my thumbs, index fingers and toes touched in perfect synchronicity with every stroke. My powers of concentration were shattered when Fuchsia adjusted her bikini top, executed a swallow dive and swam the rest of the length underwater, before flicking her hair off her face in one motion. Before she dived in, I swam breaststroke and now I struggled with doggy paddle. My co-ordination had deserted me. I had to stay in the pool until she got out.

I went for my last treatment to the spa. The friendly Thai manager was off duty and so, thankfully, was Dr Vijay. I still felt awkward about his shirt. I went into the room, which was full of glass and wood with candles and New Age music, stripped off and put on a pair of pyjamas. I took off my glasses and watch and lay down flat. I had booked a deep-tissue Thai massage, which I am convinced is the best form of massage. It has the same benefits as non-invasive surgery. Within minutes, my joints were popping like champagne corks. But while it was an excellent massage, it was difficult to switch off. Why had Devon said to Arthur that I always like someone who likes someone else? I kept playing it over in my head. My face, in the mirror, made me look as if I had been mummified. It was a struggle to get dressed.

It was dark when I left the spa for the last time. The infinity pool lights were on, the green and red ribs of the exotic plants were picked out by the up-lighters and contrasted with the romantic, dimly lit paths. The resort looked gorgeous but where had all the time gone?

Back now in my cabana, back in my home, the hotel had made a special effort with the turndown service. Every night at turndown, Devon left a hibiscus flower or a piece of chocolate. Tonight he had left a flower and some chocolates plus an updated copy of the bill, which already included my ninety-minute Thai massage but not the dry-cleaning bill for Dr Vijay's shirt. I had hoped to catch him doing turndown service, but I knew I'd catch him in the morning. My Vilebrequin linen shirt was still hanging up in the bathroom. It was beyond repair. I flung the bill on the table next to the hotel's copy of *Passionate about Travel*, my unfinished copy of Derek Percy-Ffrench's *A Time of Shifts* and Frottager's *Guide to the Coronation Islands* (2009). There was still no word from Robin.

The tree frogs croaked while my fan sounded like a series of click-top pens. I had the problem of having to shave my hair follicles while not shaving any skin off my face. I put on my last clean sleeveless shirt. I wouldn't need it for another eight and a half months, and I could always put it in the wash when I got home.

There was nobody in the Dhow Bar. I ordered a Long Island Iced Tea one last time. The bar staff had to troop off to the other bar for every ingredient apart from the Coke. By the time the drink had arrived, I wished I had ordered something else and had sat in the other bar. A honeymoon couple sat down at the bar and kept banging on about how lucky they were to stay at Omanalak for two whole weeks. I finished my drink but I didn't see anybody else to have a chat with, so I sat down on my own for dinner. I had already been replaced by a new wave of guests sitting on my sun loungers talking to my waiters. It was time to say goodbye to this world of creepy tendrils, wooden bridges, storm lanterns and kerosene lamps.

Shaggy brought me some iced water while saying how sorry he was it was my last night. There seems to be a direct relationship between the third world and how many languages the waiters can speak. Shaggy looked after Italians, French, Spanish and mongrels, like me, with relative ease. I asked him how he learnt so many languages.

'Just by working,' Shaggy said.

'But you must have learnt them at school?' I asked.

'Not really, sir.'

'So tell me Shaggy, what is your real name?'

'Shaggy, sir, everybody calls me Shaggy.'

He polished my glass and handed me the leather-bound wine list.

'But what's your Christian name?' I asked.

'I am sorry, sir, I don't have Christian name,' he said.

'Don't be daft. Everyone has a Christian name.'

'Okay, sir, I am Muslim,' Shaggy said.

'Christ Alive, I am so sorry. Of course, you are. Thick,' I said while I slammed my forehead with the flat of my palm, shook my head and tutted. Shaggy left me to look after a party of Italians. I was left to wonder whether there was anywhere in the world, in a crescent bay, where white liveried staff served black people at dinner.

There was just enough light to play 'Drunken Geography'. This is my game where you write down the names of as many countries in Africa, or names of American states, as you can remember. The answers are usually Djibouti and Arkansas, that is, if the question is which are the ones you have forgotten.

CHAPTER THIRTY-SIX

After The Love Has Gone

The uh-ho birds let me have a bit of a lie-in which was a tad disappointing. I had breakfast and tipped Shaggy. Within thirty seconds, various waiters who had poured mineral water, brought a spoon over or had taken away a plate during my stay, popped up to say goodbye. It was the most expensive breakfast I have ever had. It was like feeding fish. Shaggy was happy because he was going home in five days and would see his wife and two-year-old daughter for the first time in over two months. I bunged him extra because I was embarrassed about last night.

I put the yellow-painted coconut outside my room to thwart any further people seeking tips. I was worried about what would happen if Devon was ill, on leave, or the cleaning roster had changed. Having tried to avoid him all week, now I needed to find him.

I left my room as messy as possible so Devon couldn't clear up around me. The hotel had charged me 240 dollars for a late checkout. The idea of sitting by the pool, with my bags packed, waiting for a cab to the airport, was too terrible for words. This way, I could take my time over breakfast, have a swim in the sea, heave my bulk about the beach one last time, take a quick dip in the pool, pack, shower, ring the bellboy to take my bags to reception, slip into an air-conditioned taxi to the airport, check in at the Business Class desk, sit in the CIA lounge and finally embark with a glass of chilled champagne and a hot towel. Yesterday I was sad and today I was resigned to my fate. I didn't want to get stung early by Devon for the tip so I went for a walk on the beach. I couldn't find Arthur, but I did see Alan walking along, hands clasped behind his back, looking down at the sand.

'Cheerio Alan, all the best,' I said.

'You off then?' Alan tried to remember where he'd seen my face before.

'Off in a while. Just before lunch. Say goodbye to your lovely wife from me, won't you?' I said.

'We'll see you next year, I suppose?' He bent down to pick up a piece of coral, blew the sand off and held it up to his eye.

'Yes, I expect so,' I lied.

'Have you got my business card?' Alan asked.

'You gave it to me the other night,' I said.

'Next time you're in Lincolnshire, you must look us up.' He put the piece of coral back on the beach.

'What's that you're doing? Are you collecting something?' I asked.

'No. What I like to do is to walk around looking for stuff. If I find something interesting, I pick it up and take it back to my room. Then, at the end of the holiday, I walk onto the beach and put it all back. Been doing the same thing for years, find it relaxes me,' he said.

I shook hands with Alan, who was still trying to remember my name, and trudged over the hot sand for for one last peek at Fuchsia. I hoped to catch Fuchsia alone, but she was not to be seen. The teenager with the *Only God is my Judge* tattoo was playing music to his sisters by the pool. The sun loungers were empty. The only person I knew by the pool was Oleg. He was performing a series of calisthenics in front of Svetlana, who was already on her second bikini of the day. It was soon time to pack. I walked back to my cabana for the last time. I wondered if I could thrash things out with Devon and get into my cab and away without bumping into Alejandra and Vinnie. I wanted to avoid them or at least I wanted to avoid Vinnie, and Alejandra came with Vinnie. He had ripped my new shirt from my old fiancée.

The fresh linen and the cleaning fluids were on the trolley outside my super-deluxe sunset-beach over-water cabana, which made me very happy; I just hoped I would find Devon too. This was the first and only time I had wanted Devon to get in the way. I shouted 'hello' and walked in to find him sweeping the floor in the bathroom where my ripped shirt was hanging up. Devon grimaced and made to look busy with his mop.

'Last day today, I'm off soon,' I said.

'Maybe you'll come back,' Devon said.

'Doubt it, had a fight with the owner's son.'

'Yeah, Arthur told me.'

'That's funny, he must have found out from somebody else. I didn't tell him,' I said.

'No secret's safe out here,' Devon said.

'What about Mauritius? Are secrets safe there?'

'I suppose.' Devon picked up his bucket and went into the bedroom. I followed him. Devon knew what was coming next.

'Arthur tells me you said I always like someone who likes someone else? Why would he say that?' I asked.

'I don't know,' he said.

'Yes, you do. Please put down what you are doing, sit down and listen to me,' I said, and as I pulled up a chair, he sat down. I sat down on the bed and leant towards him as I spoke. Devon tried to avoid eye contact so I put my hands on both his shoulders until he looked up. I looked him straight in the eye, for what I had intended to be a full minute, until I spoke.

'I didn't tell anybody anything; everybody knows you and Vinnie had a fight. Alejandra must have told Arthur,' Devon said.

'I'm not talking about Vinnie, I am talking about Kay, you idiot, why would you say to Arthur that I *always* like someone who likes someone else? And hurry up about it,' I said.

'Naz told me. He showed me pictures. On his phone,' Devon said.

'Right, yes, Naz, carry on,' I said. I didn't know anything about this.

'When you used to go fishing for marlin,' Devon said. 'She used to come down to the boat club to see you off and Naz used to work at the boat club at the Aspire in Mauritius, he was a bumster, always trying to make off with the female guests, he used to pester people to go for a walk, just a walk with him and then he'd take photos on his phone. He showed me,' Devon said.

'He showed you what exactly?' I asked.

'He showed me pictures of your girlfriend when you were fishing,' he said.

'Kay wasn't my girlfriend, she was my fiancée,' I said. 'And what was she doing in those pictures?'

'You don't want to know.'

'I have to know whether you want to tell me or not,' I said.

'She was being intimate with him.'

'How intimate?'

'Oral sex intimate.'

I felt a reflex contraction in the back of my throat. All I could see was Kay on her knees, looking up at the camera at Naz with his dick in her mouth. I cleared my throat noisily and, as I waited for the nausea to subside, I wanted to give Kay and Naz such a beating their own mothers would have been unable to identify them.

'Okay... I don't know anything about this. It's impossible. How can you be sure? Why would you say this?' I tried to control my breathing.

'I'm sorry, Mr Kaganagh. I really am, but I saw the pictures myself. And I'm sorry I told Arthur,' Devon said.

'I'm sorry, too, Devon but I suppose if you hadn't told Arthur, you wouldn't have told me,' I said. I needed to go home to my friends and family.

I couldn't believe it. Why on earth would Kay do that to me? How could she be with that cunt and then meet me off the boat and act as if nothing had happened? Had a nice day, dear? Yes, actually one of the boat boys, Naz – you know him – stuck his dick in my mouth and took a picture. You see, there I am looking up at the camera.

She didn't like boats because she preferred to hang around with Naz and not with me. It had nothing to do with seasickness; it was because she was sick of seeing me. I felt guilty about thinking ill of her and felt like crying. Kay had cheated on me and now I had been robbed of her memory. I felt such an idiot.

What was I supposed to do? I couldn't bring Kay back even if I had wanted to, and I didn't. I wish she was alive, or more accurately, I wish she hadn't died, but I didn't want her for myself anymore. Assuming what Devon had said was true, it sounded like they deserved one another. I wish I had known more about her and Naz, but then, I am glad I didn't. I felt better about not being with her but I also wish I hadn't wasted so much time thinking about her. I still didn't know how Kay died but I suspect Naz may have had something to do with it. With forearms like Naz, it wouldn't have been difficult to squeeze the life out of her. But I didn't actually *know* what had happened to her. And for the first time, I wasn't particularly bothered either. Should I go to the police? And tell them what exactly? I decided, rightly or wrongly, to move on.

CHAPTER THIRTY-SEVEN

The Power

The cab was on time and, as we arrived at the Departure gates, I leapt out to help myself with my own luggage to lessen the driver's expectations regarding his tip. I avoided the people who were flying about on roller blades handing out pamphlets to passengers. I didn't want to provoke an international incident before embarkation.

I don't enjoy airports any more than I like the word 'chillax'. You spend hours waiting then end up doing everything in a rush; perhaps this explains why the young couple put the toddler through the security scanner and held onto the pram. And airport security is inherently unfair. We, the passengers, are assumed to be guilty, and are forced to strip ourselves of both dignity and mineral water as we shuffle past officials who were never made prefect at school. Meanwhile, the criminals operate on an honesty policy; if you have x or y please remove them. Have you ever seen a hoodlum standing under a sign saying *No Weapons Allowed* unloading Uzis, Kalashnikovs and a bowie knife into one of the plastic trays provided?

It was too hot inside the terminal, and my shoes made my feet sweat. I wanted to buy one of those snakes in a bottle of alcohol, but although they had been available at every airport terminal, market and even sold by hawkers by the side of the road, for some reason they weren't available at Fulgary airport. When you see something you like, you've got to grab it. You may not see what you want again.

In the business lounge, I saw a doleful milksop, with a laptop and an earpiece, wandering about and talking to people on his phone. He walked past a student, who was anotating a copy of Marx's *Das Kapital* with a Mont Blanc pen, and dressed in a DKNY jacket.

The lounge was awash with BlackBerries, laptops and magazines with titles like *Exclusive Italian Golf Vogue Collection*. A drunk with a badly gashed hand was telling everyone who'd listen that he used to live in Qatar and how it was a shithole but tax-free. I left when he asked me to guess how much his boat cost.

The trays of nibbles in the CIA Business Lounge reminded me how spoilt I'd been, while the newspapers were full of alarmist nonsense and celebrity trivia. I sat down in the comfy chairs nearest to the computer terminals. My palms were sweaty with excitement. I was about to log on to the Chairboys message board to see what had happened in the last few weeks. I raised my head off my chest and straightened my back to help to increase the supply of oxygen, while my fat little fingers pumped the keyboard... one draw away from home and a draw at home in a game we could have won. Another CEO from the football club had resigned, citing family reasons, before taking up a better-paid job with a club in a higher league, and we've got a youngster in from Wigan on trial.

Sitting in my preferred aisle seat, I paid the price as hundreds of cattle-class passengers filed past taking a swing at me with their bags. I scanned the plane for snorers and young children. As soon as it was time for take-off, I jumped up to get my hand luggage. I was fidgeting about in my seat, looking for the packets of herbal pellets my Tibetan doctor had given me, when I noticed the name of the stewardess, Anne Devine. I wondered if this was the Anne Devine, wife of Sean Devine and mother of the lovely Aoife Devine, whose house I'd been to in Kilrush. I settled down for a game of 'Doors on automatic, crosscheck and report. Cabin crew, please take your seats for take-off.'

It was an eleven-hour flight, and I was sitting on my own with nothing to do. I wondered if Kay only went on holiday with me so she could sit on the plane and watch movies. Devon knew more about Kay than I did but if he hadn't told me about her, how would I have got over it? Now I can see I was lucky to find out, it's just that it didn't feel like that at the time.

I was bored and didn't feel like reading my book. I couldn't find any films to watch, I didn't want to play quiz games, fill out a survey or listen to *Monsters of Rock* on Channel 24. I switched over to the Moving Map. I looked at distance to destination, altitude, local time at origin, distance to destination, tail wind, time to destination, estimated arrival time, outside air temperature and ground speed until I got bored. I made a point of being helpful to Anne, mindful of the need to engage her in conversation after the initial hullabaloo of drinks, headsets, menus, food and tea or coffee.

'So are you on business or holiday?' asked Anne.

'Bit of both really,' I smiled at her as I took off my headset and nodded in appreciation at every bowl she put on my tray.

'Can't be bad,' Anne said.

'No, can't be bad.' I sipped my drink and smiled.

'What do you do that takes you to Fulgary?' Anne offered me bread rolls.

'I'm in medicine,' I said.

'So you're a doctor.'

'Not really. See these?' I showed Anne my remaining packets of herbal pellets from the Tibetan doctor from when I met her husband. 'These herbal pellets are Tibetan medicine. Do you know anything about Tibetan medicine?' I enquired.

'Nothing at all, really,' Anne said.

'In Tibetan medicine, everything is done on pulses or the colour of your tongue, things like that. What I am doing is a PhD at Royal Holloway College, University of London, to see if there are any psychological applications for Tibetan medicine. Are you with me?' I asked.

Anne stood slack-mouthed next to the trolley.

'Not sure I am,' she said.

'Give me your wrist.' Anne held out her wrist while I feigned to count.

'Right, now the other one.' She handed me her other wrist.

'Your husband. Is he something to do with travel?' I asked.

'Yes,' she said.

'You, your husband, do you have a young child?'

'Yes,' Anne signalled to the other stewardess, a bustling brunette. 'Listen to this, Denise, this gentleman has told me I'm married to a man who works in travel and that I have a young child, just from my pulse.' The brunette leant forward.

'You are married, with a child younger than ten, maybe a daughter. Your house is white and has barbed wire on the top. I see the letter "a",' I said.

'Amazing,' Anne said. The brunette sniffed.

'You have a dog, a big dog?' I asked.

'Yes we do.'

'And you have a maid, but her room is smaller than the dog's?' I said.

'Absolutely right,' Anne said.

'And I can see a bridge with palm trees.'

'Oh my God, you're really good at this.'

'Thank you, can we change wrists again please as the strength of the pulse, it's wearing off,' I said. We swapped wrists. 'I can see orange, red and purple. I can see lots of orange – but orange flowers not orange trees,' I said. Both stewardesses ignored the bing-bong noises while passengers had to clamber over them to join the queue to use the toilet.

'Amazing. Absolutely amazing. I can't wait to tell Sean,' Anne said.

'Allow me to give you my card,' I said as I fished around in my wallet and presented her husband's business card that he'd given me in Kilrush.

'You bastard,' said the brunette, a little too loudly. Anne shoved me in the shoulder, while smiling at me, but too hard for it to be a joke. Her colleague sniffed and walked off.

'So you're the clever fella who thinks he can find love in places rather than in people,' Anne said as she drove her trolley into my arm.

CHAPTER THIRTY-EIGHT

Teardrops

I had little human interaction for the remaining eight or nine hours. Both stewardesses seemed to be busy whenever I asked for anything. Most of my journey was spent sitting on the cord for my headphones or on the metal part of my seat belt, counting gnat bites or bemoaning my dry nose, eyes and skin.

Fat ugly people snored. My solution to this would be to get all the travel tubbies in the same row, refuse to serve them any food so they couldn't sleep and thus ensure that everybody else could. There is always one klutz who snores constantly. He's easy to spot because he's the one who falls asleep before anyone else has had a chance to put their seat belt on.

I watched the flying cigar jerk around on the screen until I could bear no more and switched over to watch a programme about a woman from the UK who got looked after by some Indonesian islanders, and I started to cry.

I don't know why I cried. Perhaps I was overcome by the kindness shown by a stranger to a stranger; it may have been because it was the end of my holiday; or it may be because every time I go away and return, I feel I've got away with it again. Perhaps I was crying because I was relieved to be going home. I was frustrated at myself for criticising the places I visited when I was there, while at the same time dreading my return to normality and routine. Maybe I wasn't overly chuffed about going home because the ex-fiancée still wasn't there and was never coming home again. I was grateful that she wasn't, maybe she got what she deserved, I know that's not fair but sometimes it's how I feel. Or maybe she didn't deserve me. She should have been with Naz. I thought about the photos on his phone;

who else had seen and laughed at them? At the time I thought I cried because I was soppy and tired when really I was crying for myself and for the relief I felt when, for the first time, I thought of Kay as an ex-fiancée. I don't know whether Kay's death, and the revelations about her, have changed me or not, but I don't beat myself up about it anymore. The Naz factor has given me the excuse to move on. I don't feel good about what happened but nor do I berate myself. And I no longer travel the world ticking off countries.

Whether you are feeling depressed or elated at the end of a holiday is difficult to assess. Do you feel like your life is nearly over or do you just want to get home? That's the acid test of a good holiday; I suppose much depends on what you have waiting for you. And I had my birthday get-together to look forward to.

By the time you land everyone looks travel-toiled and decrepit, even the ladies who have been putting slap on since beginning the descent over Europe. You don't know how ugly people are until you wake up and see them sitting in front of you on a plane.

We had to hand back headphones, blankets, stow this piece of stuff we didn't ask for anyway, stow that menu and put our tables up. The stewardess gave me so many things to do it was difficult to remember what I had to do next.

I could see roofs with dark red tiles, houses packed in row after row of roads, the winding River Thames, trees that looked like broccoli florets, uninspiring pseudo-skyscrapers and office blocks plonked next to old church spires next to bowling greens. Then a world of storage units, sky-bridges sponsored by HSBC, chewing-gum bespattered carpets gummed together with masking tape, estuarine accents grating over the tannoy; sports teams of teenagers and people wearing facemasks queuing at passport control.

I find it remarkable, whenever I come back from faraway places, how the tree frogs still croak at night while I sit at home on the sofa. I missed the sound of the tropics after sunset. I missed the light and the colour of the sky, the sand and the sea. The hotel stays, and you leave. Arthur would be singing and feeding the tejus; new guests would be checking in and setting up camp in fresh T-shirts. The old gang replaced by fresh blood. A butterfly comes and chases the flies off the flowers, a scrawny cat stretches, yawns but makes no effort to get up. A waiter smiles forcibly for a tip. There is a new parade of bodies; the towels are changed; they're taking care of business, that's all.

I felt terrible by the time I got my luggage. I rushed to the carousel only to question whether I would ever see my luggage again. People pushed trolleys with buckled wheels over my toes. You know because you've done it yourself, you just want to get out and get home. There are blokes in shorts and women in braids, but it is cold, it is winter, it is six o'clock in the morning, it is November and it is England.

My taxi driver was on time. He talked about his wife and the spirit world. I looked out of the window, read all the street signs and asked if he had a paper. I became anxious about my home and its contents, my possessions and my family. I had jet lag and couldn't remember whether I'd paid my Visa bill or not.

With scratchy eyes, I put my key in the lock, turned off the alarm and picked the debris up off the carpet. I opened a letter from a Claire Bickerstaff in Human Capital Management. She had been instructed by Robin Hunt to invite me in for a company medical. I didn't mind trading the fear index. It didn't bother me if it was up or down as long as it was moving. What bothered me was, having spent my holiday on my own, the last thing I fancied was leaving all my pals at Fundamental to throw my lot in with a bunch of strangers who couldn't take the trouble to return my call. I had thought perhaps if I left Fundamental it would mean I was moving on. If I wanted to feel isolated I could always go on another holiday by myself. The important thing was to be on the right side of the trade. And while the money was better, the fact they didn't even pick up my call, let alone ring me back, made my mind up for me.

I put the rest of the letters on the kitchen table, carried my suitcase upstairs and opened it in the spare bedroom. I thought to myself so far, so good. I had a brief sense of elation as my feet felt the reassuring touch of carpets. It felt exotic.

Having emptied my suitcase, I picked up the ashtrays I had half-inched on holiday with my ex-fiancée. I had a ceramic one from Morocco, which I kept in the kitchen. I took the Art Deco glass ashtray, which we bought in Prague. Rather than put them in the bin outside, I walked to the recycling bins by the supermarket and slung them in there so at least they were off the premises.

Downstairs, I made tea with long-life milk. It didn't taste great but it was tea. I put away the toiletries I had stolen from the hotels. I slotted the Frottager's guide, a copy of *Playing Snooker with the Somalis* given to me by Father Terry and my unfinished copy of Derek Percy-Ffrench's book on the top shelf of my small bookcase. I didn't need to read a book for another eight and a half months.

The Tibetan herbal pellets were slung in the bin along with any business cards, and I put my matchbox, containing the world's smallest flying fish, in the top right-hand drawer of my desk. I did things so quickly it seemed as if I hadn't really been away.

I was safe home. I opened letters, threw away mailshots and used the toilet, thus breaking my final connection with the Coronation Islands. I deleted the automated sales phone calls from debt consolidators, threw the holiday bumf in the bin, checked that the heating and taps worked and rang my family. I had returned to the mundane, contrived, painful endurance of suburban life. And I have to say it felt great.

I checked my emails. I had ninety-one in my inbox and fifty-eight in trash. I wasn't interested in reading any of them; I just wanted to delete them so I could relax. I started off by deleting the trash at breakneck speed and I was just about to delete what I thought was a mailshot or a customer-satisfaction survey from the Aspire Group when I thought I'd better not in case there was a bit of customer feedback about smacking Vinnie so I opened it instead:

Hello Jack, – Remember me? The last time we met I wasn't looking my best. Anyway, I am coming over to London shortly for an interview at Aspire Group's HQ in 69, Brook Street, off Bond Street. They want to talk to me about setting up a dive centre in Okinawa in Japan and as I think you said you live and work near there perhaps we could meet up. You're already probably busy anyway but if you weren't you can contact me at this email address or ring me on 0777 290 8641. I'll arrive on the 23rd and will be around until the 28th-ish. Sorry about your shirt. I've split up with Vinnie and been asked to look elsewhere within the group which is why I'm coming over to Head Office. And to see you of course!

Bestest, – Alejandra xx

It would be nice to have something to unwrap on my birthday. I couldn't believe my luck. I'd traded up with Alejandra, switched out of the ex-fiancée and had sold my position in trading VIX, the volatility index, preferring to concentrate on my non-ethical holdings. It's the difference between wants and needs. I deleted all the previous emails regarding my trip to the Coronation Islands and deleted all bookmarks relating to my trip, including *World Travel: The Passport to Peace Through Understanding The Travelers' Century Club*. I don't have to go to any new countries, I can go back to any places I want, I am free to do what I want, go where I like and with whoever I like.

I decided against watching *Britain's Craziest Killers*, preferring to watch programmes on India, the Amazon and something about the US elections before I flopped into the scratcher.

So where to next? The Antarctic, St Lucia, the Silk Road, Montenegro or Oman? Where would Alejandra like to go? If Alejandra gets the job I could go out and visit her in Okinawa. I've always wanted to go to Japan and stay in the Park Hyatt in Tokyo where they filmed *Lost in Translation* (2003) with Bill Murray and Scarlett Johansson. But was I getting ahead of myself? The travel bug comes back after three months like a bout of cerebral malaria. I needed to look at my work-life balance; I thought about it for a moment and decided to give it all up but the alarm went off. It was 6:05 and I had a train to catch at 6:39. This is the Second Law of Travel – if you go away, you have to come back sometime, that is, if you're lucky.